EYES IN FRONT WHEN RUNNING

eyes in front when running

WILLOW KEAN

BREAKWATER
P.O. Box 2188, St. John's, NL, Canada, A1C 6E6
WWW.BREAKWATERBOOKS.COM

Library and Archives Canada Cataloguing in Publication
Title: Eyes in front when running / Willow Kean.
Names: Kean, Willow, author.
Identifiers: Canadiana 20230182925 | ISBN 9781550819755 (softcover)
Classification: LCC PS8621.E225 E94 2023 | DDC C813/.6—dc23

We acknowledge the support of the Canada Council for the Arts.
We acknowledge the financial support of the Government of Canada through the Department of Heritage and the Government of Newfoundland and Labrador through the Department of Tourism, Culture, Arts and Recreation for our publishing activities.

PRINTED AND BOUND IN CANADA.

Canada Council for the Arts Conseil des arts du Canada Canada Newfoundland Labrador

Breakwater Books is committed to choosing papers and materials for our books that help to protect our environment. This book is printed on Forest Stewardship Council® certified paper.

FSC www.fsc.org MIX Paper from responsible sources FSC® C103567

For Justin

I've got a million regrets and I'm sorry for everything
I've ever done sometimes
But it's nowhere near sunset and, baby, we've got years yet

—Amelia Curran

part one

your life is over

ice wall

CLEO GRABBED JAMIE'S THIGH SO HARD UNDER THE DINING room table, she was sure her fingers would leave imprints. Little faded pink moons on his upper thigh, under his jeans. Fran was overjoyed, blushing and stammering all over the place. Cleo thought Fran must be drunk, but that was against the rules when you were three months pregnant.

"We didn't want to say anything until we were out of the first trimester. We're a little high-risk because of my age. Things are looking great so far, but we won't know much more until the next ultrasound." Fran chugged the rest of what Cleo had thought was a vodka soda. "Anyone for an espresso? We have decaf now, of course."

She pranced off to the kitchen, holding her belly and singing to herself. Or to the baby. Could they even hear when they were that small?

Cleo was one year older than Fran.

Jamie beamed at Andrew as he pulled Cleo's clawed hand off his leg under the table.

"Congratulations, man, that's fucking great."

"No swearing in front of the baby!" Fran yelled from the kitchen.

Cleo knew Fran was only half-joking, even if the baby had no ears yet.

She could feel Jamie smiling on the drive home, hands on the wheel and little snorts of air through his nose. He turned to look at her, but Cleo stared straight out the windshield, shaking her head in the dark.

The four-way stop at Long Pond Road, another long look. The street was deserted and he let the car idle at the stop sign. She looked over and punched him in the arm.

"What?" Cleo punched him again. "What? Frig off!" She was smiling now, too.

"It's great, they're great," Jamie looked ahead and finally rolled through the intersection. "Andrew looked like he'd won the lottery."

"He seems to have conveniently forgotten that Fran slept with their accountant two years ago."

"Jesus, Cleo, they've been together fifteen years."

"If you fuck our accountant I'm leaving you and I'm getting the house."

"If I suddenly take a liking to sixty-seven-year-old men I'll be sure to give you and Clyde lots of notice. I'll give him a heads up when I drop off our receipts." The windows were steaming up and Jamie reached for the defrost button. "Don't be pissed at them because they worked through it and stayed together."

Jamie reached over to grab her knee. He squeezed and his hand moved further up before stopping on her thigh. He'd tried putting his hand in her underwear once when they were driving on the Trans-Canada and Cleo had screamed and they ended up in a ditch. They lied to the cop and said they'd swerved to avoid a moose. At the B & B that night she pounded Jamie on the chest and yelled at him for almost killing them. When he said he was just trying to be sexy, Cleo said practical was better than sexy at a hundred and twenty kilometres an hour.

The car rules now included no sudden moves while driving and no hands higher than mid-thigh.

Jamie cursed when he saw the neighbours hadn't left enough room to parallel-park in front of their house on Prospect, and pulled back out to make another cut. Cleo was lucky if she could do it in three or four. Sometimes in winter she left the car in the road and made Jamie come out to finish parking. And every year by mid-January he would bring up leaving their downtown row house for a place with a driveway and a proper backyard.

"Goddamn downtown parking goddamn neighbours fuck," Jamie said as he made a third cut.

It was Old Christmas Day and raining, and the pile of snow they'd shovelled yesterday was a solid wall of ice without much leeway, thanks to the neighbour. Jamie made it in after a fourth cut and they heard the bumper scrape against the ice wall.

"Shit, sorry, I should have let you out first," he said.

"That's okay, you can pull out again and I'll hop out."

"I just had to cut the car four—"

"I'm kidding, I'm kidding. I'll climb out your side."

Jamie got out and took Cleo's purse and she climbed over the gearshift, leaving globs of dirty slush on the driver's seat. She stepped out, then leaned back in the car to wipe off the seat and heard a group of teenage boys laughing as they walked down the street. One of them yelled out, "Hey buddy, nice purse."

Cleo grabbed her purse back and laughed at him.

"Thanks, princess," she said. Jamie slapped her on the ass and it made a soft whump over her winter jacket.

"You wouldn't have to climb out of the car like that if we had our own driveway." He put his arms around her waist while she rummaged for the keys. "And what would you do without me to parallel-park in winter?"

Cleo unlocked the door to the house and wondered how a man who had once tried to finger her on the TCH could want to live in the suburbs.

"I'd sell the car," she said. And walked on in without looking at him.

The house was freezing, so Cleo wore her "full gear" to bed, as Jamie liked to call it. Long-sleeved T-shirt, plaid pyjama pants, and wool socks.

"Sleeping with you in winter feels like camping," he said.

She climbed into bed and pulled the duvet over her head, leaving a hole big enough to expose her mouth and nose. It reminded Cleo of how she used to sleep in youth hostels, covering her eyes from fluorescent lights and her ears from snoring. She thought of the place in Berlin she stayed once, in the attic of a nineteenth-century building. The room slept twenty-six people, and for eight nights she had fallen asleep to the smell of feet and drunk English boys. It was disgusting and she'd loved it.

Jamie pulled her to his chest and put his hands around her back, then into her pyjama pants and underwear. Cleo shivered when she felt his cold hands on her bare bum cheeks. She wound her woollen feet through his.

"Aunt Cleo and Uncle Jamie," he said, giving her cheeks a squeeze.

"Jesus Christ, is Krista pregnant again? She's forty-five! I thought her tubes were tied." Krista, Jamie's sister in Clarenville, had her first baby at fifteen and she'd been on a roll ever since.

"No, I mean Andrew and Fran."

"Not related. Doesn't work that way."

"Sure it does. Mack calls you Aunt Cleo."

"That's different, Nancy's my best friend. I don't even like Fran."

"But Andrew's my best friend. That doesn't count?"

"We'll see how you feel about another niece or nephew after we get the Christmas Visa bill." Cleo's face was still covered in duvet and Jamie could only see her mouth and nose. "Next year we're getting everyone a goat from Oxfam and hopping on a plane to Barbados."

"Yeah, Sophie will love that."

Sophie was seven and the youngest of Krista's brood of five, the "Happy Accident," as Krista and Darren loved to call her. Not to her face, just around the adults at family gatherings after everyone had a few too many. Sophie was pretty sharp for a seven-year-old, and most adults don't realize how loud they are after several gin and tonics, or how kids love to listen to adult party conversations at the top of the stairs. Sophie's oldest brother Jonathan was twenty-three years older than she was. Cleo had to bite her tongue hard sometimes to keep from asking if Jonathan was the "Unhappy Accident."

"How are you feeling about tonight?" Jamie brought his face close to Cleo's breathing hole.

"Pretty drunk."

"No, I mean about Fran."

"Happy for her, I guess. It's a bit scary, though, she's pretty old."

"Naaah. Everyone's having babies now in their thirties."

"Late thirties."

Jamie lifted the duvet from around her head and face. He kissed her forehead and nose.

"I'm still cold," she said. "Bastard. I fashioned the perfect breathing hole and now I have to redo it."

Cleo kissed him and turned around, pushing her back into him to keep warm. She pulled the duvet over her head again.

"G'night."

coffee

CLEO WOKE UP TO AN EMPTY BED AND SUN LEAKING IN THROUGH the blinds they'd forgotten to close completely the night before. She smelled coffee from downstairs and wanted one, so she knew she wasn't hungover. She jumped out of bed long enough to open the blinds all the way and turn on the space heater before crawling back under the covers.

Jamie heard the space heater kick in and called from downstairs.

"Morning, babe. Want me to bring you up a coffee?"

"Yeees," Cleo shouted back. "I love you. And a teaspoon of sugar please, because it's the weekend."

"Mom and Dad are on their way in to go to Costco, they're dropping by in a bit for a cup of tea, okay?"

"*Fuck fuck fuck fuck fuck fuck fuck*," Cleo said under her breath. Coffee in bed and this was why.

"Yeah, sounds good!" she yelled, clicking an imaginary gun next to her temple.

Evelyn and Hector lived in Clarenville, a couple of hours from the city. Far enough away to feel entitled to drop in when they decided to come to St. John's on a whim. Surprise visits happened once or twice a month, usually on a weekend when they drove in for Costco or the mall, and inevitably coinciding with Cleo's hangovers. She felt fine this morning, but couldn't think of anything worse than having to put on a bra and jeans just out of bed when all she wanted to do was drink coffee and eat leftover Christmas cheese in front of the television.

Under normal circumstances, and with well-planned-in-advance visits, they were wonderful people and Cleo loved them.

She heard Jamie's feet on the stairs and when he came through the bedroom door he looked apologetic, holding her favourite mug in his hands like a peace offering.

"You don't mind Mom and Dad popping in for a few minutes?" As he handed her the coffee, some sloshed on the bedsheets. She could tell by the colour he'd put too much milk in again.

"Not at all," Cleo lied. "At least they gave us some notice." She ignored the puddle on the bed because she planned on changing the sheets later. "If we could just find a tactful way of letting them know we need a little bit more."

The last surprise visit had interrupted sex on the living room couch. There'd been cursing and a quick separation because they were afraid Evelyn would use her emergency key to let herself in. After they'd left, Cleo looked at Jamie and said, "Take care of it, or I will." She never asked what he'd said to his mother and she didn't want to know, but at least now they got a warning text message.

"I know, I know, I'm sorry."

She made a move to get out of bed, but by this time Jamie had crawled back under the covers.

"Stay for a bit, we've got plenty of time. They texted from Whitbourne."

He put his arm around her and nuzzled her neck. More coffee on the bedsheets.

"Ahhh, frig off, you!" She reached over him and put the mug on the bedside table. "Jamie, I can't rush sex when your parents are on the way."

"I'll make it quick, you know I'm awesome at that."

"Babe, later. I totally would but I have to do the dishes before your mom gets here or we'll never get rid of her. She'll send Hector to the mall and stay and clean the house. I love her, but today is a no-bra, soft pants day."

"You're no fun." He made a move to push himself off the bed, putting his hand right in the coffee puddle.

Cleo pulled herself across the bed and let her head hang off the edge so she could look up at him. "You're all riled up about babies since last night. It's very sweet, but very annoying."

Jamie laughed at that and she was relieved. It had been floating in the air between them. That was enough for now.

"Now, go get dressed so your parents don't find out we're complete slack-arses," she said. Cleo launched herself off the bed, turning back to give Jamie a brief kiss on the mouth. She pulled her shirt off over her head as she walked across the room to the closet and felt Jamie watching her bare back.

"You're beautiful," he said.

"I'm old."

"Fuck off, you're beautiful."

"My eggs are old, too."

"Fuck off."

tea

THE DOORBELL RANG JUST AS CLEO WAS DRYING THE LAST OF the dishes. She'd pre-boiled the kettle to get the tea over with quickly. Jamie was tidying the living room, running upstairs and down with handfuls of clothes, papers and books, dumping them on the bed in the spare room to deal with later. He went to answer the door and Cleo flicked the button on the electric kettle again, took out four mugs and put teabags in. She had so wanted this entire day to herself and silently cursed Jamie for not lying and saying they were on their way out.

She opened the fridge to get the milk and slid open the cheese drawer to have a peek.

"We just have to wait a little longer, sweet cheeses."

"Have you lost your head in here, talking to the refrigerator?" Evelyn came into the kitchen, carrying a casserole dish and a cookie tin. She laid them on the table and gathered Cleo in a rib-crushing hug. Evelyn hugged like a lumberjack, not a woman who barely cleared five feet.

"Hi Evelyn."

Cleo felt the tiniest pang of guilt when she looked at the four tea mugs lined up on the counter. Bags already in, kettle boiled.

"You and Hector have time to let a pot steep?" She turned to take the teapot off the shelf, grabbing the teabags out of the mugs with her back to Evelyn and tossing three of them in the pot.

"Yes, my darling. As long as we're not keeping you from anything."

"Oh my goodness, no. We're just having a lazy day. Last weekend before work starts."

"Proper thing, maid. The two of you have had a busy few months. We won't keep you too long. We gotta go up to the university to see the twins before we goes to Costco."

Karly and Bobbi were Krista's twin girls. Twenty years old and both at university, sharing a small apartment near campus with another girl from Clarenville. In her five years with Jamie, Cleo always made a point of calling them by their names instead of referring to them as "The Twins," like the rest of the family did.

"A little something for the two of you as well," said Evelyn, nodding her head at the table. "Just a tin of Nanaimo bars and a casserole. We had the crowd over yesterday for turkey so I did you up a tetrazzini. I figured you'd be busy being back at work this week so pop that in your fridge now, you'll get a few good meals out of it. Hope you're not going on a diet for New Year's."

"Definitely not. You're the sweetest."

Cleo and Jamie's deep-freeze was bursting at the seams, and here was another addition to be ignored. Jamie hated leftovers and Cleo was sick of eating entire casseroles on her own. The deep-freeze solved both these problems, and they gutted it every six months or so, Cleo begging Jamie to man up and tell his mother to stop with the casserole-delivery service. He clearly hadn't addressed the issue yet.

"Tea's ready!" Cleo yelled into the living room. From where she was standing she could see Hector on his hands and knees, checking the base of the Christmas tree to see if it needed water. Jamie was sitting next to the tree in her grandfather's old chair, elbows on his splayed-open knees, looking at his phone.

Cleo set the table with mugs and spoons, milk and sugar, and took a plate out for the Nanaimo bars. She sat at the table and reached for the cookie tin.

"My dear, don't worry about us. Those are for you." Evelyn took off her coat and placed it on the back of the chair.

The coat was off.

Hector and Jamie came into the kitchen and Hector bent to kiss Cleo on the cheek. His beard smelled like spruce gum.

"How long you two keeping that tree up? Old Christmas Day's over, be sensible now." He put milk in his mug first and then poured the tea. No sugar, just a stir that lasted too long and was too loud, clanging against the sides of the mug. He tossed the wet spoon on the table and Cleo saw the steam rising from it and brown tea pooling on the tablecloth. Something else to put in the wash with the coffee-stained sheets.

Hector blew on the tea so hard it splashed up on his moustache and he took an exaggerated slurp. He drank his tea like Cleo's stepfather, Joe. Like someone who needed a cup but had no time for one. Jamie poured tea for everyone else, doing his mug last because he liked it strong and wanted the dregs from the bottom.

"Cleo wants it up until the end of January," he said, and smirked because he knew what was coming.

"End of January?" Hector reached for the cookie tin and Evelyn smacked his hand. He reached in anyway, pulled out a Nanaimo bar and ate it in two bites. "Well, Jesus Christ, you better keep it watered then, or you'll burn down the whole goddamn block. Bad enough when you can hear someone fart next door. I suppose we'll have one of the city trucks up here the once giving us a ticket for parking on the street, will we?" Hector leaned back in his chair so he could see down the hall and out the living room window.

"Just as long as it's not Norma's spot across the street," Cleo said in her best serious voice. "She'll call the city and get you ticketed for sure. Or throw a few eggs at your windshield, depending on her mood. And she doesn't even own a car."

Jamie grinned at her across the kitchen table and took a slurp from his mug. Newfoundland Tea Genetics.

"Jesus Christ, Ev, get that tea gone fast, I just got the truck washed. Honest to God, the crowd that runs down here is something else." Hector pushed his chair back so he had a better view of the street. "Sure, take the tree down now and I can haul it away for you before we goes."

"January is depressing," Cleo said. "The Christmas lights make me happy."

"My dear, you can hang lights somewhere without having the tree up."

"Oh Hec, give up, her stepfather's the fire chief. I suppose she has half a clue about watering a Christmas tree."

"As long as you got him on speed-dial you might be all right," Hector said, as he reached for the cookie tin again. "By Christ, Ev, these are the best Nanaimo bars you've ever made."

Hector figured he wouldn't get a smack this time if he gave his wife a compliment and he was right. Cleo remembered Jamie and the coffee in bed this morning. He got it from somewhere.

"I'll water it every day, Hec, I promise." Cleo said. "Twice a day if I have to." If Joe found out the tree was still up, that would be something else to deal with.

"How was supper with Fran and Andrew last night?" Evelyn was on her feet already, clearing away the teapot and spoons, the sugar dish, putting the milk back in the fridge. Four spoons and one teapot were dirty and she started to fill the sink with hot soapy water, glancing back at the table at their half-full mugs to see if she could take any.

Cleo willed Jamie to keep quiet about Fran's pregnancy, but she had a better chance of getting Evelyn to leave the dishes.

“They’re excellent.” Jamie looked at Cleo. She shook her head and opened her eyes wide at him, but it was too late.

“They’re pregnant.” He looked like a kid ruining a birthday by saying what the present is.

Evelyn put her hand over her mouth and instantly welled up. Hector said, “Well. Now.”

“Guys, guys, we’re not supposed to know,” Cleo jumped in, knowing what was coming next. “It’s really early days, we don’t even know who knows yet.”

“Oh my, oh my, oh my,” said Evelyn and she sat back down at the table. “And after all their troubles, we never even thought they’d make it, poor souls. How wonderful.” When she brought her tea to her lips, her hand was shaking.

Cleo marvelled at how someone could be called a poor soul for having an affair. She wished Jamie were sitting next to her so she could step on his foot or punch him in the arm.

“Just imagine if you two had a youngster around the same time,” said Hector, slapping Jamie on the back. “Get on that now, and they’ll be able to go to kindergarten together.”

That had taken thirty seconds.

“I don’t know, Hec b’y,” Cleo jumped in. “At the rate we’re going, one will be in high school before the other one’s on solid food.”

And Hector roared with laughter. Evelyn laughed, too, and her eyes were sparkly with tears and dreams of future grandchildren. Like she didn’t have five already to keep herself occupied.

solo cheese party

CLEO POKED AROUND IN THE FRIDGE WHILE HALF A FROZEN baguette heated in the oven. She found some leftover pâté in the cheese drawer, smelled it, and put it on a plate with a chunk of brie that had survived the holidays. Jamie came downstairs dressed in a sweater and jeans.

"Why are you dressed? We're having a cheese party," Cleo said. She poured some oil and balsamic in a small bowl and sniffed the olive oil bottle before putting the cap back on. It smelled like being on a whitewashed patio in Greece, all fruity and sunny and warm. Cleo was so far away from a place like that she could've sat down on the kitchen floor and cried.

"I have to go to the office for a couple hours," Jamie said.

"Noooo, don't be silly. It'll be busy enough on Monday morning, wait and start everything then."

"Peter just emailed—they're sending me to New Brunswick on Tuesday. If I get in a few hours tonight I won't have to go in tomorrow."

"Fuck Peter and fuck New Brunswick."

"Save me some cheese?"

"No way."

"Let's have a baby."

"Can I finish my cheese first?

"Cleo."

"But it's a double-cream brie."

Jamie shoved his hands in the pockets of his jeans and leaned against the kitchen counter. Cleo opened the oven door to check the baguette. She squeezed it and heard it crackle between her fingers, then grabbed it and tossed it on top of the stove before it burned her fingers.

"You know we have to talk about this," he said.

"I know."

"We can talk about this?"

"We can. We totally can. I thought you were going to the office, though."

"I am, but you know. Later tonight or tomorrow."

"Okay. I'll pencil you in. Now can I have my cheese?"

Jamie kissed her forehead and headed to the living room, grabbing his winter jacket off the back of the couch.

"I love you, you know." He yelled it at her from the porch as he was putting on his boots.

"You too."

Cleo opened the fridge and prayed for booze. She found half a bottle of Pinot Grigio.

sheep

"ARE YOU ONLY BRINGING THIS UP NOW BECAUSE OF ANDREW and Fran? After five years?"

It was Sunday morning and they were having coffee on the couch. Cleo had snuck in Baileys when Jamie wasn't looking. He always laughed and called her an alcoholic when she put Baileys in her coffee, so she started doing it when he wasn't looking. Which probably made her one step closer to becoming an alcoholic. So really it would be his fault if that ever happened.

"Of course not," Jamie said. "You don't just decide to have a baby because someone else has one."

"Oh God, you're kidding me!" Cleo laughed so hard she snorted. "Sooo many people do that. Everybody does that. It's what the whole baby industry is built on. That's why kids are so messed up. Most of them are the logical next step after marriage and then the parents realize, holy shit we're terrible at this and we'd rather be on safari." Cleo drained the rest of her coffee and went into the kitchen to get some more. Jamie couldn't see her from where she stood at the counter. She poured in a huge glug of Baileys.

"You are the most cynical person I know," Jamie called after her.

"It's why you love me," she yelled back.

"If our parents thought like you did, we wouldn't even be here."

"If my parents thought like I did, my mother would still be living in Paris and I would be quite pleased for her."

"You wouldn't exist, how could you be pleased for her."

"Stop nitpicking."

"You can't tell me babies haven't crossed your mind," Jamie said.

"Every night. I count them like sheep to fall asleep."

"Can I just get you to be serious for one goddamn second."

Cleo carried the coffee back to the living room and sat back down.

"Yes."

"First off, if we get pregnant, we'll have to get a new place," said Jamie.

"Why?"

"Cleo."

"What? I'm serious! Why? We've got three bedrooms. We'd be three people. What's the problem with the house? And what's this 'we' getting pregnant thing you're talking about?"

"Don't you want a backyard? Lots of room for the kids to run around and stuff?"

"Holy shit, *kids*? With an 's'?"

"Well, you can't just have one."

"Why the hell not?"

"It would be kinda sad for it to not have a brother or sister."

"So, you're saying you're afraid it would be a fucked-up only child like me?"

"Well, yeah."

"You sound like someone's sixty-year-old aunt at Thanksgiving dinner," Cleo said. "'Oh my, sin for you, only having the one youngster.' I had Maisie and Joe all to myself and it was great. It's okay for a kid to grow up on its own, you know. You just need to socialize it a little better so it knows how to share its toys and shit."

"Look, I'm only saying I grew up with a sibling, and as messed up as it was when Krista got pregnant, Jonathan was like a baby brother, and having a houseful was nice."

Cleo had never once admitted to him that when she was young she'd always wanted a houseful like that.

"I see what you're getting at," she said. "Knocking me up is the easiest way to get off-street parking with a shed and a backyard."

"No!" He nudged her leg without looking at her. "Okay, maybe a little."

"I knew it."

"But don't you think we should look into moving now instead of when you're pregnant?"

"If Jamie, *if* I get pregnant. We haven't even pulled the goalie yet, calm the frig down."

Jamie's eyebrows shot up. Cleo knew she was being too harsh. She took a breath and started again.

"I have to see my doctor before I do anything."

"What for?"

"It's just . . . different when you're older."

"Babe, lots of women—"

"I'm not lots of women, Jamie."

"I know, but chances are it will all be okay."

"And it might not. There's always a chance it might not be, at any age. You know that, right?" She looked right at him and her eyes were serious for the first time all morning. He looked surprised but seemed to take what he could get.

"Okay. But you'll make an appointment? Just to chat with her or whatever?"

"I will. I promise." Cleo relaxed in the temporary finality of the discussion.

Jamie leaned his head back on the couch and looked at the ceiling.

"But you'd want a new place, right? If it happens?"

"Um . . ." Cleo looked around like she was doing a quick appraisal, having made up her mind anyway. "We'd be fine here, I think. There's lots of parks and stuff and we could walk everywhere."

"I don't want to raise a kid downtown."

"Well, well. Will you look at that. I don't want to raise a kid in the suburbs. We're doing *great*. Shall we start picking names?"

"Cleo, it's safer, the schools are better—"

"All right, Mr. Clarenville, downtown is just as safe, if not safer than living in the suburbs. A kid should be downtown so it can *see* all the weird stuff. We can't keep them from knowing there's bad in the world and I don't want them being afraid of everything. Like Donna, when she comes over for dinner and I have to walk her to her car when she leaves."

"Babe, Donna can't help it. She's from Cowan Heights."

"And I don't want to get in the car and drive twenty minutes to get a loaf of bread. You're an engineer, didn't you do at least one class on the dangers of urban sprawl?"

Jamie laughed, but Cleo knew he was getting tired of this. Something in him was shifting and getting serious.

"Maybe a bigger place, someday," she said, relenting a little. "But no beige neighbourhoods, none of these Sherwood-Glenwood-Pineview Terrace places where a kid's not allowed to dribble a basketball."

She reached across him and grabbed the remote from the end table, turning on the television to indicate the discussion was over.

"Fine. I give up," Jamie said.

"Fine. You should. Do you know how many people would be living in this house if we were in Cambodia?"

"You're going to tell me more than three."

"Like, probably seventeen."

Cleo pushed his feet off the coffee table.

"This would be a bed for a toddler," she said. "Have some respect."

might as well

St. John's dished out the shittiest weather imaginable, but Cleo was grateful for being able to walk to the office. She locked the front door and turned into the sleety wind and it was like a thousand tiny needles in the face. The light was dull and the sky stretched out grey, not a hint of sun burning through the clouds clustered in the Narrows.

There was a reason the women who commuted to work had the best hair and makeup and this was it, Cleo thought. By the time she got to the corner of Prospect and Holloway, the small bit of hair sticking out from under her winter hat was lashed to her face and her mascara trailed down her cheeks.

On days like this Cleo sometimes imagined that commute from Topsail or Paradise. Black leather gloves on the steering wheel of an SUV, cursing the traffic at eight in the morning on the Outer Ring Road, fighting for a parking spot downtown. One of her co-workers paid two hundred dollars a month for a coveted spot in the parking garage at Atlantic Place. Cleo would meet her in line at Starbucks on miserable mornings, Melissa in a dry, form-fitting goose-down jacket, meticulously straightened and expensively highlighted hair down to her chest. Tight black jeans tucked into high-heeled leather boots. She would lift her face from her iPhone and chirp, "Terrible day out there!" when Cleo tromped in with her full-length coat and wet mascara. If the weather was this hard on Cleo's makeup job, she couldn't imagine what it would do to the orange line of foundation around Melissa's face.

Cleo started down the hill on the sidewalk but it was a perfect, icy sheet of glass all the way to Duckworth, so she hopped up in the snowbank and trudged down the rest of Holloway. The snow was piled high but the rain had made a frozen crust on top, so every step was crunchy. This is how it must have felt to live here two hundred years ago: raw and wet and hopeless.

If she managed to get knocked up, Cleo hoped to avoid November to April. She thought about being pregnant and trying to navigate icy streets and sidewalks in winter weather. It would have to happen in the next couple of months if she wanted to avoid a pregnant winter. But then she would have to cart an infant around in blizzards. Perfect.

She was jumping too far ahead, especially considering it might never happen. Who went off the pill at thirty-eight and got knocked up right away? People like Fran, that's who. Couples with crumbling marriages who had babies as a last-ditch effort to fix things. Cleo knew enough about babies to know they didn't fix things. They only amplified the worst in people.

Cleo remembered a talk-show episode she saw years ago, with a panel of women in their thirties who were all trying to conceive. They'd waited to start families because they'd put their careers first. All of them had these fabulous jobs as doctors, lawyers, business-women. One woman had negotiated peace deals for the United Nations. Then they'd tried to get pregnant and couldn't. They had these big houses with their husbands and everyone had planned nurseries and baby names and then, nothing. A fertility specialist was sitting on stage with them and was sympathetic and speaking in soft tones and revealed to the audience that, by the way and for your information, fertility is at its peak when a woman is twenty-seven and then drops dramatically with every passing year. The women were crying and their husbands were with them and would pass them tissues and hold their hands or knees and rub their backs.

Cleo thought of some of those husbands now, with their second wives and piles of youngsters, vacationing in the Bahamas while their first wives lived alone in apartments with a cat or two and book club Sunday afternoons. That didn't sound like a half-bad deal to Cleo. She would have a cat if Jamie wasn't allergic and she'd be in a book club, too, if any of her friends were into it. But these women, their weeping faces on national television, life plans crumbling in front of a studio audience, Cleo had never forgotten that. She felt bad for the women, but she was smug and worldly and figured there were no babies in her future. Certainly no falling desperately in love with a tall redhead from Clarenville.

She reached the steps of Atlantic Place and stomped her boots and wiped the wet snow off the arms of her winter jacket before heading inside. Maybe that UN peace negotiator had been smug and worldly in her twenties, too. But if your job were that important, wouldn't you feel some kind of duty to keep at it instead of bringing another kid into the world?

Cleo's first meeting of the day was a brainstorming session about how to sell hot dog buns.

She might as well go ahead and get knocked up.

starting right now

Cleo sat at her cubicle and dialled the doctor's office. It was normally a good two-week wait to get in, but there'd been a cancellation at the last minute and she managed to schedule an appointment for the next morning. If she threw out some good ideas at the hot dog meeting in a half-hour, it wouldn't be a huge deal to miss tomorrow's session. Robert was an easygoing boss, so she wouldn't have to tell him it was for a pap smear. She wouldn't have to tell him that she and Jamie had had the talk and she needed to find out if her bits were still working.

Nancy came through the glass doors of the office, a jar of tea in one hand, tearing off her scarf with the other and throwing it on her desk. She didn't bother to pick it up when it slithered to the floor.

"Are you busting with genius ideas for the bun meeting?" Nancy asked, taking off her sopping wet coat and hanging it off the back of her chair. She took a hairband off her wrist and twisted her curly black hair into a high, messy bun.

"Naturally. There were no sugarplums dancing in my head over Christmas, only buns."

"How was your weekend?"

"Fairly eventful."

"Oooooh, do tell. First Monday back after Christmas, you need to entertain me so I don't kill myself and leave Doug and Mack to fend for themselves."

Nancy came around to Cleo's cubicle and perched on the desk.

"Proceed." Nancy sipped her tea from a Mason jar wrapped in a hand-knit tea cozy. Melissa had made fun of it once at a staff meeting, calling her "Nan" and asking if she needed a cane to go with her tea. Nancy had whipped around and said, "You need a shoehorn to get out of those slut boots?" Melissa's mouth had dropped open and Nancy had winked at her just as Robert had walked in the room.

"We had supper at Fran and Andrew's the other night. Fran's pregnant."

"Jesus fucking Christ. Is it Andrew's?"

"I'm assuming yes. Jamie's over the moon and thinks they'll magically turn into the Cleavers."

"And your thoughts?"

"We'll see what happens when she gets her first stretch mark."

"Or when she has to change her first diaper full of liquid poo. Poor Andrew."

"I know."

"God, they are completely screwed." Nancy shook her head and sipped her tea.

Cleo sat up out of her chair and looked around. She could see Rishi, her cubicle neighbour, in the office kitchen making a pot of coffee. She might have enough time to dish to Nancy before he was done. There would be no baby talk with Rishi around or the whole office would start planning Cleo's shower. She kept her eyes on the kitchen window as she sat back down and lowered her voice.

"Jamie and I had the talk."

"It's about time, Grandma," Nancy whispered back. She noticed Rishi and brought her head in a bit closer. "How'd it go?"

"Good? I guess? I don't know. Jamie's all clucky and starry-eyed.

Or at least he was when we left Andrew and Fran's. He's already talking about two kids and moving to the suburbs, like it's going to be that easy for me to get pregnant. I think he's just getting old and wants a shed."

"You can still have a shed and live close to downtown."

"That's what I keep trying to tell him. And I love our little house, you know? I'd never want to leave, even on the off chance there was a kid."

"I'm glad to hear you're being practical about it."

"Oh my God, of course," Cleo said, lowering her voice to a whisper. "Especially after all that bullshit you went through."

"Happy to have rubbed off on someone." Nancy raised her tea-cozied jar in the air.

"Besides, I'd want a downtown kid. Like, a saucy, lippy kid who's not afraid of anything. Not one who turns out to be an arsonist or anything, just one who's tough."

Nancy took Cleo's hand and squeezed it.

"Listen, you're thinking too far ahead. You've just had the talk, you're freaked out, but Cleo, if you don't relax starting right now, sister, you are fucked."

No one but Nancy would say this to her. Nancy would never be flowery about conception or babies. Any other best friend would be picking out names by now.

"I know, I know, you're right. I don't want this to be a big deal. I don't want people to know we're thinking about trying or anything. Evelyn and Hector are bad enough as it is. And I love Jamie but I don't really trust him not to drop it into a conversation, you know? God, that sounds terrible, I trust him, but you know what I mean. He doesn't get that pregnancy has to be a secret for a while."

"Doug learned his lesson the hard way when I got pregnant the first time. I told him fine, tell everyone but if anything happens you are one hundred per cent responsible for being the bearer of bad news and making sure no one talks to me about it. The first batch of phone calls after miscarriage number one fixed his ass pretty quick."

The night Nancy called her from the hospital, Cleo had no idea who it was. In twenty years of knowing her, Cleo had never heard Nancy cry like that. It was like a kid hearing their dad hysterically weeping for the first time; it was never supposed to happen. That's how it was with Nancy and the first miscarriage. Cleo had jumped out of bed so fast Jamie thought something was wrong with Maisie or Joe. "Nancy's having a miscarriage," she said, and she threw the blankets over him and ran to get dressed. She packed an electric blanket and a bottle of gin and drove to Doug and Nancy's house, realizing when she arrived she'd forgotten her emergency key, so she sat on the front steps and waited for them to get home from the hospital. Cleo made up a bed for herself on the couch and lay awake all night, listening to Nancy weep in between trips to the bathroom. The second miscarriage was worse. During the third pregnancy with Mack, Nancy was too scared to be excited. "Every day I'm not bleeding is a good one," she used to say. Cleo would stay in with her on Saturday nights and they'd watch movies. They ate mint-chip ice cream and ordered vegetarian pizza because the smell of meat made Nancy sick. Cleo would lean down close to Nancy's belly and whisper in a cartoon voice, "*Juuuust staaaay in*."

"I have to pee before the meeting starts," Nancy said, and she stood up off the desk. "Have you had a chat with your doctor yet?"

"Nope, the appointment's tomorrow morning. I haven't run it by Robert yet, but it shouldn't be a problem."

"Oh God, he won't care. Drop the pap smear bomb if you have to and he'll run screaming through the office like his hair's on fire."

Rishi came out of the kitchen with a coffee cup in his hand, just in time to hear what Nancy said.

"Uhhh. Morning ladies. Forgot the sugar." He turned around and went back to the kitchen.

"See?" Nancy said, and she headed off to the washroom.

Cleo walked down the hall on the way to the meeting and stopped to knock on the glass wall of Robert's office. He looked up and smiled and gestured with his head for her to come in.

"Well, hello Miss Cleo. How was your Christmas? Or your holiday, or whatever the hell HR tells me I'm supposed to say to you."

"Full of cheese and booze."

"Ah, so, exactly how it's meant to be then, that's good to hear."

"Yours?"

"Not enough cheese and booze, and too many relatives, I'm afraid."

"Yeah, I didn't completely escape that part either. I'm trying to convince Jamie to go down south next year but I think it would kill his mother."

"If we were smart we'd avoid the racket all together. What can I do for you this morning?" Robert crossed his arms and leaned back in his chair. Not in a boss sort of way, but in the way a favourite uncle settles in an easy chair after a huge helping of Sunday dinner. His cellphone vibrated, hidden somewhere on his desk under a pile of file folders, and he didn't bother to glance down.

"I had to make a last-minute doctor's appointment and the only time they could squeeze me in was nine o'clock tomorrow morning. If I do some prep and email it to you tonight, can I come in a bit late tomorrow? I know it's my first day back and I'm already asking favours, so feel free to be disgruntled."

"Not a problem. Everything okay?"

"Yep, everything's fine. It shouldn't take too long, I could be back as early as ten depending on the wait."

"Well, you know what you have to do if that's the case."

"Bring donuts."

"You're a good woman, Cleo Best."

"Thanks, Robert."

"See you inside, dear."

calm and clear

It was seven when Cleo finally decided to pack up and leave the office. She worked better when the place was nearly empty. It would be different if she had a room surrounded by glass like Robert did. The cubicles were a distraction and most days it was too noisy to think.

The best thing to come out of the brainstorming session that morning was "Between Two Buns: The Story of a Wiener." Robert had blamed the lack of workable ideas on Christmas turkey–brain and concluded the meeting by saying, "You're my top team, and I'm expecting some top ideas tomorrow." Cleo had filed that away and was working on a storyboard with a "Top Bun" theme. She'd never thought she'd be paying the mortgage by sketching wieners in fighter pilot uniforms.

"Could be worse, could be a coal miner," she said to herself.

She grabbed her coat and the rest of her gear and walked down the row of cubicles, waving goodnight to Melissa. She stayed late most nights like Cleo did, but they were on opposite ends of the room. They could work separately and silently without the obligation of having to keep sporadic conversation going with a person in the next cubicle.

Cleo suspected Melissa's long hours had something to do with the shitty boyfriend she lived with. They'd recently bought a house in a brand-new subdivision near Octagon Pond, high on the hill of a giant gravel pit, sod for the lawn not even laid down yet. Melissa had shown Cleo the pictures on her phone a few days after she'd moved in and Cleo had oohed and aahed and told her how much she loved the giant island in the open-concept kitchen. The kitchen Trevor had paid for with whatever money was left after a few years of hookers and cocaine in Fort Mac.

Melissa had her forehead in one hand and the phone to her ear in the other, but she looked up long enough to give a quick wave back, and long enough for Cleo to notice mascara and orange foundation in streaks down her face. She looked worse than Cleo had, coming in out of the sleet hours earlier.

Cleo was grateful in that moment for the very modest butcher block in her little kitchen. And for Jamie. Jamie, who smoked pot with Andrew on their camping trips, and who always said that sex workers made him "so sad because most of them were single moms from broken homes just trying to feed their kids."

The sleet had stopped and the sky had calmed and cleared. It was cold and pleasant and Cleo took her time walking home. The sidewalks on Water Street had been plowed and salted and even with the lights of the city you could see the stars over Signal Hill and the Narrows.

She got to the corner of Prescott and Duckworth and there was a smell off the harbour, but it smelled like it should, not like when they used to pump sewage into it. When Cleo was a student she lived in a little apartment in the Battery with her friend Jake, and every time he went to the bathroom he'd say, "Time to feed the gulls!" They lived in that spot for three years, and every New Year's Day they would bundle up in blankets and hats and sit out on their little patio overlooking the harbour. Other people drove to Cape Spear to welcome the sunrise on the first day of the year. Cleo and Jake nursed hangovers with Baileys and coffee and smoked draws, laughing at the birds circling over the shit bubble.

But there was something about the smell now that reminded Cleo of her childhood summers in Wesleyville with Joe's family. The smell was warm and clean, like the coiled rope in her step-grandfather's store. It made Cleo feel a strange mix of sadness and joy. She stopped walking up the hill to turn around and breathe deep to try and get it back but it was gone.

Cleo turned up the thermostat in the kitchen and threw her purse on the table. She ran upstairs to find her slippers and put on a cardigan and when she came back down there was a text from Jamie.

-Hey hey how's you?

She went to the fridge and poured the last of a bottle of Chardonnay in a small tumbler before she texted back.

-Good, home now was about to text. What's supper plan?

-Ended up at the Duke with Andrew. Couple pints in about to get fish and chips. Solo projects for supper?

-Yep no worries. Everything ok with Andrew?

-Totally, we're just catching up, won't be too late

-I hope you're on light beer, you're flying tomorrow ;)

-Yep. Guinness. haha

-Uh oh.

-Haha I'm good babe, promise. You want me to bring you home fish and chips?

-That's okay, gonna eat leftovers.

-Okay, text me if you change your mind, kitchen closes in 30. See you soon xo

-xx

Jamie had dropped off the car after work but she was too lazy to go out and get a bottle of wine. She'd have to nurse this last glass.

the only thing

THE TEMPERATURE HAD DROPPED A GOOD TEN DEGREES SINCE Cleo had walked home from work and the bed was cold without Jamie. She'd closed the door to their room and turned the space heater on a half-hour ago, but it did nothing to help. She cursed and jumped out of bed to find an extra pair of wool socks and saw Jamie's hoodie hanging off the open closet door.

"Fuck it."

She put it on, slinging the hood over her head, and sat down on the edge of the bed to pull the wool socks on over the pair she was already wearing. She crawled back under the covers and grabbed her book off the nightstand. It was pointless for her to try and sleep when Jamie wasn't home yet. He'd sent a text an hour ago saying he was on his way home, but it wouldn't have been hard for Andrew to convince him to stay for another pint. Cleo couldn't blame Andrew for that. If a regular Fran was hard enough to go home to, a pregnant one must be unbearable.

Whatever happened, Andrew would be a great father. He'd wanted kids for years but Fran wanted nothing to do with them. Magically, she was convinced right after the affair. Probably to lock Andrew in before he had changed his mind about their marriage. Fran hadn't worked in years and Andrew did well for himself as a criminal defence attorney. In all likelihood she was terrified of losing the house on Long Pond Road and their five-bedroom "cabin" on Thorburn Lake. Andrew would never leave her with a baby on the way; he was too good a man for that.

She heard Jamie come in the front door and could tell by the sound of his boots coming off in the porch he was drunk. Then it was the kitchen tap running and glasses clinking in the cupboard. There was a loud clang like a glass hitting the counter and Jamie swore but she didn't hear anything break. Five minutes later his sock feet were coming up the stairs, thudding softly and slowly like he was trying not to wake her. Cleo heard him use the bathroom but he didn't brush his teeth, confirming his level of drunkenness. Jamie had a fastidious before-bedtime routine that included flossing, brushing, and gargling, all of which he ignored when he'd had a few drinks. The bedroom door opened and it creaked in the cold and Jamie said, "fuck," under his breath, or what he thought was under his breath.

"It's okay, I'm awake."

"Aww, fuck. Sorry babe, I'm so sorry, I am such a drunk."

"You didn't wake me, I wasn't asleep."

Jamie stripped down to his underwear but kept his socks on and crawled under the covers. He spooned himself around her, putting one hand under her hoodie and T-shirt and moving it up to her bare breast. Cleo shrieked when thc cold hit her and her nipple hardened instantly.

"Oh, hello nipple," Jamie said, and nuzzled the back of her neck.

Cleo laughed at him and grabbed his hand to move it out from under her shirt. She tucked it between her pyjama-bottomed legs to try and warm it up, and she could still feel the cold of his hand on her thighs through the flannel.

"You're freezing. Holy shit, did you walk home?"

"Yep, it's kinda nice out."

"You're insane, it's minus twenty. Did you leave the taps in the kitchen running a little?"

"Yes."

"Are you sure?"

"No. I am not."

Cleo made a move to get out of bed but Jamie wouldn't take his hand from between her thighs and locked her in like he was practising a wrestling move.

"It's okay babe, it'll be fine, it's not that cold out."

"Jamie, our pipes froze last year in March when it was minus ten."

"Okay, okay, I'll do it. I'll flick on the taps in the bathroom, that'll be fine."

He unwrapped himself from Cleo and jumped from the bed like a child, running to the bathroom, turning on the taps, and running back to bed, all in under ten seconds.

"Hi."

He was on top of her now, and the drunk weight of him made her laugh again, even though she could barely breathe. She kept him there, wrapping her arms around his back and squeezing. He was the only thing that kept her warm on nights as cold as this.

"I made a doctor's appointment for tomorrow morning. What time is your flight? You know, the one you'll be incredibly hungover for?"

"Nine. And I'll be just fine, sank-you bery much." He slurred like he was drunker than he was and he licked Cleo's face from chin to forehead.

"You are so gross."

"Give me a lift or should I hop in a cab?"

"No, that's perfect timing. I can drop you and head straight to the clinic."

Jamie rolled off her and onto his side. He pulled Cleo in close to his face and she could smell Guinness and cigarettes and it wasn't unpleasant. It smelled like when they first started dating, when everything was booze and smokes and sex.

"You feeling okay about it all?" He struggled to pull his hoodie off her, and it stuck for a second around her head before he managed to get it free and throw it on the floor.

"Yeah, for sure. It's just a chat basically, before we make any drastic decisions."

"What do you mean drastic decisions? It's only going off the pill."

"Jamie, I've had hormones coursing through my veins for almost twenty years. There is a remote possibility things might be different when that all gets taken away. Because you know, historically, women don't deal well with massive hormonal changes."

"Cleo, it'll totally be fine. Don't get all worst-case scenario on me." He kissed her on the mouth full and slow, and she felt him go hard against her, but she pulled away.

"You mean worst-case scenario like maybe I'll get fat and grow a moustache."

"I totally dig a moustache."

Jamie kissed her again, harder this time, and he pulled her hips into his. Cleo kissed him back and then stopped and took his face between her two hands.

"Not allowed."

"What? What do you mean?" He put his hands into her pyjama pants and underwear and grabbed her behind and squeezed and now his hands were so warm.

"I'm getting a pap smear and you're not supposed to have sex twenty-four hours beforehand."

"Why not? That is the worst rule of all humanity." He was kissing down her neck and trying to lift her T-shirt up over her back.

"It needs to be . . . you know, clear sailing down there. Not . . . murky or anything. Jesus, I don't know. It's just the rule."

Jamie stopped kissing her and pulled his head back.

"But what if the plane crashes and the last moment we have is you telling me we're not allowed to have sex?"

"Don't say that, don't you dare say that, you know that freaks me out." She grabbed his face again but more serious this time. "Listen, this is for you, too. I have to make sure everything's good before, you know, before we start trying or whatever."

This sobered Jamie a little and he turned Cleo on her back and put his face over hers.

"Okay, I know. I know, I'm sorry. I get it. And I totally support you in this, I promise. You want me to go down on you?"

He started kissing over her clothes, trailing down her stomach, lifting her T-shirt to lick around her belly button in a small, neat circle. Cleo grabbed him by the head and pulled him up. She flipped him over and now he was on his back, Cleo holding herself over him, propped up on her hands.

"Lie back," she said, and she kissed her way down his chest.

airport baby

Cleo pulled up to the curb near Departures. She left the car running and put the gearshift in park, reaching for the door to get out.

"No, no, stay in the car, it's too cold. I'll grab my suitcase from the trunk." Jamie kissed her and his breath was nice, like spearmint gum and toothpaste and not like hangover at all.

"I hope everything's okay in Vagistan."

"Get out!" Cleo laughed. "Get out, you're going to miss your flight."

"Remember, the only one allowed across the border while I'm gone is your lady-doctor, don't forget that."

"All right, 1950s man who says things like 'lady-doctor.'"

"I'm serious, the troops will be home in thirty-six hours with fresh supplies."

"Safe travels, weirdo. Text me when you land."

"I will." Jamie kissed her again. "I love you."

"I love you, too."

He got out of the car and grabbed his suitcase, closing the trunk and knocking on it twice. He waved at Cleo and headed towards the entrance.

Cleo was about to pull away from the curb but she put the car back in park and pressed the button for the passenger-side window instead. Struck again by the memory of her heart beating fast against a photo of her father tucked in the front pocket of her shirt, in a plane that felt like it was falling from the sky. She never left the airport without thinking about that.

"Hey. I'm gonna come in."

Jamie turned at the sound of her voice, the automatic door open and waiting behind him.

"You don't have to, you'll be late for your appointment."

"I've got some time. It just feels shitty this morning to dump you on the sidewalk."

"Is this because you feel bad for not putting out last night and you're afraid my plane's going to crash?"

"I'm going to park the car, I'll meet you in there. And if anyone hears you say that here they're going to arrest you."

"Okay, I'll meet you in the bathroom. Quickie before we go." He gave Cleo a thumbs up and walked through the open door.

Cleo pulled into the short-term parking and cursed when she had to open the car door to lean out far enough to reach the ticket from the automated machine. Her arms were too short, or she never pulled in close enough, she could never tell which.

She parked the car and made her way back to the terminal. Jamie was at the last airline kiosk, a diaper bag slung over his shoulder and a baby in his arms. Even from a couple of counters away, Cleo could see the long, shiny string of drool trailing from the baby's mouth and attaching itself to the sleeve of Jamie's winter jacket. There was a flustered woman standing in front of him, in what looked to be heavy negotiations with the clerk. Two bags were open on the floor next to an empty stroller, and the woman bent to switch items from one suitcase to the next.

Cleo sidled up next to Jamie.

"That didn't take long," she said. "I never took you for one of those dudes who has a second family on the side."

"Well, you had to find out sooner or later."

When she caught sight of Cleo, the baby burst into tears.

"This is Rosie," Jamie said. "And her mom, Paula. I just volunteered to be the baby bouncer."

"Hi." The red-faced woman looked up from the floor at Cleo. "Your husband is very lovely. Rosie was having a fit in her stroller. My ex wasn't ever this useful."

"Thanks," Cleo said. "But he's not . . . I mean, he is, I guess. Can I help with anything?" She marvelled at how Jamie had saved the day in the few minutes it had taken to park the car. "I don't think the baby's too fussy about me, but I have two free hands if you need."

"No, that's okay." Paula was taking a stack of tiny pyjamas from one suitcase and stuffing them in the other. "One suitcase is overweight and I have to even them out or they're going to charge me a hundred bucks or something."

The woman behind the counter smiled tightly at Cleo. Jamie bounced the baby up and down, and she giggled and put her hands on his face. If anyone were looking they would think Jamie and Paula were a couple and Cleo was just some woman in line. The baby was gorgeous. So was Paula. She had the most beautiful hair Cleo had ever seen. It was like thick dark chocolate, gathered together at the nape of her neck and trickling in waves down her back. She looked so fit for someone who'd had a baby, what, five, maybe six months ago? Cleo was acutely aware of how snug her jeans felt after all the Christmas cheese.

"Next please!" the man at the next counter over called out to Cleo.

"Oh, that's okay, I'm with him." She pointed at Jamie, who was still bouncing the baby up and down and singing "The Wheels on the Bus."

The clerk cocked his head and gave Cleo a look before motioning to the person behind her.

"Okay, well clearly you've got your hands full. I'm gonna go. Have a safe flight," Cleo said. She stood with her hands in her jacket pockets, a little afraid to hug her own boyfriend and set the child off again.

"I will. I'll text you when I land." Jamie leaned in for a kiss, still holding the baby, the sweet-smelling scent of her head passing under Cleo's nose.

ice cream

It was the worst turbulence Cleo had ever experienced. She was a teenager and had been on a plane maybe a half-dozen times in her life before this flight to Paris, so that was shitty luck. This kind of thing was only supposed to happen to businessmen who travelled for work once or twice a week.

The plane had started to shake just after they'd served the meal. Some kind of chicken Kiev thing, and Cleo was disappointed it wasn't French. The first few bites were good but then the turbulence got really bad. Cleo's face got hot and her hands started to shake a little but she kept on eating.

The rest of the plane seemed normal so everything would be okay, she knew. Then the flight attendants were ordered to their seats to be strapped in, and things got really bad. There was a lurch so big and sudden the man sitting next to Cleo covered his face with both hands and the woman sitting across the aisle started to cry. Food and glasses and cutlery flew up in the air and smashed back down on trays and spilled onto the floor. The woman in front of the crying woman had rosary beads in her hand and her lips and fingers were moving, really calm with her eyes closed. It made Cleo think of Nalfie and how this was her worst fear come to life and she would never recover. This plane would kill Cleo and then it would kill her grandmother shortly after.

Cleo looked down at her meal. What was left of the chicken had been lobbed into the aisle with the turbulence, but there was a mini tub of ice cream still on the tray. She couldn't believe this was the first time she'd ever been served ice cream on a plane and now they were going to crash.

Five more minutes of armrest-gripping panic and the skies calmed. Everyone started breathing normally, and chuckling about how they all thought they were going to die a few moments earlier. The pilot came over the intercom and apologized and made some shitty joke about having eaten some bad French cheese. The flight attendants unstrapped themselves and started to clean up the remnants of chicken Kiev from the aisles. Cleo stared into space and waited for her heart to slow down.

She pulled into the parking lot of the clinic ten minutes early, before they were even open. Jamie would be in the air soon. There would certainly be no ice cream, hopefully no turbulence, or anyone falling from the sky. Planes didn't crash with babies on board, right?

They did. Having a baby was just something else that could be taken from you in an instant. Even if you did everything right.

She turned off the car and waited in the cold until she saw the receptionist unlock the front door.

flathead

CLEO SAT ON THE EXAMINING TABLE IN HER DOCTOR'S OFFICE; the scratchy white paper crinkled under her when she shifted to get more comfortable. Two years ago, Dr. Connors had replaced Cleo's family physician of thirty years, and when she met the new doctor it was the first time in her life Cleo had ever truly felt old. Older than any wrinkle or grey hair had ever made her feel. Seeing a beautiful young woman walk into a room, a woman who was younger and smarter, who was about to put a speculum in you, did that kind of thing to a person. Made you think about your own mortality.

On the upside, Cleo liked to think she would die before Dr. Connors retired. That would at least save her the hassle of finding a new family physician.

Cleo bit her bottom lip, took deep breaths, and swung her bare legs. She looked at the stirrups at the end of the table with their pink woollen covers. After years of pap smears she still wasn't sure if she was meant to take her socks off.

There was a poster with a blue-eyed baby lying on its stomach and staring into the camera, under a giant headline that read "PREVENT BABY FLATHEAD." Cleo panicked a little because she was here to talk about babies and she didn't even know something like baby flathead existed. Her baby would probably have the flattest head ever and she wouldn't even know it. Baby Flathead sounded like some kind of superhero. Dr. Connors walked into the examination room.

"Hi there. What's so funny?" She looked around like she expected to see someone else in the room.

"Baby Flathead," said Cleo, pointing at the poster. "He sounds like a superhero. Or I guess he'd be the villain because we're trying to prevent him."

Dr. Connors looked puzzled but smiled kindly before sitting down and bringing up Cleo's file on the computer.

"So, we're here for our annual pelvic exam and birth control refill?"

"Yes! 'Tis the season. And, well, no. Yes and no. Yes for the pelvic and no for the pills." Cleo started to blush, like she did when she went through customs because she was feeling guilty, even though she'd done nothing wrong.

"Any particular reason you're going off the pill?"

Cleo couldn't believe she was going to have to spell this out for someone who'd gone to university for twelve years.

"No, not really. I mean, I'm getting up there and I've been on the pill for almost twenty years so . . . so, I figured, you know, might be time to . . . stop. Stop taking it."

"You're probably fine for another few years if you like. Unless of course you're trying for a baby, in which case we should chat."

Cleo's blush deepened and she exhaled loudly through her mouth.

"Yes, well. Yeah. Let's. Okay."

Dr. Connors smiled in that kind way again.

"Let's do the exam first, I'll see how things are looking, and we'll go from there?"

"Sounds good! Let's do it. Go team."

Dr. Connors snapped off her gloves and rolled the wheely chair back to the computer.

"Everything looks good. We'll call you if the test shows anything abnormal."

"I passed!" Cleo swung her legs around and sat up on the examining table, pulling the white paper back over her bottom half.

"So, you and your partner are talking about having a baby." Dr. Connors finished typing. She grabbed a pen and clicked it several times and swung the chair around to look at Cleo.

Cleo hated the word "partner." It sounded like she was sleeping with the person she was opening a restaurant with.

"Yes. Well, it's more like, let's go off the pill and see what happens. We're pretty laid-back about the whole thing. I know my eggs are thirty-eight years old, so I've accepted it might not happen. I just wanted to run it by you because don't I have to take vitamins or something?"

Now that those first words were out, Cleo started to relax. This felt okay. She was an adult and this was normal, to talk about stuff with a completely impartial medical professional who would tell her she had nothing to worry about.

The doctor nodded and put down her pen. She folded her hands on her lap and sat forward a little in the chair.

"Now, you do realize that because of your age you're in a bit of a high-risk category."

"I know. What can I say, I'm just a high-risk kind of girl." Why couldn't she be serious about this?

Dr. Connors laughed and Cleo felt victorious, like making the doctor laugh negated anything bad she was about to say.

"Give it to me straight, Doctor. While I'm sitting here and I can change my mind about that prescription."

"First off, you need to know that the vast majority of women who get pregnant at your age have healthy babies and very few complications. You're more likely to have difficulty conceiving than a younger woman, of course, but there's a lot you can do to ensure you have a healthy pregnancy if one happens. And many women much older than you have had babies."

"I know! Look at Halle Berry."

"How old was Halle Berry when she had her last?"

"Forty-six."

"Naturally?"

"She says so. But the Hollywood types like to gloss things over to make the rest of us feel bad."

"Forty-six is pushing it."

"Yeah, I figured."

"Let's just say you're in a better position than Halle Berry."

"I wouldn't say that, Doctor."

"Well, it could happen right away, or it could take a while. There's no way to tell just yet. If conception does happen, there's a higher than normal risk of miscarriage. Being in the thirty-five-to-forty age bracket also puts you at higher risk for gestational diabetes and high blood pressure, and there's an elevated chance of the baby having Down Syndrome or other chromosomal abnormalities or birth defects. And not to scare you, of course, but statistically, you need to know that if the fetus is healthy and carries to term, there's still a risk that the birth will happen prematurely, there's a slightly higher chance of a stillbirth, and at your age, the birth might have to happen by C-section."

Cleo was quiet. She looked to the blue-eyed baby on the wall.

"What about Baby Flathead?"

"That's only a concern after the baby is born."

"Okay. Anything else I should know?"

"Women over the age of thirty-five have a greater chance of having twins or triplets."

"Oh my Jesus."

Dr. Connors laughed and Cleo noticed her row of perfect white teeth. Cleo's eyes moved to the framed picture of two babies next to the computer. The doctor's two beautiful, presumably low-risk babies.

"I know this must feel a little overwhelming for you," Dr. Connors said. “This is all information I’m obligated to tell you, but in all likelihood, everything will turn out fine. Eat well, exercise, watch your alcohol intake, and start taking folic acid.”

“What about Jamie, is he completely off the hook?” This pregnancy was so unfair and it hadn’t even happened yet.

“Exercise and eating well is important for him too. And if he’s a smoker he should think about quitting. A healthier lifestyle means faster sperm.”

“Does pot hurt?”

“Yes.”

“Shit.”

“And that goes for both of you. Now, any other questions for me before we finish up?”

Cleo’s heart started to beat a little faster and she was right back at the head of the customs line and the heat was rising to her face again.

“The termination I had a few years back, will that . . . I mean, as far as I know there were no complications, but is there a possibility it could mean something is wrong down there and maybe I won’t be able—”

“That was a long time ago, Cleo.” Dr. Connors cut her off gently. “It can sometimes be an issue, but I have every reason to believe that you’re perfectly healthy. If things don’t progress the way you like, we can chat again in a few months. For now just carry on as normal, okay?”

Just for a moment, Cleo felt much younger than her doctor. It was probably because Dr. Connors was a mother and Cleo had only come close and never followed through.

“Okay. Okay, good. Thanks.”

The doctor was gathering her things to go, to let Cleo get dressed.

“Doctor Connors, do most people leave their socks on or off? For a pap smear?”

“I’d say it’s half and half. I guess it depends on if you have cold feet or not.”

geysers

DESSERT WAS BUBBLING IN THE OVEN AND IT SMELLED NICE, A small bit of comfort on such a cold night. The doorbell rang just as the crisp was caramelizing along the edges, pink liquid from the berries oozing up from the sides and rising through holes in the topping like miniature geysers. Cleo turned off the oven and went to get the door. Donna was standing on their shovelled-out section of sidewalk, purse clutched to her chest.

"Hiya." Cleo leaned in and kissed her cheek. "Come on in, my God, it's freezing."

"My cab driver was super sketchy."

"You say that every time you get out of a cab."

Donna came in and took off her boots and coat. It was so cold and dry out that her blond hair flew in all different directions with static.

"Yum, smells good in here. What are you making?"

"That's the dessert in the oven, just a berry crisp. I'll put the risotto on as soon as Nancy gets here."

"Ooooh, fancy! What's this, Raymonds? I've underdressed." Donna put her nose in the air and flicked her hair over her shoulder.

Cleo and Nancy had taken Donna to Raymonds for a surprise birthday supper last year. She'd sat at the table with wide eyes and an open mouth the whole four hours. At the end of the seven-course tasting menu, drunk on wine and cucumber gin martinis, Donna hugged them and cried and said, "Tonight was better than my wedding."

"How's Reg?" Cleo reached in the cupboard for a glass and went to the fridge for the Chardonnay.

"Oh, he's fine. He went out for burgers and beers with the boys." Donna rolled her eyes, something she'd only started doing after her birthday tasting menu. Just like that, they'd completely ruined her. Poor Reg.

"Glass of white?"

"Yes, please. And make it a big one, I'm off tomorrow."

"Nice, wish I was." Cleo poured a glass for Donna and topped up her own.

"Where's Jamie?"

"On his way home from Fredericton. You'll probably catch him. His flight gets in at eight and he's taking a cab home."

"Oh good, I haven't seen him for ages, not even once over Christmas."

"That's because he was hijacked by the Clarenville crowd."

"I wish somebody would hijack Reg at Christmas."

Cleo heard Nancy in the porch, stomping the snow off her boots. She came into the kitchen and plunked down into a chair, putting a brown paper bag from the liquor store onto the table.

"Sweet Mother of God, Cleo where is your corkscrew? I need to start injecting Pinot Grigio directly into my veins."

"There's Chardonnay open in the fridge," said Cleo.

"Thank Christ. Hey Donna." Nancy heaved herself off her chair and kissed Donna on the cheek, then carried on to the cupboard for a glass.

"Oh, your face is cold. Did you walk?"

"I had to burn off some steam or I was going to murder my family."

"Oh my, is Mack okay?"

"No, he's not okay. He's transitioning from baby to toddler and he's a complete dick."

"Nancy! You can't call your own child a dick."

"I just did because he is."

"But he's supposed to be, right?" Cleo asked. "Like, if he wasn't a dick at this age, wouldn't you be worried?"

"That is the truth," Nancy filled her glass. "All nineteen-month-olds are dicks, and if you don't think that it's only because you don't have one."

"Well, I'm only saying dick seems like a bit of a strong word for a toddler, that's all," said Donna.

"Donna, here's the thing. If more people realized their children were dicks, and worked on making them not dicks, the world would be a better place. And while we're on the subject of people being dicks," said Nancy, pausing to take a long drink of wine. "We're getting Mack christened in a couple of weeks and you're both invited. Cleo, are you up for being fairy godmother or whatever?"

"What! You gave in? What the hell happened?" Cleo stirred the buttery rice and shallots and leaned her head in to smell the alcohol burning off. She sniffed too hard and it travelled up through her nose and made her eyes water.

"I think it's wonderful. You should have done it ages ago," Donna piped up. "Better late than never, I suppose. Are you going to get a gift registry? Do people get gift registries for christenings?"

"Either of you buy anything and I'll kill you. I basically have no choice in the matter, and I'm having nothing to do with it. Hazel's planning the affair, I just have to show up and hold my son while they indoctrinate him into a patriarchal and hypocritical institution."

"Oh, give up," said Donna. "It's only a tradition to get the family together for cake."

"So what's the deal?" asked Cleo. "Why the sudden change of heart, godless heathen?"

"Doug's nan is dying."

"Oh, no!" Donna tilted her head in sympathy.

"It's not sad or anything, she's ninety-six and miserable and she's only alive out of spite. The old bitch has been on oxygen for two weeks and the only thing she's been able to say is, 'get the baby baptized, it's my final wish.' That is literally the only thing she'll say whenever she takes her mask off. What an asshole."

"Nancy! It's her dying wish." Donna looked on the verge of tears or laughter.

"I don't care! She's a terrible, terrible woman, and she's utterly deceptive. And what's worse is, she's completely in her right mind and is faking everything so we'll take pity on her."

"Or maybe she's really dying?" Cleo said, bracing herself.

"We should be so lucky," Nancy said. "She just wants to get even with us for getting married at City Hall. Doug says to me, 'you know the quickest way for us to end all this, don't you.' So I told him fine. I'm having nothing to do with it. And as soon as we leave the Basilica, I'm taking Mack out to the backyard and turning the hose on to wash all the Catholic off him."

"Sin for you. It's January."

"The Basilica! Oooh, fancy. Do we have to wear hats?" Donna laughed into her glass. "What do you call them? The things they wear on their heads at weddings in England. Fascinators! Can we wear fascinators? Please say yes. I dies for a fascinator."

"Jesus, Hazel would love that. It's bad enough I have to put my son in a dress and dunk him."

"How did you manage to book the Basilica?" Donna emptied her glass and went to the fridge for a fresh bottle. "Isn't there a waitlist, or don't you have to book before your kid is born? If we were in London, this would basically be like booking Westminster Abbey."

"Christ, who knows," said Nancy. "Hazel is a volunteer on the board of the parish or she fucking tars the roof, I don't know. She pulled some strings or said some rosary beads or something."

"So, like, don't you have to take a course?" Donna said slowly as she sat back down, careful not to agitate Nancy any further. "I don't think Catholics let you do anything without taking a course. They told you that, right?"

"Yes, only after I'd given in, naturally. Hazel supervised and made sure I was pleasant and didn't swear."

"Do I need to do anything?" asked Cleo. "I'm a lapsed Catholic, will they let me be godmother?"

"Of course they'll let you. You don't need to do anything, I promise, just show up. You have to hold him while he gets dunked, I think? And afterwards there's a party at Hazel and Wilf's and we can drink and eat cake. I've already told Doug that if my son's going to become a Catholic I have to get really drunk after."

"I think it's really nice that you're doing it for Hazel and her mother," Donna said. "It doesn't need to be a big deal for you, just think of it as another family gathering."

"Christ, another family gathering. That's all I need." Nancy went to the stove and stuck her head over the steaming pot, holding her hair back over her shoulders and breathing deeply. "Yum, smells delish. Oh, I forgot to ask you how it went at the doctor's yesterday."

"Everything's fine. You know, just the annual pap and a chat about my old eggs." Cleo placed the scallops in the searing hot pan one after the other, making a formation like the numbers on a clock.

"Oh wow, you guys thinking about trying?" Donna asked, turning her chair around a little.

"Yes? I guess? It's been brought up. Mostly because we just found out Fran is pregnant and it's making Jamie all broody."

"Now I've heard it all. Well, if Fran can do it, you definitely should. God, that was a bit mean. I'm drinking my wine too fast, I sound like Nancy." Donna looked at Nancy. "Sorry, you know what I mean."

"I do, and I'm quite flattered."

"The baby will turn out okay if it has Andrew, I hope," Cleo said. "I think that's what has Jamie all excited, the idea of the two of them being dads together. He's a bit more into it than I am. I guess you can't blame the poor guy, he's been surrounded by babies non-stop since he was a kid. I'm surprised it took this long for him to bring it up." She took a pair of tongs from the drawer and flipped the scallops.

"So she said everything's okay? You got the green light?" Nancy reached over and gently tapped a scallop with the tip of her finger. "These are done."

"It's as green as it's going to get, I suppose. I asked about my abortion and she seems to think it won't be a problem. For now, anyways."

"Good," said Nancy. "Then you should get cooking because your eggs are going from medium-poached to hard-poached pretty quickly."

"You'll probably be fine, Cleo, most women are. I have lots of patients who've had terminations and they still manage to conceive, even at our age," Donna said.

"I can't imagine we'll jump in the deep end right away." Cleo set the scallops aside. "I think we should just ease into it. And aren't your hormones a mess when you stop taking the pill? Don't they say to use condoms for a while afterwards?"

"Nope," Nancy said, waving her wine glass in the air with authority. "That's a myth. It's actually your most fertile time. You're also extremely fertile after a miscarriage, pretty funny, hey?"

"I think you should just go for it," said Donna. "What if you're down to your last viable eggs? Or Jamie's last viable sperm?"

"Jesus, we've got no worries about Jamie if his sister is any indication. He'll probably knock me up with triplets on the first go."

"Look, it might happen anyway, even if you're not trying," Nancy said. "Remember when Heather in accounting got pregnant with twins? She got drunk at the Christmas party and told me that her husband was pulling out when they got knocked up. There you go. Poof. Instant family."

"I didn't know any of that until I went into nursing," said Donna. "I could have gotten into so much trouble in high school."

"Me too. After my miscarriages I started wondering if they happened because of all the morning-after pills I'd taken in my twenties. God, I was such a slut," Nancy said, with a smile and a faraway look of nostalgia.

Cleo gave a little laugh and looked down at the Parmesan she was grating. She pushed the chunk down too hard, felt the grater scrape against her finger, and winced.

"I'll tell you what else is terrifying," said Donna. "The number of teenage girls not using protection and trying to get their boyfriends to pull out. You wouldn't believe the stories I could tell you. Can you imagine trusting a sixteen-year-old boy to pull out?"

"Christ, I'd barely trust a thirty-five-year-old man to pull out," Nancy said, moving back to the table.

Cleo spooned out three servings of risotto in pasta bowls and put four scallops on top of each. The front door opened as she placed the bowls in front of the girls and took her seat at the table. Cleo heard boots coming off and the rustle of Jamie hanging up his winter jacket in the porch. When he came into the kitchen he was greeted by a chorus of enthusiastic hellos; Nancy and Donna both jumped up from their chairs for hugs and pecks on cheeks.

"How's it going, ladies?"

"You're just in time, the risotto is still hot." Cleo made a move to get up and make him up a plate, but Jamie touched her shoulder and sat down at the kitchen table.

"I'm going to sit for a bit. I'll have some in a few minutes."

"How was Fredericton, darling?" Nancy asked.

"It was all right. I was hungover all day yesterday. Hopefully the bridge doesn't crumble to the ground."

Nancy cleared her throat and tapped her wine glass with her fork.

"Jamie. Are you open to a very personal question?"

"Always."

"In your expert opinion as a man who was once a teenage boy, how difficult was it for you to pull out, say, before the age of twenty?"

"I never really had to. When Krista got pregnant my parents realized they needed to up the level of sex education in the household, so I got the talk when I was pretty young."

"How young?"

"Eleven or so. I didn't touch a girl until I was eighteen and I always used a condom and asked questions about her cycle, so I could figure out when she was ovulating and be extra safe."

The table went up at this and Donna almost spit out her mouthful of wine.

"You didn't!" she howled, wiping a dribble off her chin.

"I did. You learn real fast about the female reproductive system when your sister gets knocked up at fifteen. I never had sex without a condom until I was twenty-seven and I came in two seconds. Frightened the life out of my poor girlfriend."

good to go

JAMIE SCRAPED THE STICKY PINK CRUMBS FROM THE DESSERT bowls and rinsed them in the sink before loading them into the dishwasher.

"Here, let me finish that, you go on to bed, you look exhausted." Cleo stood next to him at the sink but he kept on scraping and rinsing.

"You cooked supper," he said. "I really don't mind."

"Sorry you had to come home to a houseful of drunk ladies. Supper turned out to be a last-minute thing."

"No, it was great. It was good to see everyone."

Cleo put her hand on the small of Jamie's back. "Seriously Jam, go on upstairs and I'll finish up. You should get some sleep."

"Not too tired now, actually. Come here." He dried his hands on the dish towel, put his hands around her waist and pulled her in. Cleo put her head on his chest and breathed him deep and he smelled like apple-berry crisp and clean laundry. Nobody but Jamie could smell this good after a day of work and two hours on a plane.

"How was it at the doctor? Are we good to go?"

"We are good to go," she said, her face not moving from his

chest. She was relieved she could tell him the truth, because that's what the doctor had said.

Cleo set her clock twenty minutes earlier than usual the next morning, so she could wake up slow. She went downstairs to turn up the heat in the kitchen and put the coffee on and crawled back in bed with Jamie. He was awake when she came back to bed, sitting up a little with one hand behind his head, the other scrolling through his phone. Cleo played with his chest hair, grabbing a small handful and giving it a tug. She liked it when a man had hair. She never quite understood the fascination with a bare chest.

"Mack's getting christened in a couple of weeks."

"You're not serious." He put his phone on the night table, turning to give her his full attention. "Nancy finally gave in?"

"She had to. Doug's nan is dying and it's her final wish. Apparently it's the one thing she's been asking in between puffs on her oxygen tank."

"Wow. Oh man, Nancy must be livid."

"That's not even the word for it."

"Hazel has to be in her glee over this one."

"Let's just say she's making up for the big church wedding that never happened."

"Holy shit, I bet." Jamie rolled over then, put his hand on Cleo's hip. "If we had a baby could we get it christened?"

"Nope. Not a chance."

"Not even a little one?"

"Not even the minutest of chances."

"What if it was Nalfie's dying wish?"

"Not even then, and besides, Nalfie is cooler than that."

"It would probably kill Dad. Mom might be okay, but Dad would probably keel over."

"We could have a little party with cake and a naming ceremony."

"Ugh. A naming ceremony. Hippie."

"Nothing churchy, no way. Evelyn and Hector will be happy enough if they even manage to get another grandkid out of this, so let's not get ahead of ourselves."

"We should get on that, though." Jamie leaned in and kissed her shoulder, worked his way up her neck and took her earlobe in his teeth.

"Well, we can," said Cleo, and she warmed up a little on the inside even though the clock on her night table said 7:35 and she should be in the shower by now. "I'm not saying it would be entirely pointless, but I still have a week of pills left . . ."

Jamie flipped her over and moved himself down, started kissing the bottom of her back, right in the deep groove and all the way up to the base of her neck.

"Practice run," he said. He reached around to her stomach and slid his hand into her underwear.

sunday dinner

Cleo and Jamie slept in on Sunday morning and decided at the last minute to head to Maisie and Joe's for Sunday dinner. Her parents alternated between a proper Jiggs' dinner and something international—a Greek-style leg of lamb, an English roast with Yorkshire puddings, or sometimes Joe would barbecue Indonesian satay. Sunday always held an open invitation for Cleo and Jamie, but Maisie was easygoing and they were never obligated to show up like they would be if Ev and Hector lived in town. For this, Cleo was eternally grateful.

Her mother met Joe when Cleo was two, and Maisie liked to joke that she had worked hard to turn him into her "international bayman." As a family they'd spent most of their summer vacations in Wesleyville, but when Cleo moved out after her first year of university, Maisie insisted they go a little further than a four-hour drive. She dragged a reluctant Joe everywhere, and in a short time he went from "what the hell am I supposed to eat in Slovenia" to "where are we off to next." He'd become an expert haggler, a lover of curry, and a connoisseur of international beer. Cleo saw them have the same argument every Christmas, when Maisie came home from the liquor store with a flat of Coors Light before their giant Tibb's Eve party. Joe would point out that wasn't real beer and Maisie would say that she'd created a monster.

"Is this a Jiggs'-Dinner or a Flavour-of-the-Week Sunday?" Jamie asked when he got in the car.

"Not sure, it's been a few weeks since we've been over."

"I hope it's Flavour-of-the-Week. I'm Jiggs'-Dinnered out after Christmas. I could do without one until Easter."

Maisie and Joe lived in a small two-storey house on Pennywell Road that they'd bought shortly after they married, when Cleo was three. Joe had wanted something a bit further out, but Maisie didn't drive and wanted to be able to walk to the dance studio where she taught, and to her parents' house on Carter's Hill.

Cleo and Jamie pulled into the two-car driveway and saw Joe shovelling the walkway to the house.

"Hello, strangers," he said when they got out of the car, pausing for a moment to lean on the shovel. "I suppose it's a little late for Happy New Year, but I'll wish you one all the same."

"You too, Joe," Cleo stood on tiptoe to kiss his cheek before she walked up the front steps. She could tell by the smell coming from the house that it was a Flavour-of-the-Week Sunday.

"You need some help, Joe?" Jamie headed for the open garage door and an extra shovel.

"Well, Jamie, normally I'd tell you not to be so goddamn foolish, but Nalfie's over with her walker and I'm trying to give her a bit more room to navigate. That's just what I needs now, is that splashed all over the news. 'Elderly woman falls down and breaks hip on the fire chief's front walk.' No my son, I'll not be turning down help today."

"Not a problem," Jamie said, bending into his first shovelful.

Cleo could see the tracks from Nalfie's walker in the snow on the landing of the front porch, and she felt relief that her grandmother was there, followed by a wave of guilt for having missed two of their weekly visits over the holidays.

Her grandmother was eighty-four and pretty spry despite the occasional use of a walker. Cleo couldn't remember exactly when they started calling her Nalfie. The story was that Cleo had made it up when she was a toddler, combining the word "nanny" with her grandmother's given name of Alfreda, or Alfie, as she was known by most friends and family. One of Cleo's first memories was of taking her grandmother's face in her hands and squealing "Nalfie, Nalfie, Nalfie!" then collapsing on the floor and giggling so hard she peed her pants. It had stuck after that, though whether it was because the nickname was catchy, or her family's way of reminding Cleo she'd pissed herself, she wasn't quite sure.

When she opened the front door her nose couldn't quite place what was on for dinner, but it smelled like some sort of curry. Cleo took off her gear and walked into the kitchen, where Maisie stood chopping cilantro at the counter while Nalfie sat at the table slicing garlic on a cutting board. Her reading glasses were sitting on the edge of her nose and her face was pinched in concentration like it was when she was knitting or crocheting.

"Hello my darling, how are you?" Nalfie pushed herself up off her chair, putting her two fists on the table and hoisting herself to meet Cleo's kiss on the cheek. Cleo didn't bother to tell her not to get up, that only would have gotten her a pinch on the ear.

"Hi ya, Nalf." Cleo squeezed her hard and helped her sit back down. "I see Mom's got you put to work."

"Yes, and I'll be a week getting the smell of garlic off my fingers, honest to my Jesus." But she sat back down contentedly and moved her glasses further down her nose, slicing slow and fine and precise. It was a food she never cooked with herself, but no one was going to tell her she was doing it wrong, especially in the sacred space of a kitchen.

"Hi Mom." Cleo moved to the counter and gave Maisie a quick peck on the cheek.

"Hello, love. Where's Jamie?"

"He got recruited to help Joe with the shovelling."

"That's a sin for him, sure the two of you have enough of that to do downtown."

"Nah, that's okay. Jamie loves it when Joe asks him for help, it makes him feel useful. He likes to get back to his bay roots."

"Bay roots?" Nalfie chimed in from the kitchen table. "Clarenville is about as bay as that pile of green stuff your mother's chopping up."

"I won't tell Jamie you said that."

"My dear, you go right ahead."

"What's for dinner?" Cleo asked.

She still had to stop and think sometimes about what meal it was she was about to eat. Raised on the Newfoundland breakfast-dinner-supper, she confused several classes of English students in Korea, until one of the head teachers took her aside and explained that the kids needed to be taught American breakfast-lunch-dinner. Joe laughed at her when she came home and called it Sunday lunch. "What do you think we're having, cucumber sandwiches with the crusts cut off? My dear, you don't eat salt beef for lunch," he'd said.

"Chiang Mai curry and Thai fishcakes," Maisie said.

"Your mother's trying to kill me," Nalfie said without looking up.

"Now Mom, you've had the fishcakes before and you loved them."

"Oh yes, they were lovely. And so was the pack of Rolaids I had to eat afterwards."

"Jamie will be happy. He's turkeyed out after Christmas," said Cleo.

"I daresay he is," said Nalfie. "That Evelyn would cook a turkey to celebrate a fart."

"Nalfie, you're terrible," Cleo said, but she laughed because it was true and she had a deep-freeze full of leftovers to prove it. "Can I do anything to help?"

"Pour yourself a glass of wine and then slice some of those chilies, will you?" Maisie said.

"I told you she's trying to kill me," Nalfie said, in a sing-songy voice like she was at church.

"Mom, they're only to sprinkle on top for garnish, you don't need to eat them. Cleo, your grandmother won't go near them since that time—"

"Yes, you love telling that story, don't you, Mais? Cleo, your mother never told me chilies stay on your fingers for days. For God's sake, don't touch your eyes afterwards like I did the one time I tried to cut up the damn things. One little scratch and I thought my goddamn cataracts had caught fire. God forgive me, those things just aren't natural."

"I'll be careful, Nalfie." Cleo sat next to her grandmother, knife in one hand and glass of white in the other.

"Thanks, love," said Maisie. "Don't forget to take the seeds out and the membranes too, if you can manage."

"Not natural." Nalfie in her best Sunday hymn voice.

"Yes, ma'am." Cleo turned and made a face at her grandmother.

The front door slammed and Jamie and Joe came in, stomping the snow off their boots in the porch.

"Smells like a restaurant in here," boomed Joe.

"It's almost ready," Maisie called out. "I've just got to fry up the garlic. Joe, set the table will you, when you get your gear off? You can use the nice bowls from the china cabinet, the ones we got at that antique place last summer."

"Well, she never takes those out for me so you two must be something special." Nalfie grinned and tapped her feet.

"I think one glass of wine might be enough for you today, Mom." Maisie turned from the counter and looked at Nalfie with a raised eyebrow.

"And that's what it's not. Don't you be so saucy to your mother. Sure, what odds if I go ahead and become an alcoholic now? You just wait till I takes up smoking again after forty years without a cigarette." Nalfie placed her empty wine glass in front of Cleo and gave her a nudge. "Don't let your mother pour it, for the love and honour of God."

"I'll get you one, Nalfie," said Jamie, coming into the kitchen, his cheeks red and a little film of sweat around his hairline.

"Thanks for your help with the shovelling, dear," said Maisie. "Grab yourself a glass of wine, or there's beer in there, too, if you'd prefer."

"I'm good for now, I'll wait till we eat."

Jamie grabbed Nalfie's glass from the table and went to the fridge, coming back with the glass half-filled. He plunked the glass on the table in front of her.

"Jesus, you're worse than Maisie. I'll remember this the next time you're over for dinner and nosing around for a second piece of pie," said Nalfie, looking at the glass and wrinkling her nose.

"It's all about pacing yourself, Nalf," said Jamie, opening a drawer and grabbing a handful of cutlery.

"Pacing yourself at my age is like having a shower before a shit, Jamie. Pointless."

"Oh, Mom," said Maisie, shaking her head. Jamie laughed like a twelve-year-old and went to the dining room to help Joe set the table.

"Will you look at that. Two men setting the table." Nalfie's nose was in her half-empty glass of wine and she was leaning over in her chair looking into the dining room. "I never saw your father set the table, Maisie, not once. Not even when I was laid up in bed for a month after Cora was born. Your father was useless, God rest his soul. I had to get your Aunt Peg to move in or Russell would have starved to death."

"Different times, weren't they, Mom?" Maisie came to the table and took the cutting board full of garlic, scraping it all off into a frying pan of hot oil on the stove.

"Different's not the word, my dear. If you had told me twenty years ago I'd be eating curry for Sunday dinner, I would have laughed in your face." Nalfie reached over and squeezed Cleo's earlobe, like she used to do when Cleo was a girl. "So what's all the news, my trout? Give your old grandmother some exciting gossip before I dies."

“Not much on the go, really. Back at work, that’s going pretty good. Jamie just got back from a work trip to Fredericton, you know, same as usual. Oh, here’s a bit of news,” Cleo looked over at Maisie frying garlic on the stove. “Fran is pregnant.”

“Oh my,” said Maisie. “Good for them, I suppose?”

“Fran.” Nalfie took a sip of wine, like this would help her remember, and it did. “Is that the one who cheated on her husband with their accountant?”

“Yep.”

“That shameless slut.”

“Nalfie! Shhhh,” Cleo hissed, tossing her head in the direction of the dining room, where Joe and Jamie were having a lively discussion about snowblowers while laying out the fine china.

“Don’t you worry about Jamie, he’s smart enough to know I’m right. And if he thinks I’m wrong he needs his head examined.”

“How’s Andrew taking it?” Maisie asked.

“He’s good. They’re happy about it. He’s wanted a baby forever, I’m sure it’ll work out.”

Nalfie snorted, looked at Cleo and rolled her eyes heavenwards.

“Evelyn and Hector were quite pleased about it.” Cleo grinned and glanced out at the dining room again.

“Ha! I bet,” said Maisie. “Buying clothes already, are they?”

“Probably.” Cleo could feel the heat from the chilies under her fingernails and her eyes were starting to sting. She rubbed them with her sleeve, careful not to put her hands anywhere near her face.

Another snort from Nalfie.

“They better not be at the two of you to have a youngster.” Cleo’s grandmother’s eyes were Chardonnay-bright and ready for a good argument.

“Always.”

“I’ll tell you something right now, Cleo,” Nalfie said, pointing with her wine glass at a dangerous angle. “When you have a youngster, your life is over.”

"Here we go." Maisie had heard this lecture more than once.

"Now, don't get me wrong, I love my youngsters and I'd do anything in the world for them, but my dear when you have a baby, they're nothing but a worry from the day they're born till the day you dies. Maid, if I was your age today, I wouldn't be getting married and I certainly wouldn't be having no youngsters."

"So I should get rid of Jamie, is that what you're saying?"

"Oh no, I like Jamie. There's no need for weddings anymore, though. Giant racket and a waste of money, if you ask me. Now, I don't object to settling down with a sensible fellow if you like, or even a woman like some of them does these days, sure fill your boots, what do I care. You did it right though, Cleo. No offence, Maisie."

"None taken, Mom. Not much, anyways."

"Sure if you hadn't gone to Paris and met that gutless bastard we wouldn't have our Cleo." Nalfie reached over and pinched Cleo's earlobe again.

"Thanks for getting knocked up in Paris, Mom."

"God, Cleo you're getting worse than your grandmother." Maisie's back was turned but Cleo could almost hear her eyes roll.

"And if Evelyn Pike has a problem with you not having any youngsters, you send her to me and I'll knock some sense into her. At least Maisie had the decency to get pregnant at twenty and not fifteen like Krista," said Nalfie with another point of her wine glass in the direction of Jamie and the dining room.

"All right, Mom, Jamie's only out there in the—"

"What? Sure I'd say this all to his face and more besides. And thank God you had the common sense to stop after one. My dear you'd have no hope of getting your figure back after seven youngsters like I had. I would have been wearing miniskirts with the best of them back in the day if I wasn't always pregnant. And let me tell you, no one wanted to see a pregnant woman in a miniskirt back then. Not like today, they don't mind showing off their bellies today, do they? Maternity dresses, Jesus in the garden, in my day you'd be lucky enough to get a couple of old flour sacks sewn together."

"Jesus, more wine, Mom?"

"No, that's fine dear, I'll wait and have my second glass with dinner."

"Don't you mean your third?"

"Well, it would be a third if Jamie knew how to pour a proper glass of wine, now, wouldn't it?"

"You wouldn't be allowed to drink in a senior's home, you know," Maisie said breezily, using a slotted spoon to put the fried garlic on paper towels.

"Watch your mouth, brazen boots. It's not too late to write you out of the will."

pickled

Everyone is sitting around the dining room table and the afternoon sun is coming through the window so bright that Cleo has to get up from her chair and pull the curtain across, because the light's shining directly in her eyes.

"Sure, go and get your sunglasses," Nalfie says. Her dinner is almost gone and everyone else is on their second bowl of curry. The bowls are steaming and the light from the window shines through the steam and the smell makes Cleo feel like she's back in Thailand. The sun is reflecting off the fresh snow outside, and it's strange to be eating a meal like this in a winter light.

Cleo is tipsy from the wine—the first glass she had was on an empty stomach. Not even a piece of toast this morning before they left. Nalfie is sensible and only ever takes a drink on "God's day of rest," but Cleo certainly doesn't mind taking many more drinks on God's other days.

Jamie and Joe are talking snowblowers again. Cleo catches something about downtown and "no yard, no room for a shed." Nalfie and Maisie are catching up on the latest goings-on on *Coronation Street*, and Cleo is happily quiet, enjoying Sunday afternoon with her family. Her brain has shut off a little but she knows when to throw in a few words here and there to make everyone think she is still with them.

There's a tug on something in her that she doesn't quite know what to do with. Maybe she *could* be a mom. Was Donna right? Does she have a duty to bring a child into the world to counterbalance all the crazy people having babies? If Fran's kid took after her, it was doomed to a future of racking up credit card bills and yelling at housekeepers.

What if the baby ended up with some disease, some rare genetic disorder inherited from Cleo's biological father? She didn't even know his name, let alone his medical history.

Cleo thinks she might be okay at it, but when she thinks about Jamie with a baby, with her baby, it fills her up and makes her so happy her heart could split in two. She can't figure out why it's so hard to tell him how scared she is.

She looks around the table, and maybe it's because she's a little drunk, but for the first time she thinks about Maisie and Joe with a grandchild. Maisie and Joe, who could never have kids, even though they tried. She thinks about how having a baby right now might mean the child would have memories of Nalfie before she's gone. Cleo sees a spot in the sunlight at the corner of the dining room table where the high chair would be. She sees a one-year-old with its face covered in food, banging on the chair with sticky fists. Cleo would be sitting next to it, breaking off pieces of fishcake and rice with cilantro because her child wouldn't be one of those picky eaters.

Maybe she's destined to have a baby because the collision of her genes with Jamie's might be the only combination in the world that can create the person who cures cancer or solves the conflict in the Middle East or invents the thing that fixes global warming.

Her daydream flips over to panic in an instant. Why didn't they start trying last year? Or the year before? Why have they waited so long? Her head feels heavy and sad, like the booze has turned on her. What if it's too late? What are they saying?

"Cleo? Sweetie?"

"Cleo."

"Do you want tea?"

"Uh, yeah. Yes, please."

Cleo is full of tea and dessert but the wine hasn't worn off yet so she grips the wooden railing when she walks down the front step to steady herself.

"Need any help?" Jamie's standing at the car, hand on the door, and grinning but she can see straight through him, even more so now she's a little drunk. Sometimes Chardonnay can help her read people's minds.

"I'm fine."

It's three-thirty and the light that was so bright in the dining room an hour ago is fading already and Cleo tells herself it's okay because the days are getting longer and that thought will get her through the next couple of months.

The day started out mild but it's freezing now and they wait in the car for it to warm up a little before Jamie moves out of the driveway.

"Good thing you don't have to drive." Jamie turns and winks at her.

"Hey, watch it. It's Sunday, I'm not on duty. We could have walked and you could have had a few drinks too." Cleo looks out the car window and rolls her eyes as loud as her mother.

"So, should we start thinking about stuff, now that we're going to start trying?"

"Oh, I'm thinking about all kinds of stuff."

"Maybe you should stop drinking for a while."

"Maybe you should stop smoking."

"If you got pregnant I would definitely quit smoking."

"If I got pregnant I would definitely quit drinking. Smoking slows down your sperm, my doctor told me."

"Drinking pickles your eggs."

"Who told you that?"

"That's common sense."

remnants

A WEEK BEFORE CLEO WENT ON HER FIRST OVERSEAS TRIP TO France, she'd snooped through Maisie's things to find out more about her biological father. Cleo was sixteen and had never really lied to her mother. Mostly because of the almost reverent amount of trust Maisie had in her. Cleo knew she could leave her diary open in the middle of the kitchen table at breakfast time and Maisie wouldn't so much as let an eyeball stray in its general direction.

Cleo justified the snooping by telling herself it was practically unethical to enter the country where her father was from, armed with no information about him. It was almost her country. Should have been her country. Cleo should have been the mysterious girl at her high school with dual citizenship and a second passport, but she didn't even know her father's name. *Maybe I should go live with my real dad*, she'd wanted to hurl at Maisie's face more than once. But she'd never had the guts to do it. It would have broken Joe's heart. And her real father had wanted nothing to do with her, so Joe was all she had.

It was a Saturday morning. Joe was on shift and Maisie was at the dance studio. Cleo woke after everyone was gone, sick to her stomach because she knew today was the day she would do it. She made herself tea and toast and contemplated how to go about it. She meticulously scrubbed the butter and crumbs off her hands, not wanting to leave any incriminating fingerprints on anything she might find. Like a killer scrubbing the blood off their hands after a murder, but in reverse.

Cleo looked out from behind the closed living room curtains to make sure no one was about to walk in the door before she went upstairs. Nalfie and Aunt Cora both had keys to the house. A surprise visit on a Saturday morning wasn't unheard of, but the coast was clear.

The sock drawer was too obvious, Maisie was smarter than that. There was no way she'd have a random box in the closet she shared with Joe. Would she? Cleo didn't know how much Joe knew, if he knew more than she did or if he knew anything at all. He worshipped the ground Maisie walked on, so it probably didn't even matter. The basement? The attic. The attic seemed more likely.

Cleo checked the living room window again to make sure no one was coming up the walk, carried a kitchen chair upstairs so she could reach the pull-down attic ladder in the hallway. She cursed when the rope to the small door stuck, then let go, almost knocking her off the chair. The creak of the ladder was so loud when she unfolded it, Cleo's hands started to shake, as if Maisie would hear it from the studio a few streets over.

Most everything up there was stored in giant plastic bins, but a few cardboard boxes shoved in the farthest corner caught Cleo's eye. One box was barely held together with packing tape that was dry and peeling. It was two different shades of cardboard-brown, like it had gotten wet on the bottom at some point. On top of the box was Maisie's neat handwriting, though it looked different—Cleo could tell her mother had written it when she was younger. The word wasn't sprawled across the side in black marker, like if you were labelling a box of dishes or books. It was written like a whisper in one of the corners, in faded blue pen: *Paris*.

Cleo was afraid that if she touched the box, the whole thing would disintegrate to dust in her hands, but she gently lifted the flaps anyway. A musty smell wafted out, but there were roses in there too, the smell of them like perfume from a different time and place. There were layers of brittle tissue paper, delicate as cotton candy, and hidden underneath were Maisie's old ballet shoes, the flat toes worn and soft and dirty. Cleo wiped her hands on her jeans, conscious again of the buttered toast she'd eaten for breakfast, and took the shoes in her hands, one finger smoothing across the flat toe.

Cleo found a pile of photos, badly taken. The Eiffel Tower, Montmartre, a blurry opera house. There was a picture stuck to the bottom of the box, yellowed around the sides, of two people sitting at a table. She stopped, her heart in her throat—the corner of the photograph started to rip when she tried prying it from the sticky cardboard. She went back downstairs to the kitchen.

Cleo grabbed a butter knife and ran back up the stairs. She put it between her teeth, like a pirate sneaking onto an unsuspecting ship, and scrabbled back into the attic, crossing the floor and kneeling in front of the box. She carefully laid everything out on the floor, hoping she'd remember how it was packed in the first place. Cleo put the flat of the knife between the bottom of the box and the photograph, which finally came free in her hands, leaving an outline on the cardboard where the photo had been stuck for years. She guessed Maisie didn't come up here once a week to get a dose of nostalgia.

Cleo held the photo up to inspect it more closely. The light coming through the small attic window shone through the spots where remnants had stayed behind on once-wet cardboard. The only person whose face you could really see was her mother. Sitting in a chair at a café, head thrown back in laughter, one hand off to the side with a cigarette dangling from it. There was a man, it must have been Cleo's father, leaned into her mother, his face buried in her neck, one hand around the back of the chair and the other on Maisie's thigh.

Cleo couldn't see his face. After all this, a picture, and no face. But it was a frozen moment of pure joy and love.

Cleo cried in the attic for the life she could have had. She repacked the box, stuck the photo in her pocket.

the rules

WHEN CLEO DRANK ON A SUNDAY AFTERNOON SHE WAS usually fine after a nap, a meal, and a good night's sleep. But on Monday morning she woke with a throbbing pain in the back of her head, her eyes so puffy and red she couldn't put her contacts in. Jamie had gone in to work early and she hadn't heard him get up—strange for her to sleep so heavily on a Monday morning. He'd made a pot of coffee and left it on for her, but she turned it off and made tea and toast. A hot shower didn't help much, but Cleo forced herself to blow-dry her hair and put on mascara. She dug around in her closet for something half-decent to wear, to make up for the fact she felt like a bag of shit.

The sky was clear and blue, and the morning sun reflecting off the new snow made Cleo's head throb even harder. The tea and toast hadn't fixed a thing and she was desperate for some kind of lift, so she took her chances and stopped in at a coffee spot on Water Street for a double-shot cappuccino. One sip and Cleo knew the coffee was a bad idea. She thought the hangover couldn't get worse until she saw Fran come out of a door one block up from the coffee shop.

"Goddammit," Cleo said under her breath.

Fran paused when she came out onto the sidewalk. Stood there like she didn't know where she was going, then looked in her purse and took out her phone. She walked towards Cleo, texting with her head down. Fran was so engrossed in her phone Cleo probably had time to turn around and cross the street, avoiding her altogether, but she didn't have the energy or quick thinking in her reserves to avoid anyone. She held her head up and picked up her pace, like it was some kind of busy and important day.

Fran looked distracted and was almost on top of Cleo before she noticed her.

"Cleo," she said, barely concealing disappointment.

That felt unfair, like this was how people were supposed to react to Fran and not the other way around.

"Hi ya, Fran. How are you?" Cleo tried to be chirpy, but the combined effect of hangover and Fran made it near impossible.

Cleo had never seen Fran blush before, but here she was, standing in the middle of the sidewalk, a flush creeping up her neck and onto her cheeks. Was random deep flushing a symptom of early pregnancy?

"I'm good, I'm great. Just on my way to prenatal yoga and then some baby shopping, you know how it is."

Of course I don't fucking know how it is.

"For sure," Cleo said.

"I'll let you get on to work then." Fran leaned in and gave her a pat on the arm. "Say hi to Jamie for me, will you?"

"I will."

Fran left her on the sidewalk, walking away so fast she had half the block covered in about five seconds.

Cleo had had a lot of strange encounters with Fran over the five years she'd been with Jamie, most of them exasperating, but none quite so puzzling as this one. It wasn't until she walked by the door Fran had come out of that things became clear. The door led to an office above the shop on the ground floor. The gold lettering on the door said *Richard Monaghan, C.A.*

That certainly explained the flush. Cleo had wondered why Fran's yoga mat wasn't slung over her shoulder.

"That shameless slut."

"Cleo, my advice is to stay as far away from this one as you can. The chips will fall wherever they're going to fall, especially now there's a baby involved."

Nancy and Cleo were sitting in the empty lunchroom at work. Cleo, still too unwell to eat, was making her way through a giant bottle of water. Nancy was a firm believer in a packed lunch, and swore up and down if she had the money back she'd spent buying lunches before Mack was born, she'd have enough to pay for his university education.

"That's remarkably practical advice, coming from you," said Cleo. "I was hoping to have someone to commiserate with."

"I know. I've had to learn to curtail my bitchiness since becoming a mother."

"But what if they're at it again and the affair is still happening? Andrew is a good friend and he deserves to know." It had taken Cleo all morning to calm down. Twice she had picked up her phone to call Jamie, but she didn't want to bother him at work. Nancy disliked Fran more than Cleo did but was more likely than Cleo to separate herself from the situation and give some objective advice.

"I can't believe I'm going to say this, but we have to give Fran the benefit of the doubt here," Nancy said, her mouth half-full of sandwich.

"You're giving Fran the benefit of the doubt?"

"Maybe she was tying up loose ends."

"So like, one more blowjob for old time's sake."

"I was thinking more, perhaps she was paying a visit to tell him—"

"That the baby is his."

"Jesus, woman."

"Sorry."

"Tell him about the pregnancy. Just so he knows about it instead of running into her on the street when she gets fat."

"Does she even owe him that much?"

"I have no idea. I've never had an affair, so I'm unfamiliar with the politics." Nancy pushed half her sandwich across the lunch table. "Here, eat this, you look like shit."

"So, what you're saying is, I have to put all this aside and be as nice to Fran as I can." Cleo forced herself to take a bite, felt okay about it, and kept eating.

"That is indeed the case. Those are the rules when someone is with child."

"Those rules suck."

"They do. Unless you're the one who's knocked up, then they're excellent. The world only cares about women when they're incubating humans. The rest of the time you can go fuck yourself."

Cleo took her time walking up the nightmare of a hill that was Holloway Street and turned the corner onto Prospect. She saw Jamie on the sidewalk in front of their house having a smoke. The night was still cold and clear, even calmer than it had been this morning. She could see the lit end of his cigarette and the smoke in a haze around his head, no wind to blow it away.

He saw her from three houses away.

"Hey, hey. How's it going?" he called out.

Cleo was feeling better but she was exhausted. She wanted supper, maybe a bath, then bed straight away. Normally she'd tell Jamie how shitty her day and her hangover had been, but not today. He was too sensitive about that kind of stuff these days, and according to their brief chat in the car yesterday, he was probably going to get worse.

"Pretty good."

"Work okay?

"Yep, great."

She wanted to tell him about running into Fran but she didn't have the energy. Jamie would only defend Fran anyway, tell Cleo the same thing Nancy had.

Jamie finished his smoke and tossed it in the snowbank. Cleo kept a coffee can out there for him, but he never bothered to dig it out in the winter, and she made him clean up the butts every spring thaw.

He opened the door for Cleo and followed her into the house, not bothering to lock the door, and she guessed that wasn't his last smoke of the night.

"Something smells good," said Cleo, kicking off her boots in the porch.

"Supper's in the oven. Salmon and roast potatoes, nothing fancy. I'll make a salad too, if you want."

"Look at you."

"What? I've cooked for you before, lots of times."

"I know, it's just nice to be surprised, that's all."

Cleo took off the rest of her winter gear and slung it over the back of the couch and walked into the kitchen. She saw a pile of sweet potato peelings on the counter and thought that was strange for Jamie, who was strictly a plain potato man. She'd never known him to make a sweet potato in his life. She wasn't a huge fan, but she kept quiet. She was happy to have a nice supper cooked for her after a miserable day, and Jamie's work schedule often meant she did most of the cooking.

"Want me to put the kettle on? Cup of tea before supper?" he asked, grabbing a head of romaine lettuce from the fridge.

"I'm tea'ed out after today. Glass of wine maybe."

"Shit, I forgot to go to the liquor store after I got groceries."

"You forgot."

"Yeah, I guess I was in a hurry to get home and get supper in the oven before you got here."

Cleo knew it was best to let this one go, but she was crooked and their conversation in the car kept playing over and over in her head.

"Well, that was kind of passive aggressive of you."

Jamie looked up from the lettuce he'd started to wash in the sink.

"What's that supposed to mean?"

"We have never, in five years, cooked salmon without having a glass of white." She opened the fridge and took out a big bottle of sparkling water. She didn't bother with a glass, opened it and drank it straight.

"What's the big deal about passing on the wine for one night? You drank all day yesterday, I figured you'd need a break."

"Wow. Thanks, Dad."

"Come on, Cleo."

"You mean you figured I shouldn't be drinking now that I'm off the pill."

"What's wrong with that?"

"What's wrong with that? I'll tell you what's wrong with that, Mike Pence. If we don't get knocked up for a year, I'm not supposed to have a drink. In case. Or if it never happens I'll have spent like, years not drinking. I'd rather kill myself."

"Babe, stop being so pessimistic. We can't start this whole thing thinking it'll never happen."

"And how was that smoke on the front step? Your last one, I'm assuming, before we turn those sperm into super swimmers."

"Are you actually getting angry at me for not getting wine?"

"I don't give a shit about the wine, I just think you're patronizing me."

"Do you want me to get in the car right now and go get a bottle?"

"Jesus Christ, Jamie."

"What? I will, I'll do it right now."

"Look, forget it. Let's just eat, I'm exhausted and I want to go to bed." Cleo took the bottle of water and a magazine from the pile on the kitchen table and headed to the living room to plunk down in Pop's chair.

"You need to tell me what's wrong with us having a good meal with no booze."

She turned back towards him and stood in the doorway. "It's just weird? Okay? I think it's great that you cooked, I love when you cook, but honestly it all feels a bit, 'must feed my woman healthy food now.' We never eat sweet potatoes, you don't even like them. This would be adorable if I was actually pregnant, but I'm not, and I may never be. So can we just relax about the whole thing."

"It's only supper, Cleo."

"I know. I'm sorry. I know."

no baby

It was a quiet supper and an early night for both of them. Cleo felt bad about her outburst and made a pan of brownies for dessert. They watched television for a half-hour and at nine-thirty she started to nod off, her head on Jamie's shoulder.

"I'm going to bed," she said, throwing off the heavy blanket they kept on the couch.

"Okay. I might do some work in the office before I come up."

"All right, good night." Cleo was about to get up off the couch but changed her mind and swung herself around so she was straddling him. She curled herself down and put her head on his chest. Jamie put his arms around her.

"I'm sorry for being an asshole," she said.

"You're not an asshole."

"It's because I just went off the pill. Asshole hormones."

"It's okay, I still love you."

"You fuckin' better." She grabbed his face and kissed him with something more than goodnight, even though she was exhausted.

"Hello." He put his hands under her shirt and they were warm on her back.

"Tomorrow," she said, and kissed him again. "I swear, I'm totally hot for you right now, but I'm a zombie."

"Go rest up, then. I'm holding you to it."

Cleo turned on the space heater and crawled into bed. She was a half-hour into a deep sleep when the neighbour's dog barked and woke her up. She lifted her head off the pillow and for a second didn't know where she was, the room so warm and dry she could barely breathe. She jumped out of bed to turn off the heater.

"Fuck that fucking dog." She got back under the covers and lay there, wide awake, staring at the ceiling.

Cleo had been living in Korea when she got pregnant. She hadn't even had sex until her twenty-third birthday, and she lost her virginity to Jake in their apartment when she was drunk at her party. It was a month before her overseas contract, and she'd had to reason with him. He didn't want to fuck up their friendship and she didn't want to leave the country a virgin.

Her birth control pills had run out six months into her trip. The Korean teachers at school were very hush-hush about the whole thing when she gently enquired one day in the staff room about how to go about getting some. Most shook their heads and said they didn't know, but her friend Soo-Jin took her aside at lunch and told her where to go and what to ask for. She was the Korean teacher at school Cleo connected with the most. Soo-Jin lived with her parents, like all the unmarried Koreans at work, but she had travelled the world on her own and had had foreign boyfriends. She'd lived in London for two years and her English was flawless. She cursed, she drank, she smoked. Cleo took to her immediately.

Cleo went to the pharmacy around the corner later that day, but her Korean was so mangled the pharmacist just looked at her blankly. She finally pointed at her stomach, then crossed her wrists in front of her face and said, "NO BABY." The pharmacist's face lit up and he said, “Ahhhh . . . okay!” He gave her four packs of some German brand that were sitting under the glass counter in front of her. That was it. No exam, no prescription, and four packs of pills cost her the same as one back home.

Cleo had been on the new pill for two months when she met Trent. He worked at a school on the other side of the city and they met at a foreigner party on Halloween. They hooked up that night, and when he left her apartment the next morning, Cleo sat on her bed and couldn’t stop smiling. Her second, and she didn’t care if she ever saw him again. She felt glamorous and promiscuous, like Nancy.

They hooked up a few times after that. It was casual and Cleo was fine with it, until he stopped calling and she saw him downtown with a gorgeous Korean woman. Two weeks later her period was late. She was too embarrassed to ask the Korean teachers at school how to ask for a pregnancy test so she went to the pharmacy on her own and figured it out. It turned out two pink lines meant the same thing in Korean.

She’d only slept with Trent a few times and they were always safe, but there was one time the condom broke. “It’s okay, I’m on the pill,” she said. That’s all it took. She was good, she was always so good, and for what? The pill, a condom, everything she could possibly do, and she still managed to get pregnant. The worst of it was that Trent was from Mount Pearl. She’d moved to the other side of the world to get knocked up by someone she could have met on George Street. It wasn’t even a surprise exotic pregnancy like her mother had. Her baby wouldn’t be half-Korean, or half-French; it would be half-Mount Pearl.

Something in Cleo liked the idea of keeping the baby. She turned it over in her mind, being a single mom, travelling the world with it in a backpack, raising it to be strong and independent. It was romantic for a week. Then the morning sickness started, and the exhaustion. She wept so hard every night she had to bury her face in her pillow so the other foreign teachers in her building wouldn’t hear. When reality set in, that she’d be fired from her job, that she’d have to go home to live with Maisie and Joe, that's when she went to Soo-Jin for help.

Soo-Jin was practical and efficient about the whole thing. She told Cleo, "This is very common in Korea. Mostly married women who find out they're having a girl. I'll take you, no problem."

They both called in sick that Friday and took a cab to a clinic across town where they were sure they wouldn't run into anyone from the close-knit community of teachers in their neighbourhood. The only available doctor couldn't speak English, so Soo-Jin came in with her to translate. Cleo hated how he looked at her, and the way he shook his head and spoke to Soo-Jin like he was angry. "Tell him I was very safe and it's none of his business anyway and can he please tell me where to go to get some help." The doctor calmed a little when he saw Cleo had started to cry. The last thing he wanted was a hysterical foreigner in his office. Soo-Jin turned to her after more words with the doctor. "He says actually, abortions are illegal in Korea, but there is someone at the clinic who can help you, maybe tomorrow." They left with a card saying the appointment was nine the next morning.

Soo-Jin picked Cleo up in her parents' car the next day and waited at the clinic until it was over. She drove Cleo home, tucked her into bed, went out to get food, and made up a bed on the floor of the studio apartment so she could stay the night. Soo-Jin left to go back to her parents' house on Sunday but came back that night to check on Cleo, bringing some takeout and a pint of her favourite ice cream.

By Monday Cleo was back at work. She hadn't planned any lessons, so she let every class play hangman on the whiteboard while she sat behind her desk and stared out the window.

Cleo was falling back into sleep when she heard Jamie close the bedroom door. She pretended to be asleep when he got in bed; he always felt guilty about waking her up when he came to bed late, and she'd put enough guilt on him for one day. He kissed her forehead and turned around so she could curl into his back.

Sometimes Cleo wondered what her life would be like if she'd kept her Mount Pearl Korea baby. She would have a teenager right now, a fifteen-year-old. She wouldn't have Jamie. She put her forehead to his back and wrapped her feet through his to warm them, curling tighter into him. It could never have happened.

take the plunge

"WHAT DO YOU WEAR TO A CHRISTENING? DO I HAVE TO WEAR a suit?"

Cleo was lounging in bed with her coffee while Jamie poked through the closet looking for something to wear to Mack's baptism.

"Aren't you godfather to half your nieces and nephews? You should be able to write a book on christenings, thanks to Krista," said Cleo.

"That's different, we're Anglican. If I don't wear the right thing to a Catholic ceremony, won't I burst into flames?"

"No, that will be me. I think a lapsed Catholic is higher on the sin chain than a dirty Anglican."

Jamie took his suit out of the closet and smelled the armpits.

"I didn't get this dry cleaned after Sarah and Colin's wedding. I don't think it's fit."

"You'll be fine with pants and a shirt. A suit would probably piss Nancy off, to be honest."

Jamie took out grey slacks and a light blue button-down shirt, held it up for Cleo's approval.

"Very handsome."

"Handsome enough for the Basilica?"

"Absolutely."

Jamie hung the pants and shirt off the doorknob of the closet and got back in bed.

"Do you think Hazel will be dressed up?" he asked, grabbing his coffee off the night table.

"Oh God, yes. Nancy told me she got a dress made."

"Jesus Christ. Poor Nancy."

"I know. If your parents were like that I don't know what I'd do."

"They're a little like that."

"Trust me, they're not," Cleo said. "They don't even care about us not wanting to get married. That saves us a lot of grief right there."

"Yeah, I guess so." Jamie rolled his coffee mug between his hands. "You don't mind them though, right? I know they're a bit much sometimes, but they can't help themselves."

Cleo put her empty cup on the night table and propped herself up on an elbow to face him.

"Are you kidding? I love your parents. Do you realize how lucky I am in the in-law department? Most women I know have to put up with a lot worse than I do, believe me."

"Are you sure?"

Cleo looked right at him and said, "I'm sure." She hooked her fingers tight in his chest hair. "Now if we could only get Evelyn to ease up on the frozen casseroles, she would be as perfect as my mother."

Jamie laughed like a man who was never going to ask his mother to stop making casseroles.

Cleo sent Jamie to church ahead of her and stopped by Nancy's to give her a hand with Mack. Cleo was taking her boots off in the porch when Nancy came down the stairs, Mack on her hip.

"Look at what Hazel has done to my child. How is this normal?"

Mack was focused on the toy fire truck in his hands, oblivious to the fact he was wearing a floor-length white satin christening gown.

Cleo burst out laughing so hard that Mack dropped his fire truck and erupted in a fit of giggles. The two of them went like that for a full thirty seconds, until Mack got restless and squirmed out of his mother's arms.

"I'm glad the two of you find this so amusing," said Nancy. "Come in and have some coffee, asshole."

Mack retrieved his fire truck and ran into the living room.

"I think he's totally rocking it, he looks gorgeous," said Cleo. "I thought you wanted a well-rounded little boy who wasn't beholden to traditional gender barriers?"

"That's not the point. I wouldn't put that dress on a fuckin' cat."

Mack sat cross-legged on the floor in a pile of toy cars, the white dress hiked up over his knees.

"Can I please take a picture of him? Please, oh please just one." Cleo opened her bag to get her phone.

"Fine. I can use it to blackmail him when he's a teenager."

Cleo put the phone in front of Mack and he looked up from his cars to give her a toothy grin.

"What a little ham," Nancy said. "He's worse than his father."

Cleo and Nancy went into the kitchen to get coffee, making sure Mack was still in their eyeline.

"Is Hazel here?"

"No, she's at the bloody church with Doug getting the flower arrangements ready. I told her I'd be there a few minutes before so himself out there doesn't get too restless."

"Do people normally put up flowers for a christening?"

"No! Of course not! I've never seen anything like this. The woman is certifiable. Jesus, this is worse than a wedding. This is the whole reason why Doug and I did City Hall. If we had to plan a wedding with that woman, I never would have married him. You know what? There should be a baptism equivalent to a city hall wedding. Dunk him in Middle Cove, then come home and order pizzas. But this is a nightmare."

"Nanc, you've got to calm down. It'll all be over soon, okay?"

"Mommy," Mack yelled, running to the kitchen with his fire truck in his hands.

"No running sweetie, you might trip up in—"

Mack stepped on the front of his gown, pulling himself forward and falling headfirst onto the kitchen floor before Cleo or Nancy could catch him. His head smacked off the ceramic tile and the fire truck squashed under his stomach.

Nancy threw her coffee cup in the sink and grabbed Mack off the floor. He shrieked and wailed in between giant ragged breaths while Nancy settled herself at the kitchen table and held him to her chest. She pulled him away long enough to take a look at his forehead, already showing off an angry red welt. He stuck his thumb in his mouth and buried his head in her neck.

"Do you know what I'm most afraid of? I'm afraid the priest is going to christen him Michael," Nancy said. "When we had that meeting he couldn't understand that we want him to be a Mack. Not Michael or Douglas or Ignatius, just Mack. What will I do if we're up there and he starts dunking him and calls him Michael?"

"He won't, and if he does, then it's my responsibility as godmother to intervene. Let me worry about that one, okay?" Cleo said.

"Okay."

Mack lifted his head from Nancy's neck and his face was red and wet, but he nodded and said, "Okay."

Nancy stood with Mack in her arms. She smoothed his hair and kissed his head.

"Let's go upstairs and get you changed so you don't fall down and hurt yourself again, okay Mackers?"

"Okay," he said again, and he waved at Cleo over Nancy's back as she carried him away, like he had orchestrated the whole thing himself.

Hazel met them at the side door of the church and led them into the vestry. When she saw a pair of slacks sticking out from under Mack's winter jacket she shot Nancy a look so cold Cleo imagined the statue of the Virgin Mary in front of the Basilica shattering into a thousand pieces.

"What happened to his christening gown?" Hazel's tone implied this was basically the same as showing up to your wedding wearing track pants and a pair of flip-flops.

Cleo opened her mouth to try to make an excuse or blame herself, anything to get Nancy off the hook.

Nancy didn't flinch.

"He tripped up in it back at the house," she said. "He hit his head off the kitchen floor." She took off Mack's hat so Hazel could see the large red bump on his forehead.

"I didn't want him to fall during the ceremony and ruin your day. Or hurt himself again. So I put him in pants." A victory for Nancy, who knew she had already ruined the day a little by taking Mack out of the two-hundred-dollar gown Hazel had ordered from a specialty baptism shop in Florida.

"That's fine," Hazel said, trying to hold onto what was left of her dignity. "God will welcome him into His house either way, I suppose."

Mack stuck his finger in his nose and wiped it on his winter coat. Hazel tutted at him and bent to take it off. Nancy leaned in unseen with her hands out and made like she was going to strangle her mother-in-law.

"Mommy, Mommy," squealed Mack, clapping his hands. When he was free of his coat he started running around the room in circles.

Hazel stood with her hands on her hips, shaking her head at the lot of them. "Doesn't he own a suit?"

"He doesn't own a suit, Hazel. He's two. We've got a few years to go before prom night," Nancy said, and it came out like a hiss. She was trying to keep it together, but there were tears in the corners of her eyes.

"It's completely my fault, Hazel," Cleo interjected. "We were playing and I got him a little too riled up and he tripped."

"Well, the two of you should have been a bit more careful on his special day," Hazel said, the statue-shattering stare directed at Cleo this time.

Nancy pointedly scratched her temple with her middle finger as she stood behind Hazel.

"Absolutely," said Cleo, stealing a glance at Nancy and biting the inside of her cheeks.

Hazel grabbed Mack as he ran past, propping him up in her arms and taking a closer look at the bump on his forehead.

"Let's go wash that face of yours, Mack. It looks like Mommy missed a spot or two." She walked out the door and down a small hallway towards the washroom.

"Jesus fucking Christ, just let it all be over soon," said Nancy, sinking into a chair. "I know you think your in-laws are a handful, Cleo, but holy shit. I'm not being a dick, am I? This is too much, right? And Jesus, she is so mean. I wouldn't mind if she was regular mother-in-law annoying, that would be tolerable, maybe even fun. I would love messing with a regular mother-in-law. But she is just so fucking mean."

"You're not a dick. She is something else. I'm kind of thanking my lucky stars right now the only thing I have to worry about is a freezer full of casseroles. And being walked in on when I'm banging on my couch."

Nancy slumped in her chair, resigning herself to the day. She finally cracked a smile.

"Enough with the sex jokes in church—I need you to not burst into flames until after the ceremony."

"You mean after I've eaten my weight in egg sandwiches and drunk all of Wilf's Golden Wedding."

"You are such an asshole and I love you."

"Want me to hide an egg sandwich in one of Hazel's houseplants so it stinks out the house? We'll blame it on your kid."

"Done."

Cleo sat with the immediate family in the front row. She turned around to see Jamie sitting a few rows back. She caught his eye and he gave her a devilish grin. He was sitting next to Donna and Reg, Donna decked out in an expensive peach paisley jacket and skirt. She'd forgone the fascinator, but her hair was pulled back in a sleek bun and she still looked fit for a fancy day at the races. Reg was fidgeting in a short-sleeved plaid shirt, hunched over in the pew, curling the baptism program into a tube and staring at the floor. Together they looked like a couple on a blind date, with one person thinking they were meeting for high tea and the other dressed up for chili fries at a roadside diner.

There were a few dozen people smattered through the pews, but no one looked the least bit familiar to Cleo. She spotted Doug's grandmother across the aisle with some of the extended family, oxygen tank strapped to the back of her wheelchair and plastic tubes in her nose. Cleo had thought it impossible for someone to look so smug while hooked up to that much medical equipment. Until now.

Nancy hadn't bothered to invite anyone from work, so Cleo guessed most people were friends and relatives of Doug's. No one from Nancy's side of the family had flown in from Nova Scotia, probably because they were halfway sensible. The room had a strange stone emptiness that came with weddings or funerals in big churches. If you got married here, even three hundred guests would make it feel like no one had shown up for the big event.

Mack was sitting next to Cleo, playing with one of the dinkies she'd grabbed and stuck in her purse when they left the house. He was as quiet as you could expect from a nineteen-month-old in church, but that didn't stop Hazel from shooting a look when Mack took the toy, though she kept quiet. Cleo was surprised Mack was so content, kneeling on the floor and facing the hard wooden pew. She suspected he was saving his energy for the big show.

The organist started playing and it had been so long since Cleo had been inside the Basilica that she gave a little start, forgetting how pipe organ music bounced off cold stone walls. Her Catholic reflexes kicked in, like some ancient rusty machine that didn't need oil after years of inactivity. Reflexes that sprang to life from an ingrained sense of duty, or plain old-fashioned guilt and terror. She found herself humming along to the hymn, then mouthing the words. All those years of singing in the choir, burned into her brain like a brand.

For you alone are the Holy One
You alone are the Lord
You alone are the Most High
Jesus Christ, with the Holy Spirit
In the glory of God the Father
Amen

Cleo looked down at Mack, still on his knees and driving his little truck up and down the pew.

Poor little frigger, she thought.

The altar servers walked up the aisle, ahead of a priest holding a cross. Cleo had never seen him before, which wasn't a huge surprise as she hadn't set foot in the building in close to twenty years. She'd even stopped going to Christmas and Easter Mass with Nalfie.

Cleo wondered if he was one of those don't-get-divorced-or-be-gay priests, or a laid-back one who was practical and hip, maybe had a mistress. Cleo might be more inclined to respect him if he *did* have a woman on the side.

She looked over at Nancy, who was staring straight ahead. Doug was next to her and then Hazel and Wilf, with Doug's youngest brother Dennis, Mack's future godfather, squeezed into the end of the family pew. All four were holding the *Catholic Book of Worship III* and singing along—Doug, Dennis, and Wilf not raising their eyes from the pages, like good Catholic boys, and Hazel holding the hymn book in her hands reverently but with her chin up, making a show of the fact that she knew all the lyrics by heart.

The priest reached the altar while Mack was still playing with his dinky, driving the thing up and down, crashing into Nancy and Cleo's legs like they were giant trees and mountains in his way. *Vroom-vroom* and *beep-beep* sounds echoed through the church. Hazel kept turning her head to look down at Mack, like that would get him to sit quietly with his hands folded on his lap instead of crashing trucks into leg trees.

Cleo knew immediately by the sound of Father So-and-So that he had nothing on the side. He summoned the family and godparents to the altar and Hazel found her chance. She leaned past Doug and Nancy before anyone had made a move to leave the pew and took the truck from Mack's hands. The *vrooms* and *beeps* transformed into a wail Cleo was sure had never been heard within the walls of the Basilica before, at least not from a human child.

Hazel went ashen but managed a smile for the crowd, like she was some Ativan-addled pageant mom. She pushed past Nancy and Doug, taking Mack's hand and trying to drag him out of the pew and towards the altar, but the whole weight of him collapsed on the floor in the middle of the aisle. His wails wafted down the aisle and up to the vaulted ceiling, along with a smell that hit Cleo's nose and the noses of everyone in the front row of pews. Nancy reached down to pick him up and he sobbed a chorus of "I poo, I poo," into his mother's neck, already shiny with his tears and snot.

The priest looked down from the altar at the scene like he was witnessing the birth of Rosemary's Baby.

Cleo and the family made their way up the stairs to the altar. Mack was still crying into Nancy's neck, so Cleo slipped round to her other side and whispered into her ear.

"You want me to stall so you can go change him and calm him down?"

"Nope," said Nancy. She walked up to the priest and beamed her brightest smile. It wasn't apologetic, like the sort of smile you'd flash a table of diners at a restaurant when your child was making a fuss. The grin stretched across her face with pride, like Mack was acing his part in the Christmas concert.

The priest hurried through the vows. Not the vows, the rites? The chants? Cleo couldn't remember the right word in between Mack's snotty, hiccupy toddler-screams. The priest nodded at Nancy to pass Mack on to Cleo and Dennis, and they both blinked like frightened deer when they realized they were the ones who had to hold him down during the actual sprinkling.

"Okay, Mackers," said Cleo, and she held out her arms, ready to receive the live grenade. "You've got to come up with Auntie Cleo for two minutes. Okay, buddy? Mommy will be right here."

She saw Mack's grip grow even tighter around Nancy's neck, and backed away slowly, bumping into Dennis, who was looking down at the floor with his hands shoved into the pockets of his pants.

Useless shit of a godfather, Cleo thought.

Nancy rubbed Mack's back and shook her head at Cleo; the priest barely stopped for breath or to acknowledge this breach of protocol. Nancy put Mack's head down by the basin of holy water and Cleo saw the priest's Adam's apple bob up and down in his throat as he swallowed hard and braced himself. Mack's cry when the water hit his scalp came from some deep and primal place of toddler rage. Cleo understood where he was coming from. Starting the day off in a dress, slamming your head off a ceramic kitchen floor, having your dinky taken away, and then having a strange man wash your hair in front of a crowd of people you'd never met, not to mention a giant saggy poop sitting in your diaper and not one single living soul making a move to help you. How could you blame a person, really? Cleo would have done the same. Part of her wanted to burst into tears alongside him, just for solidarity's sake.

If priests sat around and shot the shit over communion wine, this would make Father So-and-So's top ten. *Fathers, I have to tell you, it was more like performing an exorcism than a baptism.*

Cleo looked down into the sparse crowd and saw Jamie and Reg, far beyond the point of wiping the wide grins off their faces for the sake of church decorum. Elbowing each other in the ribs like two teenage boys. Donna's dream of a high-class event had died pretty quickly; Cleo suspected it might have been when the smell of shit finally reached the fifth row. Donna sat forward with one hand on the pew in front of her, ready to spring up and down the aisle in a flurry of peach to the rescue at any signal from Nancy or Cleo. Up at the altar, all the Gale men had taken Dennis's stance, looking down with hands in pockets, Doug the only one looking like he was trying to hide a smile. Hazel's cheeks were sucked in hard and she stood, silent. She was such a sickly shade of white Cleo thought she looked like someone laid out in a hospital bed.

Nancy stood beside the priest and beamed down at Mack, like she was presenting the shiniest pearl of a perfect newborn for all God's creatures to welcome into the family.

"Well, that was a hoot," Jamie said, flopping next to Cleo on the couch. He'd already changed out of his shirt and dress pants into beat-up jeans and an old T-shirt. Cleo was still in her church duds and felt like he still looked better than she did.

"Good God." Cleo put her feet up on the table. "Nancy must be so relieved it's all over." There hadn't been much of a party afterwards; most relatives had ducked out early or not shown up at all, probably hoping to avoid a family scene. Cleo had stayed for a couple of sandwiches but abstained from the Golden Wedding. Nancy had left at the same time, Mack asleep on her shoulder.

"Ooooh, I'd say it's only just beginning with that crowd. Wanna beer?" Jamie jumped up from the sofa even though he'd just sat down. A weird shift in his energy, like he'd been invigorated by spending an afternoon with a family more dysfunctional than his own.

"Sure."

Jamie came back from the kitchen and handed her an open beer. He sat again, closer to her this time, and pushed her skirt up her leg so he could squeeze his hand around her upper thigh.

"Ugh," he said. "What's with the tights?"

"It's minus twenty, that's what's with the tights."

"You should take them off." His hand crept a little higher.

"What's this? You all riled up from church or something?"

"Maybe."

"You are such a dirty Anglican."

"So. I guess those pills are out of your system, hey?"

"Yep."

"How do you feel?"

"Good. Okay for now. Give me a few more months and I'm sure I'll be your worst nightmare."

"It won't be that bad. You could never be that bad." Jamie took her beer and put it next to his on the end table. He moved his hand higher until his fingertips found the crotch of her tights and she closed her eyes while he stroked her there.

"Are you freaked out?"

"Yes." She kept her eyes closed and forced herself to shut the rest out, concentrating on his hand between her legs. After a few more seconds she pulled it away and in the same movement she straddled him, her skirt up around her waist. She leaned in and took his earlobe between her teeth and started grinding her tights against his jeans and the whole thing felt so juvenile, so like making out in a closet at a grade ten party, that they burst out laughing. Jamie started to undo his jeans and Cleo stood up to pull off her tights.

"Let's make a baby right here on the couch," he said, pulling his shirt over his head.

"That might be the unsexiest thing you've ever said to me. Shut the fuck up."

She turned then, to the sound of a car pulling up behind theirs out on the street.

"Should we go upstairs in case that's your mom?" Cleo looked up from trying to undo her skirt and smirked at him.

"Now it's your turn to shut the fuck up."

He pulled her down and she straddled him again with her bare legs, skirt still around her waist.

part two

fear and heartbreak

tangly

Cleo sat with her legs crossed in the waiting room at the hair salon and felt like she was wearing the wrong shoes or carrying the wrong bag. She was in a room full of Melissas. So many high heels, impeccable outfits, orange lines of foundation around caked-on faces. Cleo was a tangly mess, and she'd accepted a long time ago she'd never be the girl with the fabulous hair. Or effortless natural beauty of someone like Nancy, who could gather her curly black hair into a ponytail and turn around to see a trail of men drooling at her feet. Cleo had learned to live with the hair that must have come from the man who fathered her. She thanked him silently for her olive skin that shone in the summertime, but most days she cursed him for her mousy brown hair and infuriating cowlick.

Her stylist, Marina, always made her feel mildly better about herself after a haircut, and Cleo would take pains to keep that just-out-of-the-salon look for a few days, but her cowlick usually betrayed her after one night's sleep. She'd inevitably end up washing it before work and running out the door with wet hair.

The city was still under a blanket of dirty April snow and Cleo's giant winter boots were dripping brown slush all over the floor. She'd left the car home and walked up because it wasn't a half-bad night and they'd finally plowed the sidewalks between downtown and Churchill Square.

Marina came around the front desk.

"Hiya! I'm ready for you, come on over."

Cleo smiled in greeting and her eyes flicked down to Marina's belly. A question mark on a woman of a bigger size, but an obvious pregnancy on tiny, gorgeous, perfect Marina. Cleo kept her mouth shut when she sat in the chair. She could never bring herself to mention a pregnancy, no matter how obvious. She'd seen too many people do it and regret it.

"Not a bad night out there now, I hear," Marina said.

"Yeah, it's sort of nice. I walked up from downtown, sorry about tracking the mess in."

"Nah, you're fine. Not much walking around in the snow for me these days, I'm afraid. Eating for two is great, but walking for two certainly isn't."

Oh, for all pregnant women to be as quick and classy when faced with the floating unasked question. Cleo relaxed in the chair.

"I was just going to say congratulations. When are you due?"

"Not until August. A good few months yet, but sure look at me, I'm huge."

"You look friggin' fantastic." She did. Marina was one of those pregnant women that could show off a belly on the red carpet. "How are you feeling?"

"Oh, I'm good now. I was sick for the first three months, but nothing out of the ordinary."

"Well, that's good."

"So what are we having done today?" Marina picked up Cleo's hair in her hands and examined it for dryness and split ends.

"Nothing too serious. A trim to just past the shoulders I guess. And a few foils if you think my hair can take it."

"Sure thing. I can tell you don't blow-dry a lot, your hair's in good shape."

Cleo and Marina usually had lots to talk about after three or four months, but it felt strange now to bring something up that wasn't baby-related.

"Do you know what you're having? Of course if you'd rather not say, it's none of my business . . ."

"It's a girl, we just found out a couple of weeks ago."

"That's so wonderful. A little girl. Beautiful."

"You and your fella planning on it? And that might be none of my business, but once you're pregnant you want everyone else to be as well, you can't help it."

Cleo didn't mind that question coming from Marina. There were things she'd told Marina that she'd never told anyone else. It sounded better coming from her than it did her Uncle Mike, drunk at the Thanksgiving dinner table.

"We'll see what happens," Cleo said. "It would be nice, but we're happy either way."

"That's a good way to look at it. There's too much pressure these days on couples, I think."

"There's something I'll never hear my mother-in-law say."

Marina tossed her head back and laughed her sparkling laugh. "Well, if you ever have one, you'll have to bring it to me for its first haircut."

"Let's just hope it doesn't get my hair."

"Don't be silly, you're gorgeous. You relax now, I'll go and mix your colour."

Cleo watched in the mirror as Marina walked away. From back on she didn't even look pregnant.

ha ha

Cleo stopped in at Sobeys on the way back from the salon, new hair carefully tucked in under her winter hat.

This whole thing would be less stressful if she woke up with sore boobs or was suddenly vomiting everywhere. She felt fine, but her period was five days late, which hadn't happened since her first pregnancy, fifteen years ago.

Cleo peeked down the pharmacy aisle first, checking for people she knew. She ventured in and stood in front of the pregnancy tests, conveniently placed next to the condoms and spermicidal jelly. The look-what-you-should-have-dones next to the ha-ha-too-lates.

Cleo wondered how many people had stood in this aisle in hope and how many in dread. She felt somewhere in between. Jamie would be thrilled, he'd be the best dad in the world. She was still on the fence about the whole thing herself. Lately, she couldn't stop thinking about maniacal presidents, polar bears on shrinking ice floes, kids getting shot in classrooms.

She picked up a multi-pack of one of the expensive brands she'd seen on television, the know-the-instant-you're-pregnant kinds. Why any woman would need five pregnancy tests, Cleo had no idea.

"Fifty dollars, Jesus Christ," she said under her breath.

An older woman passed Cleo, hunched over a walker, and laughed at her.

"My dear, it'll get more expensive than that if you gets a positive," she cackled, tottering past the ribbed condoms and around the corner at the end of the aisle.

Cleo put the multi-pack back on the shelf and took a double pack of the drugstore brand. Fifteen bucks. She had the urge to hide the box in her purse, realized that would get her arrested, and swung by produce to grab some bananas so she wouldn't seem so conspicuous at the checkout.

She felt like throwing up on the way home and hoped it was only nerves.

After she peed on the stick she went downstairs to boil the kettle. She sat on the counter and swung her feet against the cupboard door over and over again, banging it with the back of her heels like a petulant four-year-old. She waited for two minutes and two pink lines, and went back upstairs.

The stick was sitting on the edge of the tub, one line staring at her before she'd cleared the bathroom door.

She leaned over the sink, put her face in her hands, and wept.

may

Supper was over and Cleo was working on her laptop in the living room, Jamie on his in the kitchen.

"You up for a while, babe?" he called out to the living room.

"Not really. Heading to bed in a bit."

"Okay, I'm stepping out for a second then I'll shut her down for the night."

He unplugged his headphones from his laptop and closed it.

Cleo waited five minutes for him to come back in. She knew she should leave it, but she was in a mood. She sighed and stood, went to the kitchen and opened the back door, her arms crossed against the cold. Sure enough, Jamie was lighting up a second smoke.

"You've started chain-smoking again?" She spoke loud enough that he could hear it through his headphones.

His back was to her, and he jumped when he heard her voice.

"Jesus, Cleo, you scared me."

"Jamie. Two smokes in a row? Come on." She had short leggings on and no socks and the air bit into her legs.

"Babe, I know. But it was a shit day at work."

He hadn't even taken out his headphones to talk to her.

"You can't be a smoker and have a baby," Cleo said. "The kid seeing you smoking when it's older, that pretty much guarantees it'll smoke. Have you done *any* reading at all about that stuff? A smoker in the house, even one who doesn't smoke inside the house, can be harmful to a baby—can cause sudden infant death syndrome."

"Jesus Christ, Cleo, I'd never do anything to harm our baby, never. You're being irrational. You sound like one of those people who are on the internet too much." Jamie hauled out his headphones.

"Oh, okay, *I'm* irrational? You're forty and you've been smoking for twenty-five years. Do you have any idea what an excellent girlfriend I've been for the past five years for not nagging you about this? What if we have a baby and you get lung cancer and I have to look after you and then you die and I have to raise a kid on my own? What then?"

Jamie looked at her from the back step; the wind took the cigarette smoke in through the back door, even though he was blowing it in the opposite direction.

"How were we completely normal five minutes ago? Cleo, I already told you, I got this new app for my phone that tells me how many smokes I've had and it weans you off. It's just gonna take me a while."

"I can tell you exactly how many smokes you've had today, you don't need an app. And hey, you know what else? I also know when my last period started and when the next one begins and the last time I ovulated, so a little help on your end with all this bullshit would be really great."

The ovulation thermometer Jamie had brought home from the drugstore, so proud of himself, hadn't even been opened yet. It was under the bathroom sink, next to the opened pregnancy test box with its second stick, taunting her.

Jamie opened his mouth to say something but Cleo barrelled on, knowing full well that now she did sound like a deranged person on the internet but she couldn't stop herself. "Smoking cigarettes can slow down your sperm, and pot too. So we should stop smoking pot for a while."

"Babe, Rod at work is the biggest pothead I know and he has four kids, come on. We really have to relax or it's never going to happen. We have lots of time to work on this. Most fertility issues are psychological." He started to put his headphones back in, and it was too much.

Psychological. Like all this was her fault and she had to calm down, or it would be on her if they couldn't conceive.

"Oh, I get it. So we can't do *little* things to help, that's a complete waste of time. Here's an idea! Let's not make any minor changes in our lives, at all, no effort whatsoever. We'll just carry on like normal and then do in vitro in five years. How about that? That'll be great! I would love to have a baby when I'm forty-three. That would seriously fulfill my fantasy of attending my kid's high school graduation as a sixty-year-old. So, carry on. Oh hey, maybe you'll be at the high school graduation too, you can be the wheezy old guy with your oxygen tank. Or maybe you'll be dead." She was starting to shiver now but she stayed put.

"Cleo!"

"I'm thirty-eight, Jamie, we can't just talk about this. We shit or get off the pot. It's easy for you, this is easy for you, but it's not for me and you can't be so fucking casual about it."

"I'm not being casual, there's lots of stuff we can do, lots of options . . ."

"I don't want lots of options! I'm barely convinced I want this, I'm doing this for you, I gave up everything up for you and you won't even quit smoking."

She slammed the back door in his face. Climbed the stairs to get ready for bed. Two hours later she woke with the lights still on in their room, her book open next to her on Jamie's pillow. She got up to go to the bathroom, and when she did she noticed the lights were off downstairs and the door to the spare bedroom was closed.

Cleo woke the next morning before Jamie did. She wrapped her robe around herself and went down to the kitchen to put on coffee, even though he usually beat her to it. She turned on the heat to warm the house before he woke up.

She went upstairs and opened the door to the spare room. Jamie was still sleeping, and the sight of his bare back twisted her insides. She dropped her robe and crawled into bed, curling herself around him. She started to cry and he woke with a start and turned to her.

"Babe, babe, are you all right? Is everything all right?"

"I'm sorry, I'm so sorry about last night. I'm not myself right now Jamie, I just feel so crazy and I'm so sorry." She could barely get the words out, they were coming out ragged between sobbing and gulping, and she was too embarrassed to look at him. She squished her wet face against his chest.

"It's okay, Cleo. It's okay." He held her tight and smoothed her hair.

"Can we get out of town this weekend? Can we just go?" She still wasn't looking at him, and his wet chest hair was starting to tickle her nose.

"Yes. Yes, let's do it. I can get out after lunch tomorrow. Can you swing it?" Jamie tried to gently pull her face up to his but she wouldn't budge and burrowed in even further.

"Yes," she said. "I'll make it happen, I don't give a shit if I have to quit. Can we get Andrew's place up at Thorburn do you think? Too short notice?"

"I'll call him. I'm sure it won't be a problem. They're up to their ears in baby stuff now. Can't see them up there anytime soon."

"Okay good."

"We might have to pop into Mom and Dad's for Sunday dinner on the way back . . . is that all right?" He tried lifting her face again, and she let him. He reached over her to grab her a tissue from the nightstand.

"Of course, of course. I would really love that." And she wasn't lying. Cleo could do Sunday dinner, but first let her have Jamie and the lake. A couple of nights to themselves, with some good food, some pot, some wine. She could do real life again after that.

They stayed curled around each other for a while, quiet. The sun started to beat in through the half-open blinds. The window was open a little and the room smelled like spring. Like that first real moment of the season after a long winter.

It turned out they'd chosen the best time to get away. The forecast looked unseasonably warm and they were leaving at lunchtime to beat the crowds. It was the Friday before the long weekend and the highway wouldn't be too busy so they planned on a long, lazy drive to Thorburn Lake. Andrew had dropped the keys to the cabin in their mailbox the night before.

They packed the car before Jamie went to work, and he picked her up downtown at noon. They made a Tim's run before they hit Pitts Memorial Drive and the highway. Traffic was light, it was sunny, but with enough cloud cover you didn't really need sunglasses. And no wind except what came through the open car window, because it was warm enough for that.

Cleo hooked up her old iPod and they played her favourite driving playlist, one she'd made when they'd got together and were taking their first summer road trips as a couple. Jamie's hand was on one leg, and her other was propped up on the dash, the top of her sneaker lodged in the crack of the open window. Their favourite Shovels and Rope song came on and Jamie squeezed her thigh, moving his hand up a little.

"I remember this song," he said, letting his eyes leave the highway long enough to look over and smile at her and then down at the crotch of her jeans.

"Eyes on the road, please," she said, but she was smiling too, because luckily they'd been fine and now it was a funny story. Cleo waited for the exact moment in the song when Jamie's hand had gone down her underwear and they'd gone off the road, all those years ago. It was burned into her head forever, that feeling of terror at the swerving car whenever she heard the last words of the second verse.

"Aaand there it is," she said, looking over at him.

"So sorry Mr. Police Officer, sir, there was a moose, we swerved. Um, what? Oh yeah, yeah, he went off into the woods that way." They both laughed like teenagers at the memory of it.

Cleo sipped her coffee and rolled the window down a little bit more, the wind whipping through the car so loud she leaned over to turn up the music.

This was the happiest she'd felt in months.

It felt like *them* again, like old times when everything was exciting and new and the idea of having a baby a far-off dream.

She was pretty sure she was ovulating this weekend.

They arrived at Andrew and Fran's place mid-afternoon, Cleo shaking her head at the audacity of Fran's calling this place a "cabin." Five bedrooms, a private dock, hot tub, and the dream kitchen Cleo had had in her head for years. The first time she'd come up here it had taken everything in her to keep her jaw from dragging on the floor.

"I still can't believe they never use this place," she said when they walked in the front door. Cleo marvelled again at the vaulted ceiling and giant stone fireplace. A sprawling black granite island separated the kitchen from the open-concept living and dining room.

"First time it's been used since last summer. Rick drove over from Clarenville to open the place up for us." Jamie placed a case of beer and a bag of groceries on the dining room table.

"Oh, shit. I didn't want to put anyone out like that."

"Not at all. Rick was happy to do it, he hates to see this place empty. And if it was up to Andrew they'd be up here every weekend."

"Maybe when the baby comes?"

"Maybe," Jamie said. But they both knew that when Fran and Andrew's baby was born, the trips up here would be less frequent, if that was possible.

"If we had a place like this you'd have to drag me out of it by the hair of the head," she said, packing away the groceries and beer in the nearly empty fridge, an open box of baking soda its lone occupant. She looked back at Jamie and he was rolling a draw on the kitchen island.

"That didn't take you long." She popped two beers in the freezer.

"Let's get high and have sex in the hot tub." He wet the finished joint between his lips and smiled.

An hour and a half later Cleo was lazing in the sun like a cat. Soaking up the early evening light, that last hour when the sun feels hotter than it's been all day. Jamie was standing in a terrycloth robe and a toque, giving the barbecue a cleaning and checking the propane. Cleo was wrapped naked in a blanket, her wet bikini splayed on the deck over by the hot tub. Lying in a deck chair, eyes closed and face to the sky, drinking one of the ice-cold beers they'd almost forgotten in the freezer; two more minutes and they would have exploded, but they'd caught them just in time so they were the perfect slushy cold.

"Barbecue's good to go. I'm gonna run in and take the steaks out of the fridge. You need anything?" Jamie leaned on the arms of the deck chair and kissed her, putting his hand inside the blanket and squeezing her breast.

"Ooooh, cold hands!" Cleo tried to bat his hand away but he switched and squeezed her other breast for badness.

"Another beer?" He kissed down her neck and Cleo's blanket fell around her waist, her whole torso goose pimpling in the breeze that had just picked up off the lake.

"Yes, please. And can you grab me another blanket? I just want to sit out for another little bit."

Jamie went inside and she put all thoughts of Sunday dinner in Clarenville and going back to town out of her head. All she wanted was the last of the sun on her face, a good steak, and sex with her boyfriend again. This time, in front of the fireplace.

game over

THIS WAS THEIR FIRST VISIT TO CLARENVILLE SINCE December; Cleo had banned all winter driving on the highway unless it was absolutely necessary—mostly at Christmas or if there was something pressing, a wedding or a funeral. When they'd first got together it took her a while to get used to the neediness of Jamie's family. The bewilderment of Evelyn and Hector at Cleo not wanting to drive two hours out and then back again on a snowy highway for Sunday dinner every other weekend. The bewilderment of Cleo that Jamie had been doing it for years.

But it somehow worked. They had their rhythm now. They teased Cleo for being afraid to drive in winter, and she teased right back about their fear of parallel parking downtown.

"Sure, what are ya doin' living in Newfoundland if you don't like driving in winter?"

"Sure, that's fine talk coming from a man who can't park his truck downtown!" Cleo would reply, and Hector would laugh at her sauciness.

But as Cleo and Jamie packed up the car and got ready to leave the cabin, she looked forward to seeing everyone. She was up for it now, and a small part of her felt like she could be optimistic about this. It was like the weekend had cleared the slate. At least now they knew for sure how simple and good things could be with just the two of them, if a baby never happened.

When they arrived in Clarenville twenty minutes later, Evelyn was on the front porch yelling at half of the Pike clan to come in for dinner. Twelve-year-old Marcus, the second-last of Krista's brood, was chasing Sophie around the yard. Hector and Darren were in the attached garage, a couple of Sunday afternoon beers cracked, their ball hats sitting high on their heads, on this, the first summery day of the year.

"Now, the gravy's hot on the stove but the turkey's getting cold. All of you inside, now. Well, hello darlings! You're just in time." Evelyn came down over the steps in slippered feet to hug Cleo and Jamie.

"It's been too long," she said as she squeezed the both of them, arms around both of their necks. Cleo could smell turkey dinner from the front lawn. She had secretly hoped on the way here that Evelyn had magically changed her mind and decided on a barbecue instead.

"Now, Mom, you know Cleo and the highway," Jamie said.

"Yes, I do. And I don't mind that. She's just trying to keep the two of you safe, I don't blame her one bit."

"Thanks, Evelyn."

"Here to take home my share of the leftovers, are ya, townies?" Darren yelled from the garage, as he raised his beer and pointed it at Jamie.

"Don't mind that one, sure you knows your mother made enough to feed an army," Hector said as he came out into the sun. He slapped Jamie on the back and kissed Cleo on the cheek.

"Well, there's a ton of food and enough for the lot of you to take home," said Evelyn. "We're missing a few today. Jonathan's still up in Alberta for another month and the twins both got jobs in town for the summer, bless their hearts."

"I'm starved, smells great, Evelyn," Cleo said as she climbed the front steps, strategizing in her head about how to turn down leftovers as she made her way inside, where Krista was setting the table in the dining room.

"Hi Cleo, good to see you." She gave Cleo a quick hug before getting back to the silverware, yelling across the dining room to the open front door at the kids still running around the yard.

"I'll run out and get them," said Cleo. She made a quick detour to the kitchen to get herself a drink, clocking what she thought was a strange look from Krista on her way out the front door. Cleo dismissed it as nothing unusual. Krista had always been a bit puzzled by her, so strange looks were nothing new.

Cleo knew it would be a good ten minutes before Evelyn and Krista managed to wrangle the men and the kids in from outside, so she sat on the top step in the sun, soaking up what she could before dinner and a two-hour drive. She planned on trying to catch the evening when they got home: a nice walk downtown, or around Quidi Vidi Lake. It was too nice to be inside. It was definitely too nice to be stuck inside eating turkey dinner.

"Hey guys, I think dinner's almost ready, your mom's been calling out to you for a while," she said with no real effort or persuasion.

"Aunt Cleo, look what I can do." Sophie performed what Cleo thought was kind of a shitty cartwheel on the front lawn.

"That was awesome, well done, Soph. Hi Marcus." Cleo turned her attention to the twelve-year-old. He'd stopped chasing his sister and was sitting on the bottom step, eyes glued to his iPad.

"Hi," he said, without looking up.

So this was parenthood, Cleo thought. Lying to children who were clamouring for your attention one minute, then having them completely ignore you the next.

Dinner was the usual mix of pleasantness and complete exasperation. Evelyn refused to sit and eat until everyone else was served, leaping to her feet twice in the ten minutes she did allow herself to sit down to get Marcus some more hot gravy for his vegetable-free plate of salt beef and turkey. He barely looked up from his iPad each time she put the plate in front of him and needed to be prompted by Krista to say thank you. Sophie had a meltdown because her potatoes were touching the dressing and she'd only wanted gravy on the *turkey*, not on anything else. Eventually Krista plunked her down in Hector's armchair with another iPad and giant plate of dessert. Sophie almost started crying again when she found out there was no ice cream to go with the cake but was sufficiently distracted by YouTube that the situation was defused. She sat there, crying and mewling like a new kitten, shovelling chocolate cake into her mouth.

"Friggin' youngsters, God forgive me." Krista sat back down to her half-eaten cold turkey dinner. "I have no idea how I raised the other three without iPads, I swear."

"Hand me your plate, Krista, I heats it up for you in the microwave," said Evelyn, and she was up again, her own dinner barely touched and cold.

"That dirt shouldn't be allowed anyway," Hector chimed in. "Sure when I was their age I'd be out cutting cords of wood with your grandfather."

"And that's what you were not," yelled Evelyn from the kitchen. "Not on God's day of rest you weren't out cutting wood, give it up, Hec, leave the youngsters alone."

"Do you know how many youngsters has to get glasses now because of those Jesus things?" Hec sat back with his arms crossed, finished plate in front of him. "Ev, put the kettle on while you're in there, will ya?"

"Don't be talkin'. I gave up on Marcus learning how to change a flat tire. When I was his age you couldn't get me out of the shed with father," said Darren, sitting across the table from the mirror image of his father-in-law. Marcus was out in the living room with Sophie, neither of them having looked up in ten minutes.

"Ev, come out and finish your dinner, I can do that for you," said Cleo, hoping to restore some kind of order before dessert. She kicked Jamie's leg under the table as a cue to help clear some plates; he was leaning back in his chair with a grin on his face, enjoying the banter but getting a bit too comfy sitting around like Hec and Darren for Cleo's liking.

"That's all right, my darling. Can I get you another drop of wine while I'm up?" Evelyn said as she placed Krista's microwaved plate of dinner in front her.

"Drink up while you can, Cleo. It's game over once you're pregnant." Krista looked up at her mother and the two of them sparkled with the laughter of gossipy teenaged girls.

"Ah, yep. I'll take another glass, thanks. One for the road." Cleo tried to let the comment pass over her, but there was more than a wine flush now, creeping up her cheeks.

"Ooooh, look at her, she's blushing. I don't suppose she's pregnant already is she? You're not one of those modern women are you Cleo, who thinks a glass or two won't hurt?" Krista's laugh was high-pitched and hysterical. Cleo had always hated it, but now she wanted to reach across the table and punch Krista in her fat mouth.

"Now, don't mind her, Cleo. It'll happen when it happens, won't it, my love?" Evelyn whisked around the table and cleared away Cleo's unfinished plate.

"Don't expect us to be babysitting for you, we're done with youngsters." Darren now, chuckling, his turn to get in on all the fun.

"Now, my son, you'll be doing your fair share, just like we did for you when you two were fifteen. Pour us a cup a tea will you, love?" Hector bawled out to Evelyn, who had barely made it to the kitchen counter with the stack of everyone's dirty dishes.

Jamie hadn't opened his mouth. He sat next to Cleo, eyes on the table, turning a beer cap over and over with his fingers.

Cleo was, for the first time in her five years of knowing Jamie's family, completely speechless. She felt like she was at a tennis match, watching people who weren't even her real family throw comments back and forth about her like she wasn't there. Evelyn brought a handful of mugs to the table, and bustled about like everything was normal, like this was a perfectly healthy conversation to have around a family dinner table. Cleo didn't want dessert, or another glass of wine. She wanted to get in the car and go home.

"Don't mind us, my darling. Jamie told us the two of you are trying, and we're just excited for you, that's all," Evelyn said, placing a mug in front of Cleo.

The nail in the coffin of the best weekend. The wine went to acid in her guts. Probably because it had been opened three weeks ago and had sat in the fridge ever since.

"Oh, he did, did he? Jamie?" Cleo put her hand over his and gave it a pat.

"Uh, yeah. I might have mentioned it in passing."

"Okay. No dessert for me, Evelyn. I'm fine." Cleo let go of Jamie's hand and pushed her chair away from the table.

"Oh, that'll change when you're eating for two," Krista snorted.

"Jesus Christ, Krista," Jamie said, finally looking up from the beer cap in his fingers.

"What? God, sure we're only joking around."

The drive back to town was nothing like the easygoing ride on Friday. No toes out the window, no favourite tunes blaring with memories of uncomplicated summer. Just the drone of weird Sunday afternoon CBC radio and a bank of fog so thick when they hit the Avalon Peninsula isthmus, it hurtled Cleo back to a place she thought they were finished with. It felt like a closed spare room door in her face.

Jamie's phone was in the cup holder in between their seats, dinging with several text messages every ten minutes or so. Normally he'd have it on vibrate and was fastidious about not touching the phone while driving, but the texts were coming so frequently he asked Cleo to check the messages.

"They're all from Andrew," she said. "Want me to read them to you?"

"Yep."

Cleo's anger at Jamie evaporated when she unlocked the phone and read the first text.

"Jamie. Oh Jesus, the baby's on its way."

"What? They're not due till July."

Cleo scrolled through the rest of Andrew's messages, small chunks of information thrown out in frantic short sentences.

-Fran's having contractions we think, at hospital

-You home yet?

A gap of fifteen minutes, then three more. She read the messages to Jamie.

-Baby on way we think

-Fuck

-Call you later

Jamie pulled over at the next gas station and got out of the car. He lit a cigarette and put his phone to his ear, pacing back and forth by the grass at the far end of the parking lot. He hung up, finished his smoke, and tried again with no luck. His face, when he was walking back to the car, reminded Cleo of the day two years ago when Evelyn had called to tell him about Hector's heart attack.

"No answer. Fuck."

"You might not hear from him for a while. Even if they're not in labour, it'll be . . . busy for them. But let me drive, in case he gets away for a second to ring you back," she said.

"I'm good."

"Jamie. Out. We'll switch. I'm serious."

"Okay."

He exited the car again, and Cleo got out of the passenger side.

"Just gimme a sec, okay?" he said without looking at her.

He walked back to the far end of the parking lot and lit another cigarette.

snowball

IT HAD TURNED INTO A MISERABLE EVENING BY THE TIME THEY got back to St. John's. Jamie drove out to the hospital to pace the floors, even though Cleo told him he probably wouldn't be able to see anyone for a while. She knew it was useless to say so and he went anyway. When Cleo pulled onto Prospect she got out and he hopped into the driver's seat, heading off to the hospital without unpacking the car, and without a word to her.

Cleo ate a small supper by herself and walked up to Nancy's in the rain. She tried to remember how the sun had felt on her face, how it was that forty-eight hours ago she was naked and high as bliss, wrapped in blankets, looking out over a lake as the sun set on her happiest day in months.

She arrived while Nancy was upstairs putting Mack to bed. Doug was offshore for his three-week shift so Cleo let herself in and tidied the living room while she waited for Nancy to come downstairs. She picked up piles of dinkies, books, and random plastic "garbage toys from the relatives" as Nancy called them, and stuffed them into the giant basket in a corner of the room. Cleo remembered when Nancy's house was fastidiously clean, and how she swore it would stay that way after the baby came.

Her phone buzzed from the coffee table. There was one text message from Jamie.

-baby born. A girl. 2 pounds 3 oz. They don't know much, she's in NICU call you later x

Cleo texted him back.

-Oh the little sweetheart. Give them my love and call when you can xx

Nancy came down the stairs, singing, "It's the mooooost wonderful tiiiiime of the day." She flopped on the couch next to Cleo.

"Andrew and Fran's baby came early."

"What? Jesus, what? I thought they weren't due till July?"

"They were. But it just happened. Fran started having contractions when we were driving back from Clarenville, and Jamie went straight to the Health Sciences when we got home. He just texted, it's a girl."

"How many weeks? How much did she weigh?"

"Two pounds, three ounces. Thirty weeks, I think? I'm not even sure."

"Thirty weeks is doable. Two pounds is good. Babies can survive these days at twenty-four weeks, she'll be fine. I mean, there could be complications, but she should be okay. Did Jamie say how she's doing?"

"He said they didn't know much, but he'd call. She's in the NICU."

"Did Jamie say how Fran is?"

"He didn't." A panic came over Cleo. "Should I be there? Was it wrong of me to let him go on his own?" He'd left her without a goodbye kiss, without any reassurances that he was okay without her.

"No. No you should not be there. And really, Jamie doesn't need to be there, although I realize that telling him that would be like talking to the wall."

"How long will the baby be in hospital, do you think?"

"Depends. She'll have to be five pounds before they let her out the door. A good month or more, depending."

"Fuckin' hell."

"Yep."

"How did you and Doug do this for five years? Try for a baby, I mean? Knowing all of this shit could happen. We're five months in and I'm ready to kill Jamie and his entire family. He told Evelyn we were trying."

"No, no, no, no, no, why would he do that?" Nancy sighed and leaned back, putting her feet up on the coffee table next to Cleo's. "That's rule number one, don't tell a soul. Except your girlfriends, that's different. But your mother? Especially his, let's face it."

"And it became family news, of course. We had Sunday dinner in Clarenville on the way back from the cabin, what a shit show. Krista was giving me funny looks because I was having a glass of wine. I swear she thinks I'm pregnant already and drinking to cover it up or something."

"You need to tell everyone to mind their own business. You really do. Jamie should say something too." Nancy opened her mouth to say something but stopped. Cleo could tell she was gearing up to say something serious; normally she spoke without thinking at all, no fear of consequences.

"I'm optimistic for you, you know that," Nancy said. "But I'm also the last person who would ever feed you bullshit. It could happen tomorrow, or it might never happen. And even if it does . . . you know. It still might not come to fruition, as awful as that sounds. Look at me and Doug. If Mack hadn't latched on when he did, we were done trying. Are you and Jamie both on the same page about that?"

"I don't think we are. I'd be fine if it didn't happen. Maybe even relieved. But he really wants it."

"Does he know about your abortion?"

"Nope. I don't know why I haven't told him. It feels like some kind of big deal all of a sudden. I mean, it was at the time. But. It's like a goddamn snowball now or something."

"It's an abortion snowball."

"Sounds like the name of a punk band."

"Good night everyone! We're Abortion Snowball!!"

They erupted into fits of laughter. Mack's monitor on the coffee table crackled as he stirred at the noise and Nancy jumped up from the couch to listen from the bottom of the landing, still wiping tears from her eyes.

"You know I'm not guilt tripping you here." Nancy returned and sat back down. "This is no one's business but your own. But it might be something you need to bring up with him."

"I know."

"Tell him before it turns into a big deal, Cleo."

Jamie was just walking in their front door as Cleo rounded the corner to Prospect, and he closed it behind him before she had a chance to call out. The rain had stopped and it was warming up a little; it was one of those nights when Cleo could have walked for hours. But she needed to go home to Jamie and hear the news from the hospital and then tell him it was all going to be okay. Nancy had said so, thirty weeks was good. So why did she have the urge to walk straight past the front step?

He was lying on the couch in the dark when she came in. It was quiet with no television or radio. She heard the burbling and clicking off of the electric kettle on the kitchen counter.

"Hi," she said, poking her head around the corner of the porch as she took off her shoes.

"Hey, you're home. I just texted to see where you were."

"I was up at Nancy's for a little visit. Doug started his three-week shift yesterday." Cleo lifted his legs off the couch and sat down, sliding underneath them. "How's the baby? How are Fran and Andrew?" Cleo didn't look at him, just took his hand and threaded her fingers through his.

"They're a wreck. I only saw Andrew for a couple of minutes. The baby's not great. I didn't get to see her but it's incubators and tubes and all that stuff. They'll know more after a couple of days."

"I'll make some food and stock their fridge."

"Yeah."

"Are you okay?"

"If anything happens, Andrew will never survive. They won't make it, you know?"

"I know." Cleo shifted so she was lying next to him, one hand on his chest. Jamie took a blanket off the back of the couch and hauled it over the two of them. She threw a leg around him and thought she could fall asleep like this if they lay here long enough.

"Did they pick a name?"

"Clara Jane."

"That's great, that's such a perfect name." Cleo lifted her head to look at him and smile, trying to make everything feel normal.

"It's funny," said Jamie, "Clara was my great-grandmother's name and I've always thought if I ever had a girl one day I'd call her that. Andrew had no idea, isn't that wild?"

"Yeah, that's pretty wild."

"Do you like it?"

"Like what?"

"The name Clara."

"Of course, I just said. Taken now though, so—"

"What about a boy's name?"

"Let's not get too far ahead of ourselves, here."

"It's just for fun, Cleo."

"Did you unpack the car?"

"Shit, I forgot."

"I'll do it."

Cleo pushed herself off Jamie's chest, almost tripping when she tried to disentangle herself from the blanket he'd thrown over them.

"Cleo, let me—"

"I'm good. I'll do it. Can you do me a favour, though? I really need you to not talk to your family about us trying, all right?"

"Cleo, it came up briefly, in passing. It's not like I called Mom to let her know, it was one of those things that got mentioned innocently, and for God's sake don't pay any attention to Krista."

"I love your mother dearly, but this needs to stay between us for now." She couldn't bring herself to say she loved Krista because she didn't. In fact, tonight, Cleo thought Krista was a bit of a hag if she was being honest with herself. "Even on the off chance it does happen—"

"The 'off chance.' Can we at least be optimistic? Can you at least give me that?"

"Yes. Okay. Okay? I'll give you that. If you give me a little practicality to go with it. You know what can happen, look at Nancy and Doug."

"Where is this coming from? What were you and Nancy talking about?"

"I'm tired. I am just so tired. I'm going to unpack the car, and I really need to go to bed."

Jamie stood up from the couch, picked the blanket up off the floor, folded it slowly and meticulously, and placed it back on the couch. He put his hands on her shoulders, the way a coach would when he was giving a locker room pep talk before the big game.

"Let's go unpack the car. I'll make you some herbal tea before bed. We can talk about this another time." He gave her a quick kiss on her forehead.

I don't want to talk about this another time, Andrew and Fran won't last, I hate your sister, I don't want herbal tea, I should be in France, I miss travelling and sleeping with men with accents, I had an abortion once, I don't think I even want a baby, can we please just get back to normal was what she wanted to scream at him, his hands still on her shoulders. Delusional football coach with the losing team.

"Sure," said Cleo.

breathe

THEY WERE QUIET ON THE DRIVE TO THE HOSPITAL TO VISIT Clara, neither knowing exactly what to expect. They'd only seen Andrew and Fran a couple of times in the week following the birth, mostly when dropping off food in the evenings, and even then only one of them while the other one was doing a shift at the hospital. Mostly they got text updates from Andrew, and pictures of the baby in her plastic incubator, hooked up to so many tubes and wires Cleo could hardly tell what she looked like, or who she looked like, Andrew or Fran. Or their accountant. Cleo never did tell Jamie about running into Fran coming out of Richard's office.

It was Saturday and parking at the hospital was relatively easy. Jamie held her hand as they walked through the corridors looking for the NICU. He smiled at her, and she knew he was thinking about being in a hospital with her and the next time it might happen. What she didn't tell him was that the way things were going, it might be for a nervous breakdown.

Cleo didn't like hand-holding. It felt like something only old couples should do because they'd earned it. But she let him, this time.

They found Andrew after fifteen minutes and Cleo was surprised that as soon as he saw them he hugged them both and started crying. She'd never seen him cry before and his tears were so big and fat and unselfconscious, Cleo found herself crying as well.

"Will you look at the lot of us. Absolutely useless," Andrew said, and he grabbed what looked like a well-used tissue out of his jeans pocket.

"Where is she?" Cleo's eyes scanned the giant window, behind which were a half-dozen incubators with the tiniest humans Cleo had ever seen. It was such a shock she had to breathe in slow through her nose and out her mouth to stop from weeping uncontrollably. None of these babies were hers, she didn't have the right.

"Right in front of you. There, on the left." Andrew beamed and wiped his eyes again, the tissue coming apart in his fingers.

Cleo and Jamie faced the window and peered in. Even with the layer of glass and plastic incubator between her and the baby, she could see Clara's little chest rise and fall, her heartbeat under a thin layer of skin and bone. It was the saddest and most beautiful thing Cleo had ever seen.

Jamie grabbed her hand again and squeezed hard.

"Andrew, she's perfect," he said, and he looked back at his best friend and smiled with a joy Cleo had never seen. He was crying now, too. For the first time since his grandfather had died four years ago.

"I wish you could go in and hold her," Andrew said, man-patting Jamie hard on the back, a distraction from the fact they were both crying. "Only me and Fran have been able to, really. And we need all kinds of gear on. Soon though, we're getting there."

Cleo took her hand away from Jamie's so she could rummage in her purse. They were all a mess now, and she doled out clean tissues.

"Where's Fran? How is she?"

"She's pretty good," Andrew said and he looked in at the baby, placing one hand on the glass. "It's been hard. She's really tired. She's taking the day off to get some sleep." He laughed a little but Cleo could see he was tired. Not the happy-tired that new parents were supposed to be.

"Well, I guess she should get some sleep while she still can," Jamie said, trying to break the tension that had settled over the three of them. Cleo turned back to look at the baby.

"How's Clara Jane? How much longer will she be in?" Cleo saw a welcome gratitude come into Andrew's eyes, relieved to be talking about something he knew to be sure and true.

"So much better now, thankfully. We'll be here a few more weeks, maybe even a month. Really looking forward to getting her home, though, I tell you. She's getting so much stronger every day. And when we hold her, her heartbeat evens out, the monitors say so. Isn't that something else?"

Cleo knew with everything in her, if that was her baby in its plastic house, with its tiny beating heart under see-through skin, she would never rest until she could hold her baby in her arms. Would never be able to sleep or leave the hospital until everyone was home and safe.

"She'll be home before you know it," Cleo said. She squeezed Andrew's arm, and he seemed to be grateful for her useless words of comfort, the same words he'd probably heard from every family member and friend who'd looked through this window at this perfect little creature, still so far from a normal home of any kind.

A quiet drive back to their house. Not unpleasant, only a necessary quiet to take in everything. Cleo had been relieved to get a good look at the baby. Up close she could see without a doubt that Clara was indeed Andrew's. She had a mini version of his dimpled chin, his wide-set eyes, even the beginnings of a head of dark hair.

Jamie had one hand on the wheel, and the other squeezing her knee.

"Would you dump me if I cheated on you?" Cleo looked at him.

"Holy shit."

"No, no, you know what I mean. Andrew and Fran. They're not... I don't know. Would you dump me if I cheated?"

"Of course."

What if we were trying to have kids and it wasn't working and it's possibly my fault and I'm actually okay with not having them at all.

"Then why do you think it's okay for Andrew to stay with Fran?" Cleo wasn't even sure why she was asking him this, ten minutes after meeting their kid.

"I don't think it's okay, but I have to be okay with it for Andrew. And the baby. They'll be fine. Well, they'll have to be, for a while at least."

"Would you be fine if we couldn't have a baby?"

"Hey. It'll all work out, you know that, right?" He gave her knee a reassuring squeeze.

Some days his optimism made her want to bite his fucking head off.

"Jamie, come on, be sensible. Mom and Joe couldn't have one. Nancy and Doug almost couldn't. It's pretty common, but no one talks about it."

"I guess I'd be fine." Jamie stopped at a red light and looked at her. "I don't know."

Cleo turned away from him, thinking of Clara's chest rising and falling, not quite ready to breathe on her own.

june

CLEO TIED HER BATHROBE AROUND HERSELF AS SHE TOOK THE stairs down to the living room one slow step at a time, pondering another gentle way to tell Jamie she'd just started her period.

Every month a little disappointment. They'd been trying for barely six months.

It was Sunday morning, the one day Jamie let himself be lazy. They'd lounge in front of the television in pyjamas until noon, Cleo only leaving the couch long enough to make them a greasy breakfast. But when she got downstairs Jamie was sitting at the kitchen table, a mug of tea in front of him, working at his laptop.

"It's Sunday," she said.

"It is indeed."

"It's Sunday," she said again, and the empty coffee pot on the kitchen counter made her so sad she could have burst into tears right there. "Sunday is lazy-coffee-TV day, what's wrong?"

"Nothing, babe. I just felt like tea and I have some work to do."

"I just got my period."

"Okay."

Everything was off as soon as she'd woken up. A dull ache in her back, a heaviness in her abdomen, and no smell of Sunday coffee wafting from the kitchen to cheer her. It was too much.

"You didn't put the coffee on."

"Oh, sorry." He looked over his shoulder at her, then went right back to his work.

"Jamie, what's wrong."

"What do you mean?"

"You always make the coffee on Sunday. You're sitting at the kitchen table working and drinking tea. Am I not allowed caffeine anymore?"

"Christ, Cleo. Is that what this is?" He closed his laptop and made a move to get up from the table. "I forgot to put the coffee on? Here, I'll do it now."

"No, no it's fine. Sorry. I'll do it."

"Why are you reading so much into everything lately?" He took his tea and stood up, walking away from her and heading towards the living room.

"You promised me we wouldn't do this," Cleo said, trying to keep her voice calm, but a burning lump was rising in her throat. She swallowed it down hard, not wanting him to see her cry over the very thing she swore she'd never let get to her. "It hasn't even been six months, we can't be this obsessive already. Some people have to try for years before anything happens."

"I'm not obsessive, I've just been thinking about stuff. That's allowed, isn't it?" He turned to look at her and took a long, loud sip of his tea. "Would it hurt to talk to someone and get a jump on things because of your age?"

Cleo stood at the butcher block, her arms crossed.

"Our age, I mean. The two of us." He put his tea back on the table and leaned against the kitchen door. The sun beat down on his hair through the window.

She started clanging around the kitchen, opening cupboards, trying to find the coffee grinder, trying to find the bag of coffee beans in the fridge, doing anything to distract herself.

"Lots of people can't and the doctors never figure out why, that's probably what it is," Cleo muttered to herself. Her hands started to shake a little and it pissed her off.

"Or it could be something simple that they can fix for us," Jamie said, his voice gentle, like he was trying to convince a child this trip to the dentist wouldn't hurt in the least.

"It's probably me," Cleo said with her head in the fridge, coffee beans in front of her face, pretending to search so she wouldn't have to look Jamie in the eye. Her bare feet were freezing on the kitchen floor, why was it so fucking cold in June.

"Cleo, you're thirty-eight, lots of women in their—"

"It's probably me because I had an abortion when I was twenty-three." A breath of air through her mouth. That was done, and it felt good. It felt normal. Months of curling into his back at night, her heart beating faster against his spine every time she thought about telling him. Silly.

"Maybe something got messed up," she continued. She crouched down to rummage through the produce drawer. The air from the fridge felt nice on her face.

"You had an abortion. For who?"

Cleo almost laughed. Of course, for who.

"No one you know. No one I loved. It was in Korea."

The hilarious thing was, it wouldn't be the most unusual thing for Jamie to have passed Trent in the street here at home. She'd seen him herself, six years ago at Sobeys, and ducked into the pet food aisle to avoid him.

"Was it safe there?" Jamie looked down at his tea and rolled the mug between his hands.

"Christ, Jamie. It was South Korea, I wasn't in a back alley in 1950s Arkansas somewhere. I'm sure they sterilized the instruments."

He flinched when she said that, such a slight jerk of his head Cleo barely registered it, but it was there. Like he couldn't believe she was joking about this. This of all things.

"I know, I know, but it's not uncommon to have complications later on, right?"

"My doctor said I was fine."

"Your doctor knew about this?"

"She's my doctor, Jamie."

"Who else knows?"

"Why does that matter?"

"It doesn't, I'm just wondering."

"Nancy and Donna. I never told Maisie. It's a residual Catholic guilt thing. The stuff never completely washes off you." The guilt of knowing her mother got pregnant in a foreign country and had a baby by herself, but Cleo couldn't do it when her turn came along.

"Okay. I'm glad you told me." He drained his mug.

Cleo couldn't help but think he sounded like a kindergarten teacher, disappointed in a student for not making it to the bathroom on time.

"So, we're okay?" The relief of having said it out loud weakened her legs.

"Of course we're okay. Why wouldn't we be?"

"I don't know. Maybe you're a pro-life nut and I didn't know it."

"Of course not. Jesus. Come here." Jamie walked across the kitchen. He placed his empty mug on the butcher block and grabbed Cleo into a hug before she had a chance to go to him.

She breathed in the smell of his freshly laundered robe. His heartbeat and the feel of his arms were normal and comfortable.

"Just, maybe don't tell Mom," he said, and kissed the top of her head.

summer

Cleo woke at six, determined to get a head start on the weekend without missing a second of sun. They'd booked a house in Port Rexton for three days with Nancy, Doug, and Mack; amazingly, the weather looked like it would be great the whole time.

She hadn't slept well but it was such a beautiful morning, she didn't mind. Cleo brewed a strong pot of coffee, letting Jamie sleep for another hour while she finished the packing they'd started the night before. She opened all the windows in the kitchen, turned the radio on low, and took her coffee out to the front step.

It had rained overnight, but the morning was warm and the step was dry. There were still dark splotches on the pavement that the sun hadn't reached yet. The first rays through the Narrows were only spilling up over the back of the house. A couple stumbled up Holloway Street, their night just ending, the woman barefoot and carrying her heels in her hand. Cleo smiled, remembering how she and Jamie had walked up that same hill to this house the first night they'd slept together.

She missed those days. She hadn't even thought about missing them until they'd gone off the pill and everything became so complicated.

It would be good to have other people around this weekend.

When Jamie came downstairs an hour later, Cleo was packing the cooler with food and beer, cutting the plastic rings from two six-packs with a pair of kitchen shears.

"Good morning," Cleo said, putting down the scissors and taking a bite of toast. "Coffee? I made it strong and dirty because it's early."

"What are you doing?"

"I'm cutting the rings."

"Craft project?"

"No, I'm cutting the rings so the seagulls don't choke."

"What?"

"The seagulls at the dump. These are perfect gull-neck-size holes, there are a million of these at the dump and the seagulls get their heads stuck in them and they choke and die. They shouldn't even be legal. It's complete bullshit."

"Can I have my coffee first before we figure out how to save the world?"

"Listen man, I'm just trying to save the gulls."

"I thought you hated seagulls ever since you saw one eat a baby duck at the park."

"It's all part of the food chain Jam-Jam, and we really have to get serious about trying to save the world if we're going to procreate."

"If we ever manage to procreate." He reached past her head to the cupboard for a coffee mug.

"Yep. That's right." Cleo moved out of his way. She should have been relieved to finally hear him sounding practical, but it felt like a kick in the stomach.

"Well, this is a bit ridiculous, isn't it?" Nancy put her sunglasses up on her head, closed her eyes and raised her face to the sky.

They were sitting in deck chairs drinking beer in the sun, watching Doug and Jamie run around the field with Mack.

"Yes, a bit. The sun is actually glinting off your child's blond hair. It's like a fancy tourism ad out there."

"Can you believe that kid came out of me? Look at him. Doug spit right out. It's so unfair. I get a wrecked vagina and that one hemorrhoid that refuses to go away. It's a good thing he's so fucking adorable."

The beer was ice cold and the breeze was warm. All Cleo wanted in the world was a place like this to get away to. Somewhere quiet in the sun, near the ocean. A kid running around. Maybe, maybe not. Probably not. It was impossible to turn that part of her off now, especially watching Jamie running around with Mack.

"How are things?" Nancy pulled her glasses back over her eyes and turned to look at Cleo. "In Babyland, I mean."

"Ugh. The same. Exhausting. Hopeless. The usual. The sex is blah, because we have to."

"Did you tell him about abortion snowball?"

"Yup."

"How'd he take it."

"Fine, I guess. He wanted to know for who."

"Jesus, of course."

"He's so impatient. We haven't even been at this for longer than a few months. I guess he thinks because his sister got knocked up at fifteen it'll be easy for the two of us in our old age. Like fertility runs in the family or something."

"Remember when sex was just for fun?"

"Nope."

Mack ran towards them, cheeks red, gold hair shining in the sun. Jamie and Doug were behind him, smiling like boys, sweaty with exertion and joy. There was a stupid perfection in all of it that made Cleo's heart swell, half with love and contentment, but with fear and heartbreak too, that it would never happen for her.

Doug came back downstairs after a twenty-minute bedtime with Mack.

"That was it? That was bedtime?" Jamie asked over his shoulder from where he was standing at the kitchen counter, opening a pack of chicken for supper.

"Yep," said Doug. "New record."

"I've never seen that in my life. Krista's kids were always a nightmare to put to bed. And I remember because I had to do a ton of babysitting."

"It's the fresh air." Doug flopped on the couch next to Nancy and put his hand on her leg, his long fingers splayed over her entire thigh.

It was always a shock to Cleo how big Doug was. She didn't know if it was because his offshore schedule meant that she rarely saw them together, or because Nancy's personality made her seem bigger than she was. When she looked at them slouched on the couch, relaxed from the sun and the prospect of a few hours together without their child, the difference in size was almost comical.

"It's also because we were heartless and sleep-trained him as a baby." Nancy reached out her hand to Doug and they fist-bumped. "He goes out like a light most nights. I know for a fact it's the only thing we've done right as parents. At those annoying playgroups I get to say, 'Oh no, he goes to bed great.' I just leave out the part where we had to let him cry in a dark room by himself for thirty-two minutes the first night. I'm afraid the other mothers might report me."

"Oh God, I don't know if I could do that." Jamie laughed, poking around in the kitchen drawers, looking for a good knife.

"It's funny, usually only the moms say that," said Doug. "Don't mind this one and all her tough talk. She cried so hard when we did it she had to leave the house." His hand squeezed Nancy's leg and he turned and beamed at her.

Curled in the easy chair across from them, Cleo felt the strangest pang of envy. The way Doug looked at Nancy, how proud he was of her.

"It's true. I went out and got us a pizza. Then I sat in the car for ten minutes, I was too afraid to go inside."

"Remember when you did?" Doug was sitting up now, like he was really getting into watching a football game.

"The sweetest silence I have ever known," Nancy closed her eyes and put her hand to her chest.

"She literally fell to her knees and started to cry again. It was awesome. Then we drank beer and ate pizza like old times."

"And we started having sex again because I was getting more than two hours sleep a night."

"It was good times, brother."

"So, what you're saying is, when the time comes, we should call you two for support." Jamie said.

"We'll do it for you. We're hardened veterans." Nancy gave him a mock salute.

"At the rate we're going, Mack will be old enough to do it," Cleo said. Day drinking in the sun had left her tired and surly, and she didn't have the energy to be fake hopeful.

"It'll all work out. It's a rough go for sure," Doug said, clearing his throat a little after he spoke.

"Hopefully. I mean, we're trying to relax and let things take their natural course. If it happens, it happens. I don't think we're the kind of people to spend all kinds of time and money on fertility stuff," Cleo said, her eyes on Jamie at the kitchen counter. She examined his movements as she spoke, the stiffening, almost imperceptible.

"Of course that kind of thing works out great for some people, and more power to them," she continued. "But we're not up for it. And who has the money for that these days, anyways?"

"Yeah, we'll see what happens." Jamie was chopping, head down, concentrating on deboning the chicken thighs. "It's only been a few months. We'll give it a bit more time and go from there."

"Like, go on a really fancy trip to the Maldives with all the money we've saved from not doing a bunch of in vitro. Sounds like a plan!"

Cleo got up from the easy chair and walked over to the counter.

She stood on tiptoe and kissed Jamie on the cheek. She felt bad about bringing up the fertility stuff, especially while he was cooking them a nice supper. She went back to the living room, standing at the window to take in the last of the evening sun. It lit the whole room pink and dark orange. Suddenly, it felt wasteful to be inside when the evening was so calm and the sunset this perfect, and Cleo felt frantic to get out the door. She went to the porch to find her sunglasses and sandals.

"Look at poor Vanessa at work," Nancy said. "It took them seven rounds before they had Jasper."

"Seven rounds? They let you do it that many times?" Jamie turned to the living room, his hands in the air, dripping chicken juice all over the kitchen floor.

"If you have the money, they do."

"Jesus, the stuff people have to go through." Doug shook his head. "I thought two miscarriages was bad enough."

"I'm going to sit outside and watch the sunset." Cleo stuck her head in from the porch. "Anyone wanna join?"

"But they got a baby out of it," Jamie said.

"Yeah, she's super sweet. It's too bad about their divorce," Cleo said on her way out the door.

Everyone was in bed by eleven, tired from the day's drive and the sun. Cleo took a shower in their ensuite bathroom before sinking into the king-size bed; she couldn't bear getting into those fancy expensive sheets with a layer of the day's sweat and sunscreen on her skin. Nancy and Doug had insisted they take the largest bedroom, telling them it was their reward for agreeing to come on vacation with a toddler.

Jamie stripped off and got into bed, pulling Cleo in close and kissing her forehead. The tip of his nose was sunburned; his summer freckles had appeared in full force.

"Hi there." His hand slid down to her bottom and squeezed.

"Hi."

"I heard a rumour you're ovulating this weekend."

"I am indeed. Was that meant to be a turn on? Because you've been much sexier with hints in the past."

"Whatever works, right?"

He kissed her a little harder, but Cleo gently pulled back to look at him.

"Jamie, we can't."

"What? Why not? We'll be quiet, no one will hear."

"I can't, it would just be too weird. Mack's bedroom is just across the hall."

"Toddlers sleep like logs once they're out, it's all good."

"We can't, and . . . and I'm not really in the mood. I'm really tired. Maybe we can sneak off somewhere tomorrow?"

"But you're ovulating."

"We'll still be good tomorrow."

"I thought there was a window."

"There is, but it's a couple of days."

"But what if we need to do it right now, and tomorrow is too late and we miss our chance and then have to wait till—"

A wail from across the hall so loud and terrifying the two of them sat up in bed. Cleo heard Nancy fling open her door and run down the hall to Mack's room. A minute later and Nancy was carrying him down the hallway, until his crying and Nancy's shushing faded behind the click of her and Doug's bedroom door.

"See? It's like he heard us talking about doing it." Cleo cuddled into him, sure that Mack's freak-out would lighten the mood and let them go to bed content and looking forward to tomorrow.

"I guess he did. Okay, then. Good night." Jamie kissed her on the forehead, and switched off the bedside lamp. He turned on his side to face the wall.

laundry

THE CLOTHES WERE STILL HOT WHEN CLEO DUMPED THEM ON the sofa in the space between them—she burned her finger on the metal button from a pair of Jamie's jeans. It was strange for her to go to the basement and get laundry fresh from the dryer. Maybe this was unconscious training for washing baby clothes. She could be pregnant right now and this was her homemade pregnancy test. The hormones had kicked in and were manifesting themselves in household chores.

Some days she had to run down to the basement after a shower to get a pair of clean underwear. When Jamie saw her opening the basement door in her towel he would say, "Why don't you just fold the laundry as soon as it's dry," and Cleo would say, "Why don't you put the dishes away when they're dry instead of stacking more wet dishes on top." That's as far as their division-of-labour arguments went, which didn't seem so bad, according to the horror stories she'd heard from some of her married friends.

"I hate sorting socks," Cleo said. A pile of mismatched ones laid across her lap. "I'm going to throw out all my socks and all your socks and buy all black ones."

"I'll let you throw out the socks if you let me get rid of this." Jamie was holding up her favourite towel, the one she got in Mexico when she was eighteen. It was orange and green and had a giant cactus wearing a hat and sunglasses and holding up a drink. "Tequila Sunrise" was written on it in giant letters shaped like puffy clouds.

"You seriously want to throw out my Tequila Sunrise towel? You're lucky I don't have it framed and hanging over the fireplace. That thing's been to thirty-two countries."

"Yeah, it looks it."

"The towel stays. Or you can find someone else to fold your underwear." Cleo held up a pair of his boxer briefs and smiled sweetly before folding them in a neat little square and putting them in the underwear pile on the coffee table.

She didn't tell him the towel had been used for beach sex with the hottest man she'd ever slept with. A stupidly good-looking Greek bartender she'd had a month-long fling with when she travelled to Crete in her early thirties. That was mostly why she couldn't throw it out. When she wrapped herself in it she remembered how warm it could be at night, and how good olive oil tasted when it came from two farms down the road.

Jamie held the towel up to the light. "You can almost see through it."

"I like old towels." Cleo grabbed it from him. She put it to her face and breathed deeply. It was still warm from the dryer and smelled faintly of laundry detergent, but years ago it was always warm from the sun and smelled like ocean and sunblock. "They dry you off better. The best towels are old and nubby. Like you and your sperm, ha."

"Jesus, Cleo," Jamie muttered. He got up from the sofa and walked off into the kitchen. His leg brushed the edge of the coffee table, knocking a pile of folded underwear onto the floor.

"What? What! I was joking! That was a joke. Come on Jamie, don't be like that."

"Be like what?" he said on his way to the kitchen, his back to her. He grabbed the orange juice from the fridge and closed the door hard enough that the pair of hula salt and pepper shakers they'd bought in Maui wobbled precariously back and forth from their perch on top of the freezer. Pepper fell off and smashed behind the fridge. They both started at the sound of the glass breaking.

"Jesus, sorry. I won't bring up your sperm again."

She didn't think it was possible for someone to look so intense while they were drinking juice. It was like watching a terrible pitch. Cleo could see all the ad execs sitting around the table saying, *No, no, no, he's too angry.*

She bent to pick up the pile of underwear and refolded them silently while Jamie drank his juice at the kitchen counter.

the fall

It's Jamie's birthday and they've driven to Clarenville for the whole goddamn day. He is now forty-one and his mother still insists on a day-long celebration in the family home, like he is a child. His birthday is on a Saturday this year so they have to go, there is no excuse, and Cleo is so sick of telling her boyfriend *you can do what you want, it's your birthday, you're a grown man* that she shuts up about it this year because everything feels fragile so she does what he wants. She does what his parents want, she does what everybody wants.

They left town at ten in the morning, which meant Cleo missed one of her lazy weekend mornings and she is so crooked by the time they get to Evelyn and Hector's because there's a houseful of people and the house smells like turkey dinner and sweet God can the woman cook anything except turkey when there's something to celebrate. Cleo had wanted to take Jamie out this year, take him to Raymonds, splash out, make up for everything. But it is turkey again; it will be turkey until the end of time.

Hellos and hugs and Cleo runs to the bathroom because she's had an extra large Tim Hortons on the way here, which she never does but she needed the caffeine, some kind of mood elevator to get her through the onslaught of pregnancy inquiries from Jamie's family. And it doesn't take more than ten minutes when Cleo has to pee again shortly after arriving. When she comes out of the bathroom for the second time, Krista and Evelyn are standing there expectantly. What is wrong with this family.

"My oh my, you're having to pee a lot," says Krista, standing at the kitchen counter peeling carrots with her mother.

"Still not pregnant!" Cleo says it loud enough for everyone to hear, including the men having pre-dinner drinks in the living room and Sophie and Marcus, who are so engrossed in their iPads they probably don't care.

Darren finds hilarity in this and he elbows Jamie sitting next to him in the loveseat.

"You shooting blanks or what, Pike?" He laughs so hard at this, like he's the first person to ever use this expression, laughs like he invented it.

He's an idiot and his only real goddamn accomplishment is fathering five children and Cleo bites her tongue hard to keep from telling him so.

Jamie laughs a little to break the tension, all the men do, and for once, the women are quiet in the kitchen.

Jamie is having a light beer because he's driving back, even though it's his birthday. Hector and Darren are drinking hard liquor, rum and Cokes. Cleo has no stomach for the stuff but she rummages in the fridge and miraculously finds tonic and there is gin in a small kitchen cupboard that serves as a liquor cabinet so she pours herself a double gin and tonic. She can't find any lemons or limes but there's a large bottle of that store-bought lemon juice in the door of the fridge and she puts a squirt in her glass. Cleo doesn't ask Evelyn and Krista if they need help, she leaves them like two hens to cluck and tut and judge her. She joins the men in the living room for banal conversation about the weather, the news, Darren's latest shed project, interjecting only enough to make it seem like she's in the world. Mostly she's quiet and enjoying the slow burn of gin mixed with too-lemony lemon juice that lights a path to her stomach.

Everything's a bit more tolerable now that Cleo's a few drinks in. There's a tiny tug of guilt that she's the one getting drunk on Jamie's birthday, but she tells herself that he's the one who dragged her to Clarenville so she deserves to enjoy herself more than he does.

The gin on an empty stomach has made her famished so she wolfs down a helping and a half of dinner, and she lets Evelyn and Krista clear her plate. Cleo is sick of the men not helping, not even Jamie, even though he shouldn't have to clear up on his birthday. She doesn't quite get how not helping will get any kind of point across, but she's too tipsy to help clear anything from the table anyway. She turns down Krista's offer of a cup of tea and keeps on with the gin.

There's a mangled chorus of "Happy Birthday" and Sophie brings Jamie's cake to the table, flanked by Krista and Evelyn who are terrified she'll drop it. Hector and Darren are holding iPhones so the twins and Jonathan can FaceTime in from town and Fort McMurray.

There is no event in this family that is not monumental. If Cleo had a baby she'd need security to keep them from rushing the delivery room doors, everyone holding camera phones high in the air. Except Evelyn: she'd be holding a giant platter with a turkey on it.

The cake is served and there's ice cream this time, so Sophie doesn't have a meltdown and everything is really delicious. Cleo thinks she might get through the rest of this day and then it happens.

"Just imagine," says Evelyn, her mouth half-full of cake. "This time next year you might have something else to celebrate on your birthday. Or someone, I should say."

The whole table laughs, everyone except Jamie and Cleo. Even Sophie and Marcus are laughing, and Cleo doesn't know if it's because they know about the baby stuff too, or if they're feeling left out.

"See, here's the thing, Evelyn." Cleo shoves a giant spoonful of ice cream into her mouth and it makes her head and teeth ache with the sudden cold. "I had an abortion in Korea when I was twenty-three and I'm pretty sure my insides are a mess so we probably can't have kids. I guess Jamie forgot to call and give you the latest developments." And she looks at Jamie when she says the last part, his face like he isn't awake but his eyes are open and he's not able to move in his sleep.

This isn't so bad, she thinks. It feels kind of good to have it all out in the open. She keeps going, raises her third double gin and tonic.

"Ah well, we can't all be as fertile as Krista. My eggs aren't exactly fifteen years old, you know."

The room goes like one of those educational videos from the '50s, where a mushroom cloud appears on the horizon and the next shot is all the kids running out into the hallway at school and putting their heads between their knees and covering the backs of their necks like there is any way in this world to stop the nuclear shitstorm about to hit.

Evelyn drops her dessert fork and the thing that surprises Cleo the most at this very moment, is this is the first time she's ever seen dessert forks in the Pike household. No one licked their dinner fork and laid it back on the tablecloth to wait for dessert. Cleo keeps talking, even though she can't connect between her brain and tongue, and her face is so hot it's sweaty.

"No, no, no, I'm not being mean. I'm not being mean! That's how it's supposed to be. Like, evolution. You pop out a bunch of youngsters starting when you're fifteen, and you get your tubes tied after the last 'Happy Accident.'"

"That's me!" Sophie shouts from the end of the table. She eats a mouthful of cake and bounces on her bum up and down in her chair, happy to be included in the adult conversation. Marcus sits across from Sophie and he's just old enough to know exactly what's going on. His cheeks redden and he drops his head. Hector and Darren are the same, with their arms crossed. Three generations of mortification, it's like a weird painting.

There's a sober blip on Cleo's radar that there's a child in the room, two children, but she can't stop. Somewhere in her head she's pleased with Sophie for being so smart, and grateful she's not old enough to fully understand the disaster unfolding at the dinner table.

"Krista gets it! She said, fuck it, I'll start early, and look at her, everything fell back into place." Cleo points at Krista's chest from across the table, her arm hovering above the tub of Eversweet margarine with crumbs in it from breakfast and she says, "Those boobs are like, look at me! I breastfed five babies. Five babies! And all my shit fell back into place." Cleo hits herself hard, with one pointy index finger thumping her breastbone. "It's all for the best, really. I'm thirty-eight, so if I had a baby now I'd be fuuuuuucked."

Krista's mouth drops open but no sound comes out and Cleo remembers Krista didn't breastfeed at all, so she's probably justified in feeling some indignation at Cleo's making an example of her.

Jamie grabs Cleo by the arm, pulls her from the table, and hauls her out to the living room. Everything is quiet except for Evelyn crying softly.

duckish

THEY DROVE FROM CLARENVILLE TO GOOBIES IN COMPLETE silence. Cleo was still drunk on gin but the sauciness was gone. She felt guilty, but she was proud of herself. If anything good came out of the evening, it was Evelyn and Hector leaving her alone from now on. If there was a from now on. She wasn't sure there would be after that.

It was just getting duckish. Cleo leaned forward in her seat a little to watch for moose. She thought she might welcome a set of antlers coming through the windshield at this point. That would stop them from worrying about everything and make them happy to be alive and childless. If the moose didn't kill them, of course.

"That wasn't fair, what you just did," Jamie said.

He couldn't even look at her.

"Yeah, well, life's not fair, and you shouldn't have told your mother we were trying. That was fucking stupid." Cleo's head pressed against the window and the condensation was making her bangs wet. It was so quiet she could hear Jamie swallow.

"Some couples can't have kids, Jam-Jam. What are you gonna do."

She never used that nickname when she was angry with him. She sang the last part, *What are you gonna doooo*, to try and defuse everything but that only made it worse.

"Cleo, anyone can have kids if they give a shit and try to figure it out."

"I don't want to figure it out! So, what, are we supposed to re-mortgage the house for in vitro? What if we ended up with fucking triplets? I don't want to go through all that. Jesus, can't we just be happy on our own?"

"I can't be happy when you don't care enough to want to figure out what's wrong with us."

"What's wrong with me, you mean."

"Well, you're the one who had the abortion."

She turned her head away from the passenger window and looked at him and his face said he regretted the words before he even registered what he'd said. He stared straight ahead with wide eyes and that little muscle clenching and unclenching in his jaw.

"I didn't mean it like that."

Cleo had never been hit by a man before. She imagined only for a second that this is what it must feel like. What he'd said was like a man slapping a woman hard across the face in a movie.

"Fuck sake."

"Why didn't you tell me sooner?"

"Because it's an abortion. Everyone's had an abortion. Maybe not Nancy, but she took the morning-after pill, like, ten times in university, which has to be scientifically equivalent to at least two abortions. Melissa at work had one, your boss Kim had three and I know this because she got drunk at one of your Christmas parties and told me. So, what does it matter that I didn't tell you right away? It's my own gynecological business. And besides, I told you, didn't I?"

"If it's no big deal then why didn't it come up in conversation ever? We could have done something about this years ago if you'd only told me."

"What the hell is that supposed to mean? We could have done something? This could all be you, you know. This could be your sperm.

Or it could be that you're so uptight about this it's stressing me the fuck out and my uterus has shut down out of spite."

"I mean, if it turns out it is something that's connected, at least we would have had a heads-up."

"A heads-up, Jamie? Fuck!"

He touched her arm like they were out for a Sunday drive. His eyes went soft as a puppy's and Cleo felt like throwing up. She jerked her arm away from him in a way she'd never done, and she meant it.

It was quiet in the car until Whitbourne.

"Sometimes I think you don't want any of this." Jamie eased onto the two-lane highway.

"Sometimes I think that too."

part three

first buds of spring

we'll see

"Cleo, could I speak with you for a second?" Robert's head poked out his office door.

Cleo resented her co-workers in that moment: the way they shamelessly peered around their individual cubicles, thinking she wouldn't notice everyone staring at her like she'd just gotten called to the principal's office. Idiots.

"Sure!" She said it with every ounce of normalcy she could muster. It wasn't unusual for Robert to summon anyone to his office for an impromptu meeting. So what if she'd just ended a five-year relationship. No one blinked an eye when Melissa came to work with smudged mascara and orange foundation streaks on her face at least once a week, but Cleo couldn't go through one goddamn breakup? She couldn't have a week or two of being listless? She hated everyone. Except Nancy. Nancy, who'd essentially kept her alive since she'd left Jamie. Nancy, who Cleo heard chastise everyone, with "Nice and subtle, guys, good work. Jesus Christ," as Cleo was closing Robert's office door behind her.

"How are ya, duckie?" He was on his feet, hands in his pockets, staring out at the harbour. This alarmed Cleo a little; it gave the meeting an immediate and serious feel. Robert was usually bumbling at his desk under a pile of papers, looking for his cellphone or a half-eaten sandwich. She sat down and folded her hands in her lap. Preparing for the worst. So, she'd get fired, so what. Get all the awful shit over in two weeks and be done with it.

"I'm okay. I've had better days. I apologize if I seem out of sorts and if you think the work's been suffering."

"Jesus, maid, your work this week has been better than anyone out there on the best of days."

"Okay, good. I thought you were calling me in to fire me." Cleo unfolded her hands and relaxed a bit in the chair.

"God, no. I just wanted to check in and see how you were doing . . . and I wanted to run something by you."

"You've opened an office in the Cayman Islands and you want to transfer me? Sign me up."

"When I do, you'll be the first to know." Robert left the window, sat back at his desk and was quiet for a moment.

Why did he still look like he was going to fire her?

"Cleo, I need you to tell me if I'm overstepping boundaries here. I won't lie and tell you I don't know what's going on."

"Okay."

"I know you've moved back in with your folks for a while."

"Yep." She really did feel like she was in the principal's office now. She raised her eyes to the ceiling, taking a deep breath and exhaling with a puff.

"Now it's none of my business," Robert said. "We've all been there. Christ, I had to move into my parents' basement when I was thirty after I lost my job, and I had a wife and two kids with me. You take the time you need and do what you have to do, yeah?"

"Yeah." Where was this going?

"Now, I don't know what your plans are, again, none of my business, but my sister has a spot she's looking to rent, and when she mentioned it in passing, I thought of you. It's a nice place, and you can probably get it for a great price. I would have felt bad if I didn't let you know, in case you were looking. I hope that's okay, and I hope you don't think this is inappropriate."

"No, no, of course not Robert . . . that's . . . that's really thoughtful of you. Of course." If Cleo didn't think he'd be mortified, she would have leapt over the desk and kissed him on the cheek for his overwhelming decency. "I hadn't really thought about it yet, but if something is out there and available, I'd be silly not to consider it. Where, and how much and all that?"

"A nice place up by Quidi Vidi Lake. Two-bedroom basement apartment, but it's above ground, lots of light. I've been there, it's great, looks out over the lake. Nice chunk of backyard they never use because they got a huge deck upstairs."

Cleo's heart sank a little at the word "basement"; she had it in her head that she'd get a place downtown. Maybe a place like her old spot on Bond, with a view of the Narrows. Quidi Vidi was walkable, but much farther from work. So far from good coffee. But it was Robert and she had to follow through.

"That sounds great," she said. "I don't really need two bedrooms, but it wouldn't hurt to have some extra space if the price is right. Did your sister say how much?"

"Well, here's the thing, and I'll be honest with you. Marsha's a bit of a case." Robert leaned back in his chair and folded his arms over his chest. He looked left, then right, like someone else was in the room with them. "The woman has a ton of money and a lot of time on her hands. The basement was a bit of a pet project for her, a space for relatives to stay when they came to town. Now she can't get rid of them and wants to rent the place so she'll have an excuse to tell everyone to frig off."

"She sounds like my kind of people." Cleo thought of Evelyn and Hector, how relieved she always was that they refused to stay at Prospect because of the parking. She'd give anything now for the normal she used to know. For a cup of tea over a casserole and chats with Evelyn.

"I'll vouch for you. She's adamant about no partiers and pets, no smokers and all that. You could probably get the place for seven, eight hundred bucks all in."

"Robert, that's it?" Eight hundred bucks all in couldn't get you a decent thing these days, especially downtown.

"I'm telling ya, she doesn't need the money. She's just sick of babysitting relatives every weekend. You'd be doing her a favour."

"Could I get her number or email? I'd love to see the place."

"Let me give her a call first. I'll tell her you're interested and I'm sure she'll be in touch to set something up."

Cleo had held herself together at work all week. But this act of kindness from Robert, and the finality of getting her own place, felt like it might send her into an abyss, one she couldn't climb out of without a good cry.

"Robert. Thank you." She stood, quicker than she wanted.

"Not a problem, my dear. You go on, now."

Everyone kept their eyes on their screens when Cleo left Robert's office and made a sharp right, heading to the washroom.

Three days later, Cleo had the keys to her new place. It was a good half-hour walk from work, but it was newly renovated and Marsha offered it to her for eight hundred dollars a month, everything included. There was furniture, two big bedrooms, and even an island in the kitchen, bigger than the little butcher block at her old place.

The view from the kitchen window was of the lake. She could look out over it while she was doing dishes. Stare out of it while she was eating takeout and drinking whiskey.

Marsha made no bones about what she was looking for in a tenant.

"I'll be straight with you," she'd said, after looking Cleo up and down when they met at the entrance to the apartment. "I'm looking for someone quiet, clean, no drama. Robert said I wouldn't have a problem with you, but he did say you're just out of a relationship. If a drunk ex-boyfriend shows up pounding on your door at three in the morning, this probably isn't going to work out."

"It's not like that. It was a very civil breakup."

"Yes. Well. We'll see. I've got family coming in to finish their shopping, but the place should be ready a few days before Christmas. You can take the keys now and move your stuff in when I finally get rid of them. I'll have the place cleaned and let you know as soon as it's done. No need for rent until January."

"Oh. I can pay some rent for December if you—"

"No need. First of January is fine." Marsha waved a dismissive hand at Cleo.

"Thank you. I appreciate it."

"Just remember. No funny business."

tea II

It was Saturday afternoon and Maisie and Cleo were drinking tea at the kitchen table. There'd been a few snowfalls but nothing had stuck. Sloppy wet sleet and rain that made everything icy and miserable, or dry sharp snow that felt like sand on your face in the wind. Cleo held her mug in her hands and stared out the window. There was a thin layer of powdery snow on the brown grass.

"What a terrible time of year for a breakup," Cleo said. "At least if it was sunny and warm, things wouldn't feel so awful."

"I don't know. A beautiful day might make it worse, in a weird sort of way. You hungry?"

"Not really."

"Cleo, you have to eat."

"I know. I'm just not hungry."

Cleo had always gained weight after breakups, usually after comforting herself with hard carbs and beer. Even when her high school boyfriend had broken up with her, she'd burst in through the front door, kicked off her boots as hard as she could, and gone straight to the fridge. She ate half a tray of leftover lasagna and drank a litre of chocolate milk before going to bed in the middle of the afternoon and crying herself to sleep. After Jamie she was lucky to choke down tea and toast.

"Well, I'm not having it. I'm making you lunch. Something simple to settle your stomach," Maisie said, draining the rest of her tea and making a move to get up.

"Maisie."

"Cleo."

"Fine."

Maisie got up and rummaged in the fridge, then moved to the cupboard to have a look. She stood back with her hands on her hips.

"Got it."

She took a container out of the freezer that looked like it was soup and put it in the microwave to defrost. There was a fresh loaf of bread on the counter from the Georgestown Bakery. Cleo had heard Maisie up at six-thirty to make coffee and walk there for a Belgian when they opened at seven, like she did every Saturday.

"A grilled cheese and tomato soup. You'll eat that. I have a nice smoked cheddar in the fridge, it'll be a like a grilled cheese for grownups."

Maisie took the soup from the microwave and poked the sides of the container with a spoon. She dumped the soup out in a saucepan and reached for the giant wooden cutting board to slice some bread.

"Joe has the big firefighters' Christmas banquet at the Armoury next weekend," Maisie said as she cut the bread in perfectly even slices. "We know you're wanting to lay low these days but we got you a ticket anyways. In case you feel up for it."

"Thanks. I mean, I probably won't. But thanks."

"No trouble. Ticket will be here if you want it. Supper and a dance. Might be nice for you to get out."

"I'll think about it."

"Good."

The smell of freshly cut bread and soup was tempting. Maybe she could eat.

"This was your favourite meal when you were little," Maisie said. "I must have made this thousands of times."

"It was the last thing you made for me before I got on the plane for Korea, remember?"

"I certainly do. I came home from the airport and your dirty dishes were still in the sink. I cried for two days."

"You didn't."

"I did. I wasn't as bad as Nalfie, though. She was pacing the floor saying the rosary for a month straight, praying to the Virgin you wouldn't get kidnapped by the North Koreans."

Cleo laughed and it caught in her throat. That was before anything bad had happened. She would give anything to go back to that.

"She's giving you her car." Maisie said it without looking at Cleo, clanging the spoon on the pot as she stirred the tomato soup.

"What? No. Mom."

"Cleo, she wants to give it to you."

"I can't. I won't, I don't need it."

"But you will, and she wants you to have it. She hasn't driven in two years and she knows she can't anymore."

"She always swore she'd never get rid of it."

"I know, but in her mind this justifies it. She's helping you, so it's not like saying she can't drive anymore. If you take the car, it'll save us all a lot of grief, you know that."

"I know."

"It's paid for, it's only eight years old and it's barely been driven. If you let her do this for you, it will make her very happy."

"All right." Cleo knew it was pointless to argue with Maisie, and it would be completely futile to try and reason with Nalfie.

"If you need help with money for insurance or anything we'd—"

"I'm good. Honestly."

"But you'll tell us, if you need help, right?"

"I will. I promise. I got a real good deal on the apartment, it'll be fine."

"All right then. You want some pickled hot peppers on your sandwich?"

"Always."

A car. She had a parking spot at her apartment. This might work. How could she ever repay Nalfie? Cleo dropped her head on the table. Her mother put down the jar of pickled hot peppers, crossed the kitchen and sat next to her. Maisie reached over and smoothed Cleo's hair.

"Happy birthday, my sweet girl."

newbie

"You look nice," Maisie says to Cleo on her way back up the stairs to finish getting ready. "That dress looks great on you."

"Thanks. You're looking at a primo Value Village purchase."

"Well you'd never say it. It looks like it's from a boutique in London somewhere."

"All right Maisie, I wouldn't go that far," but Cleo smiles because this is the first time she's so much as put in her contacts since Jamie, and she feels the tiniest bit better, mostly because she had a glass and a half of Chardonnay while getting ready, she can't face this night without a little help. She's looking forward to baskets full of homemade rolls wrapped in cling film, laid out on the long tables, next to bowls of those little foil pats of butter, too hard to spread on soft rolls. When she was twenty she went to the Christmas banquet and sat with some of the senior firefighters' daughters. They were all drunk and her friend Joanna took a handful of butter packets and put them in her cleavage to warm up. She managed to fit five in there, without any of them falling into her bra or onto her lap. The girls all cheered when the butter was softened and Cleo remembers looking down at her own cleavage and thinking she'd be lucky if she could hold two pats without losing them.

Cleo wants to eat stuffed chicken breasts with bland vegetables and gravy that tastes like nothing. It would be a strange, familiar comfort to her now. She is determined not to get loaded and sad. She won't be that newly single woman, drunk at the Christmas party. She will be a mysterious thirty-eight, okay, thirty-nine-year-old single woman who is happy with herself and who can't have babies and doesn't even care. A single woman who is going to a Christmas party with her parents. Is it an open bar? Probably not. Cleo knows firefighters can drink more than anybody, or maybe a bunch of them have to stay sober in case something catches fire or there's an emergency in the middle of the banquet. Wouldn't it be great if it was an open bar because half the firefighters couldn't drink anyway and they thought what the hell, Merry Christmas firefighters, and also to your single stepdaughters.

Joe and Maisie come down the stairs and Cleo stands up from the couch.

"Well, now. Aren't you a vision." Joe scoops her up in a giant hug like he used to when she was a little girl and it catches her off guard and makes her want to cry.

"Thanks Joe."

"I'm really glad you decided to come with us tonight, sweetheart."

They pile out the front door into the snow. Cleo grabs Joe's arm on the icy walkway so she doesn't fall in her heels.

Cleo hasn't seen a lot of Joe's co-workers in a few years, so the banquet is like a big family reunion. There are hugs from giant men who are like her uncles and their wives, with their mall hairdos and high-heel shoes worn once a year, twice if they have a child getting married. But it's nice and Cleo likes the manly bear hugs and perfumed hugs from the women. It makes her float above it, if only for tonight. No one asks about Jamie, which is a relief, even though she was ready for it, but it's been so long since she's seen everyone maybe they have no idea who Jamie is anymore, or who he was.

Supper is dry chicken breast drowned in gravy, making it go down easier. Cleo is sitting with her parents this time so there's no butter in anyone's cleavage. The staff is collecting plates and Cleo stands to go to the bar. Her high heel catches on the table leg so she looks wobblier than she feels.

"You guys need anything?"

Maisie and Joe exchange glances and say no.

"You want coffee or tea when they come around with dessert, love?"

"Tea please. Thanks, Ma."

Cleo makes her way to the bar and these goddamn heels, she wishes it was summer so she could have slipped flip-flops in her purse for later on in the evening when everyone is drunk and no one cares what's on your feet. They're not obnoxious pointy heels, they're a little chunky, but she'll still have blisters later tonight. There's something lovely in the relief, though, that makes it worth it, just for that moment the shoes come off and your real heels, not the high heels, hit the ground.

There's a crowd at the bar and everything around her smells like beer and Old Spice, it reminds her of summer weddings in Wesleyville when she was little. A man walks towards her from the crowd of suits and loosened ties, carrying two bottles of beer in each hand. His head is turned and he's shouting and smiling at someone across the room. He twists his torso to let someone by and raises his hands slightly to give them more room, but he's jostled a little by the crowd and beer spills over Cleo's arm. He turns back around and sees her, beer dripping off the ends of her fingers.

"Oh shit, oh shit, I'm so sorry, let me go grab you a napkin."

"You've got your hands full, it's okay, don't worry about it."

"I'm such an idiot."

"Honestly, it's beer, it doesn't even stain. If you were carrying red wine you might be in trouble."

He laughs and sounds surprised that Cleo made a joke, like he knows it's never this easy when you spill booze on a woman. He appears relieved that she's alone, with no drunk boyfriend to get angry, though by the looks of him he could easily take care of himself. It's noisy now that supper's over and everyone is looking for drinks before dessert is served and the speeches begin, so he leans in to Cleo's ear and she thinks she hears, "Let me drop these at my table and I'll come back and get you a drink." Cleo wants to say no but he's gone already, walking back to his table. He lays down the drinks and there is a cheer and a clink of bottles and thank yous. He turns and heads to the bar once more without looking back at his friends, who don't appear to notice he's left them now they have their beer. He's close to Cleo's ear again, and there's no Old Spice smell, he smells like vanilla but a masculine sort of vanilla or sandalwood or something, and clothes off the line. Like Jamie used to. He's so young he probably still lives at home with a mother who does his laundry.

"What can I get you?"

"White wine."

"Any kind in particular?"

"I'm pretty sure they only have one."

He reaches out to shake her hand.

"I'm Francis."

"Cleo. Nice to meet you."

"I don't think I've seen you before, are you a firefighter?"

"No. Oh God, no."

"You here with your partner?"

It's nice how he asked if she was a firefighter first, she likes that. The kids are so politically correct these days.

"No, I'm here with my family. Joseph Best is my stepdad."

"Joe! Joe's my boss! Well, I can't buy you a drink and not buy one for Joe and your mom. What are they having?"

"I think they're probably okay."

"Let me buy a round for everyone, if they don't drink it that's okay."

"Mom drinks red and Joe will have some kind of light beer, he's not picky." Joe eases up on his beer snobbery when he's at events like this, knowing it's pointless to be angry at the bar for not stocking a wide selection of his favourite Asian lagers.

"Okay, red, white, and beer. Be right back."

Francis moves his way through the crowd at the bar and there are handshakes and slaps on the back and he sees a firefighter around his age and now some "heeeeeys!!" and big back-thumping hugs. For a second Cleo thinks he'll forget about her and the drinks, and she starts to move into the bar herself but he gives his buddy one last hard grab on the shoulder and keeps going. He's loosening his tie as he's shouting out his order and the bartender smiles at him because she thinks it's for her. Cleo doubts the Armoury had any trouble finding staff for this evening's banquet. The three bartenders on duty are all women under thirty, dressed like they're at a cocktail party.

He's coming back with a wine glass and a beer in the one hand, but his hands are so huge it's not a big deal for him. Cleo looks down at his shoes and they are pontoons, good for his girlfriend, she thinks. Or hey, maybe boyfriend. Probably girlfriend.

Francis is handsome, but not in that hard sharp way; he's softer somehow. If he were in a movie, one of those awful frat boy comedies, he would be the misunderstood one, the nice guy, the one who stops his friends from roofying girls' drinks at parties. He would end up with the really hot girl after she realizes her quarterback boyfriend is a complete asshole. But this guy, this guy is the one who will stick by your side and give you lots of babies. Cleo's never understood the firefighter thing. With Joe as her stepdad she was never really allowed to. The men at the station from childhood through to adulthood were like her brothers or her uncles and no one made the slightest indication of a move for fear of pissing off Joe. This Francis though, as he's walking to her she can envision an old lady slung over his shoulders in a fireman's carry, or cradling a soot-covered toddler, running out of the smoke of a burning building, and she gets why women freak out. She smiles and thanks him and goes to take the drinks.

"I'll come with you, say hi to Joe and your mom," he says, leaning in, his manly vanilla smell wafting under Cleo's nose again.

Francis. What a strange name for someone his age. He looks like he should be called Mike or Rob, or he's probably young enough to be a Tyler. He walks with Cleo to the table with an easy confidence, like he's forty-five and been at the job for twenty years, not a young firefighter on his way to give his boss a beer. There's no way he's even thirty yet and he's had this job for more than a year or two.

"Good evening, Joe," he says. "Mrs. Best." He's not nervous at all Cleo notes, probably because he's had a few. Good for him, most of the newbies are terrified of her stepfather. Joseph Best is a teddy bear inside the body of a bull, but the guys at work don't see that, except during Fire Prevention Week when there are field trips to the station and Joe helps the kindergarteners climb up into the giant fire trucks.

"Hello Francis, how are ya?" Joe reaches across the table and shakes Francis's hand.

"I accidentally spilled beer on your stepdaughter when I was in line at the bar, and when I found out who she was, I figured I'd buy a round for your table before you had me fired."

"Ahhh, Cleo's tough, it would have taken more than that," Joe says.

"Well, I'll give this to Mrs. Best for safekeeping then." Francis places the glass in front of Maisie.

"Thank you, Francis."

His penance done, Francis nods at the table and puts his hands in the pockets of his pants, all loose and easy.

"Enjoy the rest of your evening, folks. Nice to meet you, Cleo."

"You too, Francis." Cleo watches as he heads back to his friends a few tables away.

"He seems like a nice young man," says Maisie.

"Francis Fitzgerald. Been with us a year. Good kid. Bit of a show-off, but that won't last long in this business."

Cleo sits back down and looks over again at Francis's table, full of what she figures must be freshmen. She can tell by the way the table reacts when he returns that he's the leader, the funny one who tells all the good stories. Joe and Maisie have tucked into dessert and Cleo hasn't even noticed it's in front of her. She's still looking at Francis, and he glances up and sees her, then nods in her direction and smiles. She smiles back and snaps her head down, grabs her dessert fork. *Fuck fuck fuck fuck fuck.* She went there in her head for only a second. She is ridiculous.

She shovels a forkful of pie in her mouth. It had looked so good, but once it's in she realizes it's canned pie filling and not the real thing at all.

Cleo leaves the banquet early, shortly after the speeches and before the dance begins. She has to call a cab in front of Maisie and agree to have Joe walk her out to make sure she gets in before Maisie will let her go.

Joe gets her jacket from the coat check and brings it back to the table. She kisses her mother on the cheek, and Joe holds the jacket while she slips it on. They walk directly by Francis's table; Cleo feels his eyes on her but she pretends not to notice—in a nonchalant way, she hopes, not bitchy. She's still mortified that he caught her looking at him during dessert and she wants him to think it's not a big deal and it's not, of course.

They're on the sidewalk waiting for the cab and it's started to snow that Christmas movie snow, the kind that almost makes winter lovely. Joe doesn't have his jacket on and the snow is settling on the shoulders of his suit.

"I'm good, Joe, you go on in, you'll freeze."

"No, no, I'm fine, I'll wait."

"Is Maisie afraid I'll ditch the cab and try and walk home in these heels?"

"She wouldn't put it past you. Neither would I, for that matter."

The glow of the yellow cab light is coming down the road and Joe raises his arm. Anyone else would look silly doing that, like they thought they were in New York City, but it's an authoritative greeting that works coming from a man of his size and demeanour.

"I had a nice time tonight. It was good to get out of the house. Thanks for the ticket."

"Not a problem, my trout. You sure you're all right now?"

"Best kind. Tea and toast and bed."

"I'll have to stick around for a while, but we shouldn't be too long."

"Take your time. Make a night of it."

"I don't know about that. Once I switches over to rum and Coke your mother will start giving me the look."

Cleo laughs and Joe opens the cab door for her. Puts his hand on the roof of the car and peers in at the driver.

"Just a ways up Pennywell, my buddy."

"Yessir," says the cabbie and he nods. Joe has that easy way of making people feel like they're old school chums.

"See you later on, Cleo. Or probably in the morning."

"Probably in the morning."

"You've got your key? And some cash."

"Yes, Joe."

"All right, my love, see you at home."

Joe closes the cab door and knocks on the roof twice, turns and walks back to the front doors of the Armoury.

She's only thought of Jamie once this evening, when she got the smell of clean laundry off Francis and now it's that January morning when she dropped Jamie off at the airport, him knocking twice on the trunk before walking away. How she changed her mind and ran in to say goodbye.

toast

Cleo goes upstairs right away to take off her make-up before she gets too tired. It's only ten-thirty but she hardly slept last night. Sleep will be a relief, better than being awake. How much longer will it take for being awake to be okay? Christ, if anyone heard what was going on in her head they'd have her committed. Nancy thinks she should find someone professional to talk to, but Jesus Christ, she's not that far gone yet, is she? She'd never be able to afford therapy anyway, and she's not going to ask Maisie and Joe. *I can afford car insurance but can you guys spot me some money for therapy so I won't drive it off a bridge?*

Maisie and Joe will be out late because Joe needs to see the night through to the bitter end. Those two were always the last to leave the Christmas banquet, the last to come home from weddings, anything that involved a few drinks and a dance. She hopes she's like them when she's their age and not a single sixty-year-old woman who's getting drinks bought for her by young firefighters, but fuck it, there could be worse things when you're sixty.

She puts her hair up and scrubs her face clean, puts on her pyjamas. It feels like twenty years ago, like living at home during her first year of university.

Downstairs, Cleo puts on one of Joe's old Motown records. She pours a tall glass of ice water and puts some bread in the toaster. She gulps down half the glass and then holds it to her forehead to stop the throb she knows will start soon. Maisie and Joe renovated the house five years ago and put heated floors in the kitchen; the heat is so good right now Cleo didn't even bother putting her slippers on when she got changed. She loves the feel of the warm ceramic tile under her bare feet, it feels like it did when she lived in Korea. When she moved there she was so surprised they heated their homes like that, they'd been doing it for a thousand years. She would come home from work on bitter winter nights and lie on the floor to warm up, so she does that now. Puts the glass of water on the counter and sits on the floor, then lies back with her hands behind her head. Her pyjama top has ridden up and she can feel the heat on her bare lower back and nothing has felt this good in a long time; she could fall asleep right now. Her legs are flat on the floor but she bends them so her knees point up and the arch in her back is touching the ceramic tile.

She thinks about Jamie and what he's doing now, then forces him out of her head before the good buzz disappears and she's sunk in sadness again. Instead she makes herself think of Francis, she sees his face in her head, how he looked at her when she left the party. Which was a coincidence. It was a coincidence, when someone is leaving a party and they're in your eyeline, you look to see who's leaving, that's what you do, you look to see if it's a friend of yours, if it's someone you should say goodbye to. He bought her a drink, but he was being a nice guy, he would have done it for anyone. Or would he, twentysomethings don't do that, aren't nice like that. But this one is, he's an overly chivalrous firefighter, he has to be, it's in his fucking job description. Why is he in her head, this is fucking stupid, but she lets herself think that it was nice to have someone watch her walk away. Is Jamie thinking ahead already, is he eyeing women at his office, all the women he couldn't do that with before, or maybe he did and Cleo didn't know it. Will he find someone and get her pregnant and if it happens soon

Cleo will die, if it ever happens she thinks she'll want to die.

The last month they had together, they didn't touch each other. Cleo spent every night lying next to Jamie, awake for at least an hour after he had fallen asleep. Thinking how afraid she was to tell him outright how unsure she was, how she knew he wanted this more than she did. It feels like ages since anyone's touched her and she hasn't touched herself, doesn't care about it because it's like she doesn't exist down there anymore. Her hand is on her stomach and fuck this, now it's in the waistband of her pyjama bottoms. And Cleo thinks, if Francis walked in here right now she would fuck him, she would fuck him on this warm kitchen floor. She thinks of him loosening his tie at the bar. She gets his smell in her nose again and slides her hand into her underwear and it's a shock how wet she is. She comes so hard and fast the coming down isn't a resolution, it's like hitting a wall of shame and regret. She rolls on her side, her hand still tucked between her legs, and ugly cries until she can't breathe, the heat of the kitchen floor on her cheek.

bond street

Cleo didn't feel like heading out for drinks with everyone. The childless at her office, especially the childless singles, would gather every Friday after work, religiously, for a couple of drinks. There would be plans to go home after one or two, for supper. Some nights the work drinks turned into spontaneous work parties, happy hours stretching into denial stretching into standing in the slush outside the chip van waiting for a poutine at midnight. Especially this time of year, December days were an excuse for everyone to train for upcoming Christmas parties.

Cleo was avoiding work gatherings these days. Too many heads tilted in concern, too many hands reaching across tables to pat hers and ask how she was doing with it all, after a few drinks had loosened everyone into a false sense of familiarity.

She was glad to be finished work, but she didn't want to go home. It was mild and last night's rain had cleared the streets and sidewalks of whatever light snow had fallen. Cleo wanted to walk and breathe in the air that smelled like spring, but carried with it the threat of horrendous winter. Like December was messing with your head, secretly whispering to enjoy it while you still could.

She got a hot chocolate and puttered around Gower Street, King's Road, Colonial. The few squares of downtown the tourists adored, those lines of brightly coloured houses that bridal parties posed in front of every summer. The only place left untouched by condos and badly designed office buildings. There were a few Christmas lights up and trees decorated in windows, it was nice. She walked up the hill and decided to cut down Bond, her old neighbourhood. She had lived in the top-floor apartment of an old row house for five years before moving in with Jamie. She joked with him they couldn't ever break up because she'd given up such a great apartment for him. Even when they lived on Prospect she still missed the place. That view of the harbour with her morning coffee, or sitting in front of the window during a storm when there was no view at all. Wrapped in a blanket in Pop's armchair, the wind and snow whipping against the window in the dark, hiding everything except the top branches of the tall trees in the backyard.

Cleo paused when she reached her old front step. Ran her finger over the lid of the mailbox. It was the same one but too rusty now, it needed replacing. She tilted her head back and looked up at the third-floor window facing the street. She could see plants and fairy lights, the shadow of someone in the kitchen. Her chest suddenly felt heavy and her stomach sick with longing for the time before Jamie. She was grateful to have lucked into her new place; the view was great, she liked the lake and the crows, she liked that having a rich, bored landlady meant she was getting the place for a song. But she missed those days before everything got so fucked up. Starting at the agency with Nancy and getting to work with her after all those years away. Boozy weekend brunches and dancing at the Ship, late night whiskies with scruffy men in her apartment. It had all been so easy and so good. Now she was thirty-nine and getting drunk by herself, staring at crows out a basement apartment window.

And Jamie fucking still had her grandfather's chair in their living room.

His living room.

fling

Cleo liked sitting at a bar by herself. Not in the way you'd sit and shoot furtive glances around, trying to catch someone's eye, but in the way you'd sit and have a nice beer or a glass of wine with a meal. She'd never felt the insecurity she was meant to feel as a woman eating out by herself.

She even liked sitting on her own years ago, pre-smartphone, when you brought a book or a magazine with you. There was only once she'd let someone distract her: a tiny beachside bar in Thailand. He was Northern Irish, an accent on him like chocolate with crispy toffee bits. Sidled up next to her before her book was out of her purse, before she'd even ordered her beer. Four hours later they stumbled back to her hut and began a sunny, boozy week-long fling. Her last, before she met Jamie.

Book or phone or staring off into space, Cleo had spent the past few weeks perfecting the art of building invisible armour.

Today she looked like everyone else, scrolling through Twitter on her phone, hanging off the end of the bar at the Ship with a pint and a plate of fish tacos. Only a couple of weeks into getting her appetite back, she joked with Nancy she was trying to gain back the five pounds with beer, not food, and already she felt her jeans snug on her thighs the way they were when she still lived on Prospect. The only thing that felt normal was her jean size.

It was one-ish on a Saturday and she was one of a small handful of people in the place. It was a bit too early for the hangover crowd; they usually needed a twelve-hour turnaround before they returned to the sticky floors of the night before. There might be a few Christmas shoppers later. Suburbanites coming downtown on Saturday for the free parking and the adventure of eating fish and chips somewhere that wasn't in a strip mall. She was face and eyes into her second taco when she heard a gaggle of men come in the door, the gust of cold air reaching Cleo all the way over at the bar. The sound of people swooping into a place usually turned her head, looking for anyone she knew, but that reflex had stopped. All she wanted since the breakup was quiet and anonymity and a little buzz to get her through the day.

Cleo took a huge bite of her taco and the men settled at the table closest to the ladies' washroom, in plain view of her stuffing her face and drinking alone. She didn't give a shit. She wiped hot sauce off her face with a napkin and took another swig of beer.

There was something about their banter that sounded familiar, and when Cleo looked sideways she saw one of them slap another hard on the back and crack a joke.

Sweet Jesus, it was Francis the Firefighter.

The tacos were spicy and her eyebrows were sweaty and now the heat intensified as she realized she was in plain view of the man, the *boy* she'd masturbated to on her parents' kitchen floor the night of the Christmas banquet.

Cleo had that feeling of running into someone you kind of knew from high school, and the split-second decision to either speak to them or avert eye contact to save you both the effort no one really wanted to make. Except she couldn't think of anyone from high school she'd masturbated to, so in that way the situation was a little different.

It would be easy enough to pack up and leave, but Cleo was pissed at herself for letting some random twentysomething who meant nothing to her ruin her day. She wanted another beer, then she would go home to nap and watch Netflix.

The bartender was close enough that she could order another pint without being heard across the bar. Even that worry felt a bit ridiculous—that Francis would remember the sound of her voice, a woman he'd chatted with for five minutes over the din of two hundred drunk firefighters. Cleo relaxed and kept eating, trying her best to feign lack of interest in anything not food-or-drink-related.

Francis stood to go to the washroom a few minutes later and spied her when he got up. His face broke out in a genuine grin of recognition, or at least that's what Cleo picked up from her sideways glance.

"Cleo?" He said it with uncertainty, and who could blame him.

"Hey! Yeah, hi. Francis, right?" She tried the same uncertainty but wasn't sure if she pulled it off. Like he was no big deal to her, with his muscles moving like butter under his casual yet well-fitting plaid shirt, dark day-old scruff on his face that might chafe a bit if you were making out with him on the couch.

Jesus Christ.

"Yeah!" he said, like he was surprised she remembered his name. "How's it going?"

"Not bad. Just came for a bite and to get some work done." The words out of her mouth before she realized she was at the bar with an empty plate and two thirds of a pint in front of her, no laptop in sight. "But the tacos and beer won out, as you can see." Saved. Nice one.

He laughed, his eyes crinkled. He had a nice deep laugh.

"Do you recommend the tacos?"

"God, yes," Cleo said, and it felt like there was still hot sauce on her face so she reached for the crumpled napkin on the bar and wiped her mouth. And he laughed again. How was it he found her so funny.

"What are you up to today?" she managed. Too casual, she didn't even know him. What had Joe said his last name was? Something with an F.

"Not much, here with the boys. I have the weekend off, out now trying to find a cure for last night."

God, those twentysomethings and their effortless hangovers. He was the picture of health, standing in front of her with his hands in his jean pockets and his skin all glowy.

"How's Joe and your mom?"

"They're good. Nice of you to buy them a drink the other night."

"Least I could do. Don't forget to send me your dry cleaning bill."

"Ha! It was only a minor beer spillage. Lucky for you. All good."

"Well, I'll leave you to it. Nice to see you. I'll see you around."

"You too."

And that was his polite firefighter good deed for the day. Back to his table of handsomes nursing their adorable hangovers.

Cleo took her laptop out of her bag, to begin the work she hadn't intended to look at today.

An hour later Cleo is on her third pint and there are honest-to-goodness chunks of time where she forgets Francis and the Handsomes are there. She's buzzed, probably a bit closer to proper drunk, it's true, but the ideas are flowing and there's some good stuff. She wonders what Robert would say if he knew she was sitting at a bar, two and a half pints in with hot sauce under her fingernails, doing all the work she couldn't do this past week because she was too sad and sober. No wonder so many of the world's great writers are alcoholics, she totally gets it. She's churning out the ideas right now like nobody's goddamn business. And besides, three pints is a business lunch in England or someplace, isn't it?

She's completely ignoring Francis across the bar and the stretch of floor to the ladies', which she has been desperate to use for the last twenty minutes but she won't, and that must mean she isn't *actually* ignoring him.

The Handsomes have inhaled their food; they are hungover cavemen. They put on their jackets and trundle up to the bar to pay their bills and they are all so young and the smell of their cologne reminds Cleo of Korea and backpacking. She's right back there again for a nanosecond, pulled back into a sudden sadness of lost youth and regrets.

"Getting anything done?" Francis leans on the bar next to her, credit card in hand, waiting his turn to pay.

He's old enough to have a credit card, that's good.

"Yes, weirdly. Getting lots done."

"What are you working on? I mean, what do you do?"

"Advertising." Cleo rolls her eyes when she says this. "I think you win in the virtuous jobs category. Mine is mostly to annoy people."

"I don't know about that, it sounds pretty exciting."

"I'm working on a campaign for cat litter."

"Hey, I love cats."

"You have a cat?"

"Nah, I struggle to find the right brand of cat litter, so I've never bothered, you know?"

His buddies leave and he stays for one more pint. Three hours later they're walking back to his apartment on Gower Street.

Well, he has his own place, that's good.

highly flammable

SHE WANTS THIS SO BAD SHE COULD CRY BUT SHE THINKS THAT might freak him out because he's only twenty-five. Jesus fucking Christ, he's only twenty-five. He's stripping off her shirt now and it sails over her head and he throws it across the room and it's hanging off the lampshade. She worries for a second that it might catch fire because it's a cheap shirt she bought at the mall and it's probably highly flammable but she pulls Francis onto the bed on top of her and she doesn't care if the whole fucking house burns to the ground. Then she laughs out loud when she remembers she's about to fuck a firefighter.

Francis stops.

"You okay?"

He's twenty-five and he doesn't know Cleo's laughs.

She pushes him off her chest and rolls him over on his back. Straddles him and undoes his belt.

coffee II

"You don't look like a Francis."

The morning after, and Cleo was surprised she'd slept so well in a new bed. She'd woken with Francis curled around her. Her first thought on waking was how nice the sheets smelled for a guy who lived on his own.

They were lazing now, and nothing felt forced and Cleo was relieved.

"What do I look like?"

"Like an Ethan."

The sheet only came up as far as his hips and when Francis laughed Cleo saw his stomach muscles contract. She had never once seen Jamie's stomach muscles. There was one time that came close, when they came back from Hawaii and he'd had that awful stomach bug for a month. He'd been so excited to eat again when he got better that he gained extra weight.

Stomach muscles had never been important, not even when Cleo was in her twenties and it was supposed to matter. But the fireman's were impressive, she'd give him that.

Francis rolled from his back onto his side, held himself up with one elbow on the pillow.

"I think the Ethans are a few years behind me."

"What do you mean?" Cleo knew what he meant, she just wanted to hear his take on things.

"You know, how names go in cycles? Like everyone your age is a Jennifer or Tracy or Greg. Now all kids are like . . . a Sophie or a Jackson. My niece Ava is four and there are five of them at her daycare so they call her Ava F."

Cleo thought of Jamie's niece Sophie and it made her stomach hurt.

"Were you Francis F?"

"Nope. The only one. But there were three Tylers in my grade five class."

"So, why Francis?"

"I was named after my grandfather. He died two days before I was born."

"Jesus. That's awful."

"Yeah, Mom was pretty devastated. But the silver lining is that he saved me from being named Brandon."

"You could have pulled that off. Although Fireman Francis has a much better ring to it."

He smiled and leaned in, put his hand through Cleo's hair at the back of her head and pulled her in for a kiss. His morning breath was sweet, like they hadn't been drinking whiskey last night before going to bed together, after hours of pints at the Ship. Cleo could still taste the sourness of it burning her throat and stomach and she pulled away from the kiss quick as she could without alarming him.

"Coffee?" Francis jumped out of bed and grabbed a pair of track pants from the top of his dresser.

Cleo wasn't sure if her hangover could stomach coffee but she felt it would be rude or awkward to say no.

"Sure."

"What do you take?"

"A little milk. And a teaspoon of sugar because it's the weekend."

The bile rose in the back of her throat then, and it was full of whiskey and regret. What had she done.

Francis pulled on a pair of vamps and a T-shirt.

"Why only on Sundays?"

"I'm thirty-nine. It's a weekend treat thing. Never mind, long story, tell you later."

Get out get out get out get out! She needed to throw up so badly her forehead broke out in a sweat and the inside of her cheeks started to water.

"Cool. You stay here, back in a few minutes."

When he was safely downstairs Cleo jumped out of bed and ran to the bathroom. She shut the door as fast as she could without slamming it, fumbled for the lock, and turned on the bathroom sink at full force so he couldn't hear her getting sick.

saucy and brave

CLEO DRINKS WHISKEY AS SHE UNPACKS IN HER NEW APARTment because she wants something strong and clean and she's sick of white wine. It's all started to taste like vinegar to her, even when she splurges on a twenty-dollar bottle instead of her usual fifteen.

She likes drinking whiskey straight, the look she gets from men when she orders it in certain bars where they expect you to be drinking wine or a cooler or a White Russian. She likes the raised eyebrows when she says, "double Jameson's," like, who would fuck with her now? She likes what it does to her more than wine. It makes her feel saucy and brave.

It's the first real stormy evening of the season, five o'clock and pitch black already, the days still getting shorter for another week. Cleo is grateful that Robert's forced her to take a couple days off. "To unpack and get your head back on straight." She laughs and pours another shot over the ice cubes in her glass. She loves that she doesn't have to go into work tomorrow. Her own little long weekend, how special. She peeks through the living room window and she can't see the lake because everything is horizontal and white, she can't even see her car. She has her very own spot and doesn't have to parallel-park and worry about beating off the side mirror on an icy mound of snow. She's kept Nalfie's medal of St. Christopher pinned to the visor and there's a little travel bottle of Febreze in the console that she'll never use, but she keeps it there anyway, because it makes her feel like the kind of person who has her shit together.

"Ha ha, fucker, I have my own parking spot, have fun on Prospect," she says as she turns from the window and puts her nose back in her glass.

But now she has to shovel out her own spot and Jamie was better and faster than she was. She always gave up early when they had to shovel out after a storm. "You keep at it and I'll go make us something good to eat," she'd say, and she would make them homemade scones and hot cocoa with Baileys and massage Jamie's shoulders when he came inside, and he always said, "Let me shower first," but she made him sit until she kneaded the shovelling knots out of him.

She shoots the rest of the whiskey to erase all thoughts of scones and Jamie, promising herself she'll slow down, that was only her third, it's okay.

Christmas will be here soon and at least she doesn't have to go to fucking Clarenville, there's one small blessing. Although this year would have been Cleo's turn to have Jamie with her family for a Christmas in town. Evelyn must be thrilled to get Jamie every Christmas now, instead of every second one, imagine that.

Cleo snorts to herself. She hopes Jamie enjoys Evelyn's five traditional turkey dinners between Tibb's Eve and Old Christmas Day.

Maybe she could ask Maisie for a curry this year instead of a turkey. In fact, Cleo is certain her mother will cook whatever she wants if it means making her wreck of an only child happy.

Cleo peeks out of the window again at the horizontal snow and thinks of the shovelling she'll have to do in the morning. Fuck that, in the afternoon. Her laptop is sitting on top of two cardboard boxes marked *books* and it's playing hip hop as loud as the tinny speakers will allow, but not loud enough to piss off her landlady on the second day after moving in.

The apartment is furnished but there's an empty corner that would be the perfect spot for her grandfather's chair and she considers texting Jamie in a haze of whiskey anger, then stops when she realizes it would probably give him the satisfaction of thinking she's a full-blown alcoholic after the breakup and she's not, she's just developing better taste in booze.

Cleo takes her laptop from its perch on the cardboard boxes to the small kitchen table. Peruses the IKEA website and picks out the most gorgeous wingback armchair she can afford. She reaches across the table to grab her credit card, still sitting in the crumbs of pot where she'd been rolling a joint earlier.

When the chair is ordered she bundles up in her winter gear and stashes the joint and a lighter carefully in her jacket pocket. She'd stomp through the snow and head to the lake, find a little park bench out of the wind and smoke a draw. Something about smoking by herself in the middle of a storm feels perfect right now, like it's the most exciting thing she's done since before meeting Jamie.

Fuck it.

She texts Francis.

-Unpacking in my new place. Drinking whiskey. You at?

Her phone is buzzing in her mittened hand before she's closed the front door.

gulp

"I SLEPT WITH SOMEONE."

Nancy's wine glass nearly slipped out of her hand, like something beautifully timed from a movie in one take, a slosh of white wine hanging in the air for that split second before spilling over her hand and falling to the table, just as the waiter walked by. He took her half-empty glass and moved back to the bar without missing a beat.

"Could you wait, next time, and tell me that when my hands are empty, please?"

"Sorry. I didn't think you'd be so surprised. And I'm not quite sure how I feel about that, thank you very much."

"I'm more surprised by the fact that you waited until lunchtime to tell me."

"I figured I'd wait and tell you when we were out of the office. Those cubicles aren't soundproof. And Rishi is like a bay nan for the gossip, so here we are." They were taking an hour and a half lunch for a Christmas treat, and were allowing themselves one glass of wine to "add some European to their lives," as Nancy liked to put it.

The waiter returned and wiped down the table, placing a fresh, full glass of wine in front of Nancy and winking at her before heading back to the bar.

"That one's a bit cheeky," Nancy took a sip and turned her head around to smile at the waiter. "I like it. He's getting a great tip. Anyways, who? And how was it? And how did all this happen without so much as a hint of me knowing anything?"

"One of Joe's firefighters, God help me."

Nancy whooped so loud she turned heads. Cleo expected as much and steeled herself for further reaction. She hadn't even got to the good stuff yet.

"Who is he?" Nancy lowered her voice when the waiter returned with their appetizers.

Cleo waited until their waiter was out of earshot. He looked to be about the same age as Francis, and wouldn't that just be her luck.

"His name is Francis. I met him at the annual Christmas banquet. Then ran into him at the Ship. There you have it."

"That's adorable."

"He's twenty-five."

"Cleo Best! Holy shit, my sweets, good for you. Lunch is definitely on me today." Nancy shook her head in genuine admiration, laced with what looked to Cleo like relief.

"When I was in junior high, he was in diapers." Cleo cut a scallop in half and ate it, starving. She hadn't had breakfast, and a few sips of wine made her remember how hungry she was.

"Fuck that. You know as well as I do that if you were twenty-five and he was thirty-nine, no one would bat a goddamn eyelash."

"I know. It's just, you know . . . weird. So soon after Jamie and everything."

"It's certainly not, and I'm sorry if my initial reaction led you to believe that. I was trying to convey overwhelming happiness, not surprise that you're not letting cobwebs grow around your vagina."

"Oh, Nanc." Cleo shoved a whole scallop into her mouth.

"And?"

"And what?"

"Cleo! Jesus, how was it?"

"Great. Really, really great."

"Good. Just what you needed."

"Something like that." Cleo didn't feel like spoiling the story and telling Nancy she'd thrown up afterwards and gone home and cried for two hours.

"Most importantly, is it going to happen again?"

"We'll see," Cleo lied. And she thought about the string of texts from Francis, unanswered on her phone.

oh, shit

CLEO STOOD AT THE KITCHEN COUNTER AND DRANK HER COFFEE while Francis finished his shower. She'd been careful last night, just enough whiskey and pot for a quick buzz, so she was good for a giant cup of coffee before she left for work. She'd let Francis stay the night for the first time; they alternated sex between her place and his, and she'd stayed at his place on Gower a few times, but she couldn't bring herself to wake up next to a man that wasn't Jamie in a bed that was her own. But they'd finished sex late last night and it was snowing. Francis was on shift in the morning and he said he'd have time to shovel her out if she was able to drop him at work. Practical, nothing else.

Francis knew the whole Jamie saga and wasn't bothered by it. Cleo figured this was exciting for him. He was young, he was building a repertoire of women and stories and this one was deluxe. Older woman breaks up with long-term partner because he wants kids more than she does. Older woman loves whiskey and pot and wants fling with no strings attached. She knew this wouldn't last, he'd be bored soon enough or maybe she would, but for now, he listened to her, enthralled, over a series of drunken nights when Cleo told him everything. Not out of love or investment, but because she didn't give a shit anymore. He was interested, he listened, he commented and sympathized at all the right times. Like her Northern Irish fling in Thailand: by the time their week was over they knew each other's life stories. Something about brief, intense physical connection opened the floodgates for free therapy.

Francis said he didn't think Joe was on shift this morning but Cleo texted Maisie to be safe.

-Hey are you and Joe around today, I might pop up after work for a visit. What's Joe's schedule, would love to see you both it's been ages

Cleo's phone went off with Maisie's reply.

-Joe is on at eight tonight. Pop up for supper if you like!

She was in the clear. She'd pull up across the street from the station and drop Francis. She'd barely have to touch the brakes.

-Thanks Ma! I'll text you later this afternoon xo

Francis came out of the bathroom and walked past her to the bedroom, a towel around his waist.

"Coffee's ready, you want one? Thanks for shovelling me out. And hey, we're in the clear, I just texted my mom, Joe's not on till eight tonight," Cleo said.

"That's okay, I'll grab one when I get to work," Francis called out from the bedroom. Through the open door Cleo saw him pick his clothes up off the floor, scattered around the room from where she'd tossed them the night before. He gave them a smell, shrugged, and started to pull them back on.

"Would it really be so bad if Joe knew about this?" Francis stood in the doorframe and pulled his shirt over his head.

"Think about what you just said for a minute," Cleo said, dumping the rest of her coffee in the sink and heading to the bathroom to brush her teeth.

"We're both adults."

"Well, I'm heading to Mom and Joe's for supper tonight, you want to come over and be the one to tell them?" Cleo said, with her toothbrush in her mouth.

"Uhhh . . ."

"Exactly. Don't be silly. Keys are on the counter, you can run out and warm up the car if you're ready to go, I'm right behind you."

~~~

It was the car that gave it away. Nalfie's Corolla was bright red and due for a muffler check-up. Joe was leaning on the wall by the side door as soon as she pulled up, with a coffee in his hand, chatting with a couple of the boys who'd popped out for a smoke at the end of their shift.

Why hadn't she stopped around the corner and made Francis walk? What was Joe even doing here?

Out for a morning drive with his Tim's and stopped for a yarn with the b'ys, of course.

She was such a fucking idiot.

She didn't need to look over to see him. He towered over the other men and she could see his salt-and-pepper hair and moustache from her side vision. Francis clocked him when he was halfway across the street. *Don't look back, don't look back, don't look back.* Francis did, and Joe looked her way at the same time, before she had time to gun the car and get away. Cleo leaned her head back and closed her eyes. She couldn't bear to see Joe look at him, to see what Francis would do.

She took a deep breath and glanced over, and Francis was gone. Presumably inside already, or knocked out cold in the snowbank in the ten seconds Cleo had her eyes closed. There was nothing to do but look at Joe and wave.

When she did, he nodded and took a sip of his coffee.

~~~

When she got to work, she was dying, but she was early and Nancy wasn't in yet. She waited a half-hour and texted Maisie.

-Shit, sorry Mom, evening meeting. Maybe next time? :(

Another text, to Francis. She sent it before Nancy arrived and had a chance to talk her down.

-We should chat later. Call me after your shift.

signals

Sometimes Cleo wishes she could feel two pints in all the time. Two pints in and a walk downtown with the sun on her face and it all seems okay. Even if it's minus ten and her fingers are cold through her red leather gloves that never really keep her hands warm, they're only for looks and driving. Cleo goes to Rocket Bakery after pints by herself at the Ship and buys a coffee and an almond croissant. She usually goes straight for the chocolate ones, but something in her wants sticky sweet marzipan instead. She walks her coffee and croissant down to Harbourside Park, the only part of the waterfront these days not cordoned off with ugly wrought-iron fences or giant chain restaurants.

She sits on a bench, takes off her gloves, and eats her croissant with freezing fingers. The wind whistles through the plastic cover of the coffee cup in her other hand. Cold coffee dribbles down her chin and icing sugar from the croissant covers her jacket. She shrugs and keeps eating. When Cleo's a little drunk by herself and walks downtown, she wonders if this is even a tiny bit of what homeless people feel. She totally understands why they would want to be drunk all the time and feels a sudden indignation towards every person who's ever said,

"I don't give them money because they'll only buy booze."

"Of fucking course they're gonna buy booze," says Cleo to no one but a seagull watching her from a wooden post. There's always one who's abnormally patient.

"You eat baby ducks, you're not getting any croissant." But she throws him an almond anyway when she finishes, and gets up to leave before he emits that weird food signal to all the other seagulls that will come. Stupid seagull. Keep it a secret and eat all the food yourself.

slowly, slowly

CLEO WAKES UP AND HAS TO PEE SO BAD, IT'S THAT KIND you've been holding in all night because you're passed out so hard from all the booze. It's still nagging in the back of her mind but she knows it can't be possible because she can't have kids and they used a condom every time, and even that one time it broke it was fine because it was the day after her period ended. She thinks about Jamie then, and how when they first got together she was so terrified of getting pregnant she wouldn't let him come inside her except on the Sunday after her period had ended and they called it Come Inside Me Sunday, even though she was on the pill, but she'd been on the pill in Korea, too and look how that turned out. This is stupid—she's a week late but probably just fucked up from stress. She puked at work but only because she ate a burger that was off, from that new place across the street from the agency. She remembers a box of unpacked toiletries under the bathroom sink and how the pregnancy test is still there, the one left in the pack of two that she'd used when she thought she was pregnant for Jamie. Cleo doesn't even know why she kept it, maybe because she is her grandmother spit right out. *Better to be looking at it than looking for it*, she hears Nalfie say in her head. Might as well, to ease her mind. Pee and go back to bed, sleep off the rest of the whiskey, she feels her eyeballs still floating in it.

She opens the test but she has to pee so bad it won't come out and she can't concentrate. She remembers from that first time testing for Jamie's almost-baby that you can pee in a glass and put the stick in it, so she goes to the kitchen with her underwear around her ankles. She hears the seams ripping as she's walking but who cares they're old and not sexy, like she feels right now anyway. Back in the bathroom, she squeezes her eyes shut and leans over a bit and it's easy to pee in the glass, but she pees all over her hand, too. She goes enough to fill the glass halfway and clenches to stop, puts it on the counter and then she finishes.

Cleo pulls up her underwear, puts the toilet cover down and sits on it. She sticks the pregnancy test in the glass, with the fibre tip down in the yellow cloudiness. The little plastic window on the test, where the line or lines are supposed to come up, but of course there will only be one line, that window changes colour, fades from a white backdrop to pale pink, won't it take three minutes, why is the colour change happening so fast. And it fades upwards, it changes upwards, like mercury rising in a thermometer slowly, slowly, one dark pink line on the pale pink backdrop and slowly upwards and Cleo is so tired and drunk she almost falls asleep sitting up and then the plastic window fills up to the top with pale pink and in the pale pink window there are two dark pink lines. There are two pink lines fuck fuck fuck fuck, no. She is pregnant with Francis's baby, it's not a baby yet really, it's okay, and she's told herself that once before.

She's pregnant for Francis and the test came from a box of two, the box she used for Jamie. She picks up the test and it drips urine over the counter and the floor and her hand looks so old holding it, she is too old to have a baby. She will go to bed, she needs to sleep, she is not pregnant, not really, she can't be pregnant, she is still drunk from the night before.

Cleo woke at ten and didn't think about taking the test at first. There were two whole minutes of lying in bed without pink lines even entering her mind. Then something went off in the back of her brain and a solid brick of panic sat in her stomach. The feeling that hits when realizing you've slept through an important meeting, or worse, remembering someone has died and you've forgotten. Cleo was jolted out of that blissful few moments of temporarily forgetting.

She had this same feeling the morning after Pop died. A thirty-second long stretch and then a piano dropping from a high-rise apartment building and Pop was gone again.

Did she dream last night? Her brain felt fuzzy. She lifted the blankets and saw her ripped underwear sagging down around her hips and she remembered taking the pregnancy test for real. Cleo looked at the clock. Not last night, just four hours ago. She sat up and jumped out of bed, ran to the bathroom.

The test was sitting on the counter in a puddle of dried pee. The two pink lines staring up a good morning at her.

two for joy

It was raining when Cleo decided to walk around the lake. A "sly rain" Joe called it, the kind that was so misty it didn't seem to be there and then soaked you to the bone in five minutes. It was warm, though, and feeling spring-ish and enough snow had melted that the path around the lake was mostly clear. A few icy patches still remained, so Cleo picked her way along carefully. She knew at her age you didn't need to tumble down a flight of stairs to lose a baby. Most days she was afraid to sneeze.

Maybe something was telling her to go on this walk for that very reason and the universe would take care of it. She couldn't be a mother, what was she thinking? She hadn't been thinking for the last three months and that was the problem. That's how she got here.

The lake was a whole different ecosystem in the rain. The ducks were normally pretty mellow, but with no joggers or dogs around, they swarmed the new patches of grass, looking for worms. They must have known something Cleo didn't, because she thought it was still too cold for the worms to come out. She never saw any baby ducks up here, and wondered if they all got eaten by seagulls before they had a chance to grow up.

Cleo heard a rustling in some alders when she got halfway around the lake and she stopped and peered through the bush. A giant crow, she didn't even know they came that size. It was so close it was like the shock you get when the moon is just at the horizon and it's that huge moon from National Geographic you think only exists in Africa. The crow couldn't have been farther than two feet away, and it clicked at her as she looked in. It stared back at Cleo, right in the eye and cocked its head. Crows were different in the rain, too. They got closer to you, watched you harder.

One for sorrow, two for joy, three for a girl, four for a boy. When Nancy got pregnant for the third time and it looked like things would be okay, it seemed the crows always came in groups of four. Murders of four, Cleo knew was the term, but that seemed so wrong when you were thinking about babies. There'd been lots of fours, and then came Mack. She hoped this lone crow wasn't a bad omen. It felt like it. She turned away and kept walking, quicker this time.

Cleo had almost made the entire loop around the lake when she became tired and had to rest on a bench across from the dog park. The bench was wet but Cleo didn't care. She was soaked through, but the rain wasn't cold and she wasn't far from home.

If she went through with this, she'd be a single mother raising a baby in an apartment.

At least they would be closer to the ducks. How was she thinking "they" already? She wasn't carrying anything bigger than a lentil inside her. Don't get attached. It might be an empty sac, like Nancy's was the second time. Or if it took, there might be something wrong with it because she was so old and then there would be no question.

Or if it took and everything was fine, what then? She was old enough now to see through the romance of it immediately.

Cleo was surprised to see a few people in the dog park with their sopping wet animals. There was an older man leaning on the fence of the enclosure, looking out at the dogs and their owners. Cleo sat and watched him for a good ten minutes; the only time he moved was to shift his weight onto the other foot. There was something so sad in that, a whole sad story about loneliness and a dog dying, and him on his own in the rain, remembering happier times. She felt a quiet kinship with him and decided to stay until he left. She was soaked to the bone now and getting cold, but she didn't want to leave the old man staring at the dogs on his own.

After five more minutes he turned to leave, and as he walked past Cleo he tipped his hat at her and said, "Hello, miss. Lovely day." When he tipped the hat a pool of water fell from the brim and spilled over his face and he laughed and winked at her the way her grandfather had when she was little. She smiled back at him and tried to speak. No words came out though, she just inhaled sharply through her nose in little jagged breaths instead, almost bursting into tears, but she held it in, held on to it until he was out of earshot. She didn't want to scare the old man, because that little moment they'd just shared seemed like the kindest, most beautiful thing that had happened to her since everything went wrong.

He had called her "miss." That was nice. She knew she was closer to "ma'am." She was a pregnant single ma'am. And soon she would be fat.

She needed to go home and warm up. She wanted a bath, but her apartment didn't have one so it would have to be a long hot shower.

Cleo finally burst into tears, sitting on the park bench, soaking wet, shaking with cold and sobs. She was pregnant and she didn't even own a bathtub.

the second one

"I'M PREGNANT."

Nancy snorted, then made a *pffff* through her lips.

"You're funny. Are you going to finish the rest of that?" Nancy made a move to grab the last corner of Cleo's croissant. Cleo grabbed her wrist.

"You can't eat the rest of that. I'm going to finish it, and then I'm going to get another one, because almond croissants are the only thing I've been able to eat for two weeks without puking everywhere."

Cleo was still holding Nancy's wrist. Nancy made no move to escape.

"I . . . no. What? Jesus Christ." She bent her head and shut her eyes tight. She didn't open them when she said, "Congratulations?"

"You don't need to say that. It's me. I'm not even sure what I'm doing yet. Please don't say that."

"Well then what the fuck, Cleo." Nancy opened her eyes and stared at Cleo, shaking her head.

How different her reaction would have been if this was six months ago, Cleo thought.

"Didn't you use something? Anything?"

"I'm still off the pill but we used condoms every time. I mean, we were usually loaded when we did it, but Francis was pretty paranoid about pregnancy, even though I told him I couldn't have kids. Ha ha."

Nancy looked at the floor. She brought her eyes back to meet Cleo's and they were wet and shiny. Nancy stared and was quiet for what felt like a good two minutes. Cleo ate the last of her croissant and looked out the window of the coffee shop.

"It wasn't you."

"Guess not. We never got tested or anything. But I guess I'm fine. Like, super fucking fertile fine."

"Does Jamie know?"

"Fuck, no. You're the first person I've told.

"How long have you known?"

"Three days.

"Oh, Cleo."

"I mean, my doctor. My doctor knows, I've made an appointment."

"Donna doesn't know?"

"Nope. I can't tell her till I know what I'm doing. I don't know. I don't know why I can't tell her yet. I mean, she's a nurse, this shit is her job."

"Jesus, I thought you just had food poisoning that time you puked at work."

"I know. Me too."

"So you don't know if you're going to—"

"I don't know."

"Whatever you decide, I love you."

"I'm glad someone does."

They left the coffee shop and went back to Nancy's after picking up Mack from daycare. Nancy cooked while Cleo sat at the kitchen table holding Mack in her lap. She breathed in his two-year-old head and wondered how long they smelled this good. It probably all ended in kindergarten. Then came other people's children with their snotty noses and head lice and peanut allergies and stomach flu all the time. No sweet-smelling heads then. Heads smelling like sour milk and sweat and Play-Doh, probably.

"How far along?" Nancy was reheating a giant pot of chili and making Cleo plain butter and cheese pasta on the side. Cleo breathed harder into Mack's hair to cover up the smell of the simmering meat.

"Six weeks or so, I guess. Not out of the woods yet. And Christ, the drinking I've been doing."

"It'll be fine. If you decide—"

"Nancy, you of all people know it might not be."

"It'll be fine."

"How do you know?"

"Pregnancies are like pancakes. Sometimes flipping the first pancake gets messed up. You know, pan's too hot, or not hot enough, too much oil. First one's a tester. Second one usually works out. In our case, the third."

"But this is my first pancake."

"Nope. Your second, technically."

Cleo didn't care anymore about keeping it all in, even in front of Mack. She was so relieved to have said it out loud, she couldn't stop the tears. She inhaled sharply and sobbed, crying into the back of Mack's head, soaking his blond hair with tears.

Mack didn't move; he'd never heard Cleo cry before. He stared at his mother across the kitchen with wide eyes, Cleo's head still buried in his hair. Nancy smiled at him and shrugged, like nothing was wrong in the world.

"It's okay, Mackers, Auntie Cleo's having a bit of a hard day. Sometimes mommies and aunties have to cry, too. Do you think maybe a hug might help her feel better?"

Mack nodded and turned on Cleo's lap, wriggling around like a puppy until he was facing her. He grabbed her face with his hands and kissed her on the nose, then wrapped his arms around her neck and squeezed hard.

"S'okay, Key-o. I sorry."

"Thank you, Mack. Thanks, sweetheart."

Cleo returned his hug and breathed in his warmth and felt his little heart pounding against hers.

~~~

Cleo was so nauseous and tired when she returned from her doctor's appointment that she collapsed on the couch without bolting the door or taking off her coat and boots. She woke twenty minutes later when a gust of wind blew the door open and frightened her to her feet, in such a stupor she had no idea why she was still wearing her winter clothes. She stumbled to the door and closed it, stripped off her gear, and went to put the kettle on when she felt her guts lurch. She had ginger tea somewhere and needed to brew some to settle her stomach before she threw up everywhere. Like she did yesterday at work, again, barely making it to the washroom in time.

She'd called in sick to go to her first doctor's appointment, telling Robert she'd caught the stomach flu that was going around. A very reasonable half-lie. He'd seen her run past his office on the way to the washroom, so he'd never suspect her of lying, even after the "food poisoning" incident two weeks earlier.

Cleo was still reeling from the embarrassment of her doctor's appointment. Dr. Connors congratulating her before Cleo burst into tears with the truth of her breakup, convinced she couldn't have kids, an unexpected pregnancy with someone she hardly knew, all the drinking she'd done, all the pot she'd smoked, would the baby be okay, please say the baby will be okay, do I have to get rid of this one too. Dr. Connors had hugged her to calm her down and joked that this was how half of all babies were conceived anyway, and if everything went according to plan, and if she wished to proceed with the pregnancy, the baby would be just fine.
~~~

Cleo poured her ginger tea and brought it to the kitchen table, sitting it in front of her to let it steep a little. She wrapped her hands around the mug to warm them and stared out the window at the giant backyard she never used.

Maybe she could do this.

Another sip of tea and she urged again, with no time to run to the bathroom. Cleo stood and threw up, circles of undigested Cheerios spilling over the sides of her kitchen table and onto the floor.

like hope

"TEA?" MAISIE GOT UP FROM THE TABLE TO PUT THE KETTLE on. She didn't wait for an answer.

"Yup. You have anything herbal? With ginger or something in it? Not feeling orange pekoe today." What Cleo meant was, milk in tea smelled like wet dog to her now.

"Let me take a look in the hippie cupboard." Maisie stood on tiptoe to reach a tiny shelf that was mostly filled with odds and ends Cleo had brought back from travelling. She removed several boxes of tea and laid them on the counter before finding one marked ginger-lemon, and Cleo saw a box with Korean writing on it, green tea she'd given Maisie years ago.

"That one's probably ready to go," said Cleo. "Been a while."

"Tea don't go off," said Joe. He wasn't looking at her while he drank his. He kept his eyes down, slurp and clang, the cup back on the saucer. Something was wrong. The smell of the milk hit Cleo across the table and her stomach churned and she swallowed hard.

The kettle came to a boil and shrieked on the stovetop. Cleo had hated that thing her whole life. It used to make her cry as a child and she would wail at Maisie, "It sounds like witches coming to get me." She had no idea why anyone would want a kettle that screamed incessantly when you could just plug in an electric one and have it cut out on its own when it was done.

But now she didn't want the kettle to stop, she wanted it to make noise enough for her to slip out the back door unnoticed. Maybe she would go straight to the airport and take a nine-month "trip to Halifax" like girls did when they got pregnant in Nalfie's day. Except those girls weren't hovering on pre-menopausal and sleeping with firefighters young enough to be their nephews. It would even have been possible for her to have a son close to Francis's age if she'd been an outrageously slutty teenager. Like Jamie's sister.

"You're gaining weight," said Maisie. "You look good. You needed that."

"I'm pregnant."

Joe's look across the kitchen table was one that Cleo had seen a hundred times. How his face went when there was an emergency at the station. This time, he didn't grab the car keys and his jacket, he jumped up and said, "Lord thunderin' Jesus," put his hands on his hips and then ran them through what was left of his hair.

Maisie couldn't seem to move her face. She didn't get pale, she went red, like Cleo did when she was upset or mortified.

"Who?" Maisie squeaked out. "I thought . . . is it Jamie? Are you back together?" And when she said that her eyes lit up with something small like hope and Cleo wanted to disappear.

She didn't care about Joe right now, Joe was Joe, but her mother. Her mother's first grandchild and Maisie didn't even know who its father was. Of course, Joe too, it was Joe's grandchild too, but her *mother*.

Joe crossed his arms and leaned against the kitchen counter. He was breathing hard but looking resigned at the same time. He stared past Cleo and out the window.

"Is it Francis?" he asked.

"It's Francis," Cleo said.

"Who's Francis," Maisie said, like she was resigned now, too.

man up

"I DON'T UNDERSTAND."

"There's nothing to understand, Francis. I'm pregnant. And believe me when I tell you there's no one more shocked than I am."

Cleo wasn't sure if that was true and she took no comfort in it. He'd never looked younger to her than he did right now. Sitting on her couch, leaning forward like he was getting ready to run, white-knuckled hands grasping his knees.

"I thought you called me over here because you wanted to get back together. I mean start things back up again or whatever. Or that you like, missed having me around or something."

He was like a teenager, being admonished by his parents because he'd been caught smoking pot and they were concerned for his future. How fucked was his future now? A twenty-five-year-old with a thirty-nine-year-old pregnant ex-fling, or whatever she was to him. His boss's daughter, pregnant. Cleo had the realization at that moment, with this kid who looked like he was going to throw up all over her living room, that this might actually be easier for her.

"How long have you known?" Francis straightened and folded his hands in front of him. An unconscious effort in his body to man up.

"Three weeks."

"Why didn't you tell me sooner?"

"Because I didn't know if I wanted to go through with it."

"You were going to have an abortion?"

"I was considering it, yes."

"But you can't—"

"Yes, Francis. I can."

"Yeah, yeah, sorry. I know. I just . . . yeah." He nodded and looked down. "But you're not?"

"I've decided to keep it."

"Okay," he said, and Cleo thought he might cry.

"You're off the hook, you know," she said.

"What—what do you mean?"

"Francis, you're just a kid." Cleo took a deep breath to start again when she saw how his face fell at this, how someone could even consider him a kid when he rescued people from burning buildings.

"Look, you know what I mean, you're not a kid, but to me you still kind of are, and this whole thing was my fault because I told you I couldn't have kids. You did everything respectfully, and right, and I was the one who fucked up here, okay? You are so young and you have so much ahead of you." Everything out of Cleo's mouth sounded like something from a terrible TV movie of the week and she hated herself for it.

"Cleo, Joe would murder me if I was off the hook, if I didn't—I mean he's going to murder me anyways. Oh fuck." Francis's head collapsed into his hands, the reality of knocking up his boss's daughter hitting him for the first time.

"I don't want the only reason for you helping me out to be my stepfather." Cleo tried her best to make her voice reassuring but they both knew there was no way around this. As awful as it was telling Joe she was pregnant, she knew Francis was rightly terrified.

"It won't be like that, that's not it, I just . . ."

"Francis, it's okay." Cleo cut him off and tried to ignore the fact that his voice was cracking. "We'll let it sit for a while. We don't have to make any decisions right now. I'm not even really out of the woods yet, especially for someone my age. I just really had to tell you."

"I know. Yeah, I know." Francis leaned back on the couch, ran his hands through his hair and let out a long slow breath. "Does anyone else know?"

"Just Nancy." If she told him Joe and her mother already knew, it would break him.

"Jamie?"

"Christ, no. I can't even think about telling him. I can't even think about that. God, I'm sick just thinking about it."

"Yeah. That'll be pretty awkward."

"Awkward's not the word."

They sat there on the couch in silence for a while. There was a fleeting moment of relief that neither of them was Jamie.

breathing for two

Cleo had called ahead to let her grandmother know she'd be by and would use her key to let herself in. It was easier that way, in case Nalfie was having a bad day and had trouble getting around. The front door was at the bottom of a long flight of stairs that led to the second floor with the kitchen and living room. Nalfie left her door open for years, back when you were able to do that downtown. "My dear, you can't be at that now with the pack of dogs that runs down here these days," she'd said once to Cleo over Sunday dinner. "They'd break down an old woman's door to steal a pack of Rolaids thinking it was the Oxy. Alberta got this city ruined, maid. Your poor grandfather's probably up there on Newtown Road rolling in his grave."

The week had been warm and the sidewalks were finally passable, the first really warm day the city had seen since late September. That day in St. John's that made people forget there'd be two more months of misery before you could sit on your front stoop and have a cup of tea without a jacket on. It was nice enough to walk from the lake and Cleo felt like she should go outside. She hadn't left the apartment all weekend, and she had a duty to get some fresh air.

It took her an hour and a half to get to Carter's Hill. She wanted to delay this visit as long as possible, so she took her time. She walked around the lake and took King's Bridge Road to downtown. Wandered down Duckworth and Water before making her way to New Gower and turning up Barter's Hill and then onto Cabot.

When she reached the middle of Carter's Hill she was sweating and had to stop to take off her fleece. It was already starting to tighten around the middle. She made her way to Nalfie's door and stood on the front step, considering the weight of the set of keys in her hand. She didn't realize how long she'd been there with her forehead resting on the door and the keys dangling off her fingers until Mrs. Keough leaned out her window and yelled from across the street.

"My dear, you can go on in, your grandmother's home! What are you doin', havin' a spell are ya?"

Cleo started and lifted her head off the door. She turned and waved at Mrs. Keough, then let herself in before she had half the neighbours out, wondering what was wrong with "Maisie's young one, you know, Alfreda's granddaughter with the French father and the queer name."

Cleo closed the door behind her and bolted it shut. She bent to untie her hikers and wondered how much longer she'd be able to do that without difficulty, and now no one living with her to help. She felt like tying them back up and running as fast and as far away as she could.

"Hello, my love, come on up," Nalfie yelled from the second floor. "I heard Patsy bawling at you across the street so I knew you were here. I got the kettle put on."

The smell coming down the stairs was Mr. Clean and molasses buns. Claire must have been by to clean the house. Maisie and Joe paid for one of the neighbourhood girls to come every couple of weeks and give Nalfie's house a good going-over. It had taken them five years of convincing to let them do that much for her. Cleo breathed in the scent of molasses and relished not having to throw up. That smell would have sent her tearing off for a bathroom a few weeks earlier, but thankfully her morning sickness had calmed down. She was worried that meant something was wrong, but her latest blood work had come back fine.

How had Nancy done this three times?

Cleo padded up the stairs. Nalfie was sitting at the kitchen table. It was still cool enough that she had to wear a pair of wool slippers, but her usual heavy sweater was replaced with a light cardigan that she'd put on over a floral housedress. She was sitting in the chair on the side of the table where the sun flooded in through the kitchen window.

Cleo had to bite the inside of her cheeks to keep from crying when she saw her grandmother sitting in the patch of sunlight, looking like some saintly, matronly pillar of everything good. Because now Cleo had to pretend she'd invited herself over for a casual cup of tea and tell the woman she loved more than anyone that she was pregnant and alone and fucking terrified. Her heart broke right then, and it hurt more than the night on the highway coming back from Clarenville, when she knew she couldn't make it with Jamie.

It burst out of her right before the tears did.

"Nalfie, I'm pregnant."

Nalfie looked at her and smiled, bright and knowing.

"I know, my darling."

Cleo's knees felt weak and she crossed the kitchen to Nalfie's chair. She knelt down and put her head on her grandmother's flowered lap and sobbed, gulping in great breaths of air while Nalfie said, "Shhhh" and pushed Cleo's hair back and tucked it behind her ear.

"I'm sorry, Nalfie, I'm so sorry, I messed up. I really, really messed up."

"Yes, my trout, you did and that's okay. You're not the first woman who has, and you certainly won't be the last."

"I'm so sorry."

"I know my darling, I know. Don't cry too hard now, I got the window open and you'll have Patsy over the once."

Cleo sat opposite Nalfie's chair, the afternoon sun inching its way to her side of the kitchen table. They were waiting for the tea to steep in the ceramic teapot placed in the middle of the table. No bags in mugs here, that "wasn't proper," Nalfie always said. Cleo hadn't unpacked her teapot since leaving Prospect Street. She'd only ever taken it out for Nalfie or Evelyn, and it was unlikely to see the light of day now. Her hands were cold so she wrapped them around the tea-cozied pot.

The table had been in that same spot ever since Cleo could remember. It was old-fashioned Formica, with a leaf that came out of either end, though Cleo couldn't recall the last time it had been fully extended—even when Jamie was around and they were five for Sunday dinner. Nalfie always kept it covered with a tablecloth and a plastic cover over that. She replaced the plastic every couple of years, and this one was near its end. Dozens of partially melted rings from too-hot cups of tea dotted the surface, and there was a pattern of large rings in the middle of the table where the teapot always sat.

Cleo sat with her arms wrapped around her knees and her heels on the chair, toes out over the edge, like she did when she was a kid, watching Nalfie make pies. Today it was molasses buns. There were already some piled on a serving platter at the far end of the counter and another batch cooling next to it on a rack. Nalfie was bent at the oven, taking out the final tray. She took a handful of buns off the rack and put them on a smaller plate for the two of them.

All this was done in silence, without a word between them. It was a good kind of quiet, the kind you worked out with someone after years and years of knowing them. There was just the squeak of the oven door and the shuffle of Nalfie's slippered feet back and forth across the linoleum floor.

The quiet kitchen sounds brought Cleo back to a place that wasn't so complicated. She wanted to sit here forever, with her arms wrapped around her knees and Nalfie's pink ruffled curtains billowing in lazy gusts. Of all the places she'd been, of all the scents that had been in her nose, the smell of molasses with the spring breeze coming through the open window was her favourite of them all.

"How did you know?" Cleo finally asked her grandmother.

If Cleo looked at Nalfie long enough, she could see her in the kitchen thirty years earlier. In her fifties, fierce and lithe and strong. She was stooped now, her eyes deeper in her face, but the same woman was still there. Her mind was still there, at least. For that, Cleo was grateful.

Nalfie was at the counter, standing side-on so Cleo could only see her profile when she smiled.

"Cleo, I might not be the sharpest knife in the drawer, but I'm not the dullest either. You've been avoiding me like a case of tuberculosis, and you only avoid me when you feel guilty about something. Yours isn't the first pregnancy I've guessed, maid. Some of us can do that, you know. The only reason I never guessed your mother's was because she was in France."

Nalfie turned on the hot water and reached for the giant bottle of green Palmolive, squeezing in more than she needed for the amount of dirty dishes on the counter.

"So, my dear, do you have it all figured out yet?" Nalfie sunk her hands into the steaming water without flinching. "Do you have a plan?"

"No plan yet. Trying to let the idea settle in, I guess."

"But you're keeping it?"

"Yes, yes of course."

Cleo's ears went red at this. In all her years, she'd never heard her Catholic grandmother so much as mention anything to do with abortion. Cleo didn't think the word existed in her grandmother's vocabulary, and she was pretty sure Nalfie believed it shouldn't exist in anybody else's.

Nalfie turned to look at Cleo, her hands still in the soapy hot water of the sink.

"No need to look surprised, Cleo. I might be eighty-five, but there's not much new under the sun, you know."

Nalfie finished the last of the dishes, leaving them on the drying rack. The water was still so hot the dishes sent up plumes of steam. She dried her hands on the tea towel hanging from the oven door handle and reached into the cupboard for teacups and saucers. It was the good set, the kind that only ever came out after Sunday dinner.

"Well, I know this is probably a very confusing time for you, but I'm pleased for you, if that's okay to say."

"Of course, Nalfie, that's totally okay. I'm just a little worried about doing it on my own."

"Your mother did it for a couple of years before Joe came along, and she did just fine."

"I know. But she had you and Pop."

"And you'll have your mother and Joe. Maybe not me for too long, but I'll certainly do what I can to help."

"Don't say that, please don't ever say that."

"I'm old enough to say what I damn well please, thank you very much."

She placed Cleo's cup and saucer in front of her, and the clink of china and one click of the tongue ended that discussion before it got started.

"And what about this fella of yours?" Nalfie picked up her teacup and smiled like a schoolgirl.

There was no going back now. Cleo had nothing else to hide.

"We're not really together. But he's a good guy. He's going to help out as much as he can."

"Well, there you go. That's a damn sight more than Maisie ever got from your biological father."

"I'm not too fussy about raising a baby in an apartment."

"My darling, this house isn't very big and I raised seven youngsters in it. Most people my age were reared in small quarters with not much privacy. Young ones today are spoiled rotten, sure. Two bodies in your place is nothing at all, don't go getting foolish on me, now."

"You're right, I know, you're right."

"The smaller the place the less you have to clean. That'll really mean something in a few months."

Nalfie winked when she said that, and Cleo couldn't help but smile. She was suddenly starving and reached across the table to grab a molasses bun.

Nalfie poured Carnation milk from the creamer into each of their cups first before lifting the pot and pouring in the tea. Cleo watched the dark brown turn to beige in a swirl and remembered how, when she was little, Pop would always pour a bit of tea in his saucer and let Cleo sip it slow, only when Maisie and Joe weren't looking. The same way he'd let her have the tiniest glass of Baby Duck on Christmas Day with her turkey dinner.

Pop's tea was always barky and strong and not very sweet. Like Jamie's. She didn't know how Francis took his tea, or if he even drank tea, and she was going to have his baby.

"Does Jamie know yet?" Nalfie brought the teacup to her lips and blew on it softly, even though it had steeped in the pot long enough that it wasn't scalding anymore.

"No. I don't know what to do. I don't want to tell him."

"Cleo, I'm not telling you what to do, but it's better to tell him early on. It's a small place and you two have so many people in common, he's sure to find out sooner or later. But God forbid he doesn't know and you end up running into him when you're seven or eight months pregnant. No one needs that shock, least of all you and the baby."

"I know. Christ. I know."

"I'd say your best bet would be to tell him on the email. You know, not ideal, but at least he'll know and it'll be done."

Cleo rubbed her face hard and rested her chin on her hands. She nodded and looked out the window.

Nalfie put down her tea and reached across the table. She put her hand around Cleo's forearm and squeezed it. When she spoke her voice was gentle but more serious than Cleo had heard it in a long time.

"Don't go upsetting yourself. You got to look out for number one, and you know who that is now, right?"

Cleo nodded again and pointed down.

“That’s right.” Nalfie let go of Cleo’s arm, picked up her teacup, and took a sip without making a sound.

hey

To: Jamie Pike (jamiehectorpike@hotmail.com)
From: Cleo Best (cleobest@gmail.com)
Sent: April-28-17 2:31:00 AM
Subject: Hey.

Hi Jamie. Hope things are going okay at your end. Sorry to bother you . . . I know we decided to not touch base for a while, and I promise after this email I'll leave well enough alone. But something's come up that I thought you should know. I actually don't want you to know. But you should know. And I couldn't work up the courage to call you. Anyway. So, you may or may not know that I was seeing someone. It was very casual and has since ended and I'm not sure if I was supposed to tell you that earlier, I'm not very good at this. It's been over for a few weeks now, but as it turns out I'm three months pregnant. It was obviously a massive shock considering this past year and I'm pretty fucked up about it. And it's beyond fucked up that I'm telling you this in an email like we're business colleagues, but I didn't know what else to do. My biggest fear was you hearing this through the grapevine, or if I ran into you a few months down the road and it was obvious. Please know this is the hardest email I've ever had to write and I am fully prepared for you to hate me forever and never want to see or speak to me again. I would like it if you didn't tell your parents, I don't think Evelyn could handle it right now, but I don't need to say that, I'll leave it up to you.

I am so sorry for this fucked up year and how awful I've been.

Cleo

She stared at the screen for a half an hour, her finger almost clicking Send a dozen times, until she finally saved it in her drafts folder and went to bed.

tell him to his face

SHE RAN INTO HIM AT HALLIDAY'S, OF ALL PLACES. WEEKS OF urging at the smell of any kind of meat, and now a craving for lamb shanks so bad she stopped on the way home from work and forced herself to parallel-park on Gower Street. She was too tired these days to walk everywhere, and if she was going to make a go of this on her own she had to get used to driving more. To what, to play groups? Piano lessons? Hockey practice? Not hockey. She'd never be able to afford hockey, and she could never handle seeing her child being slammed up against the boards by some little asshole who happened to be bigger. Fuck hockey.

Cleo knew the risk, it used to be their local shop. It was only his now, but she also knew Jamie's schedule and didn't think he'd be there in the two minutes it would take her to run in and get the lamb after work. It was five-fifteen and he'd never show up at home before six. But when she left the butcher's counter and headed to the cash he was there in line, holding a carton of milk. He turned around so fast there was no time and nowhere to run, and she would have. She wasn't above running away from the man she used to live with, their old house a two-minute walk from the very spot she was standing in right now, wishing it would open up and swallow her.

"Hey."

He smiled when he said it and looked happy to see her. His face lit up the way it used to when she finally came downstairs on Saturday morning after a girl's night out with Nancy and Donna. She half expected him to kiss the top of her head and hand her a cup of coffee.

"Hi, how are you?"

Like it was no big deal, like she wasn't still in love with him and pregnant with someone else's baby. Something dropped in her, her stomach or something lower and she panicked, suddenly wanting to call Nancy to ask her what a miscarriage felt like, maybe this was how it started. The danger still felt real because she hadn't had her first ultrasound yet; she wasn't even sure if she was incubating a tiny person or an empty sac. She *felt* like an empty sac, though, staring at Jamie with a two-litre of milk under his arm. And it was out before she could stop herself.

"You're back on the two per cent?"

He laughed like it was the most normal thing in the world, like she was a roommate who'd moved out and not his almost-wife. Mother of Almost-Baby.

"Ha, yeah. I never could handle the skim stuff. Just waters down your tea."

"Good for you."

It was the only thing she could think to say and possibly the most awkward, she realized, as they sat on the silence that followed the first moment of running into each other.

"How's work?" She fought rolling her eyes at herself, standing here asking the question she hated most in the world when it came from anyone and he knew it.

"Good, good. Just got back from Fredericton again."

"Exciting."

"Yeah."

He grinned and looked down because he knew they were both

thinking of the last time he flew to Fredericton. The morning she brought him to the airport before she went to see Dr. Connors.

Cleo squeezed her eyes shut and stopped just short of telling him right there. It almost spilled out of her, a bag of frozen lamb shanks in her hand and a baby in her belly, and the man she wished was the father standing in front of her. He turned and paid and she was behind him, *don't wait don't wait oh God please don't wait*, but he did because he was always braver than she was and just a better person, really.

She paid and he held the door for her when they left the store together. They stood on the sidewalk staring at each other. Cleo could see the roof of her old house.

"You look good," he said. "Things are okay?"

"They are. They're good." She wanted to throw up. She was off the lamb shanks already.

"Listen, Cleo, do you want to come down for a cup of tea? This is just weird."

"I can't. I told Nalfie I'd stop in before I head home. But maybe another time."

"That would be nice. I'd like that. And I still have your pop's chair. We should, you know, figure something out or chat or I could—"

"You love that chair. You should keep it." She cut him off before he said what it felt like he was thinking. Something about the way he was carrying himself, the way he'd held the door for her.

Jamie leaned in for a hug and he kissed her on the cheek. Cleo sucked her stomach away from the embrace, like he'd be able to feel what was going on inside her.

"I'll call you," he said.

"Okay."

Cleo would go home this very minute and send the email sitting in her drafts folder, before she had the chance to get her boots off. Before the adrenaline stopped pumping in her veins.

Jamie made the turn to walk down the hill to their old house, his house, and Cleo felt a surge of relief run through her, followed by maybe-baby kicking the words into her throat and out her mouth.

"Jamie, I'm pregnant."

He stopped moving, but didn't turn around. He didn't stiffen, no whirling around in a fury. It was like he was stopping to look at a nice sunset. The same way Maisie had stopped to do the mental math in her head before the realization set in, Jamie was doing that, too. There was a whole two-act play, with intermission, in his back, in a single instant. The rise and crushing fall of hope in his shoulders and then the awful truth of what she was telling him.

That there was a baby, but it had nothing to do with him.

Jamie turned to face Cleo, so calm it was a bit scary, but there was a look on his face she'd seen before.

Cleo's face was flaming red, and a single drop of sweat ran down the curve of her back and into the top of her too-tight jeans. Her turtle-neck felt like it was trying to strangle her.

"It's . . . I'm not with anyone. I was dating, seeing someone. Very briefly, more like a fling, no one important, I mean."

"Oh, well that's good."

"It's over now. But I just found out. I'm sorry. I'm so sorry."

"I can't do this now," he said, so quiet she could barely hear him.

"Jamie, I thought I couldn't get pregnant."

"I can't fucking do this now, I have to go," he said, louder now, and he finally started down the hill. "I can't believe you did this."

"What do you want me to do? What?" Cleo hated herself, and the big fat tears rolling down her face, spilling off her chin and onto her coat. An elderly woman across the street stopped and was staring at them.

"I thought I couldn't, I didn't know," Cleo said, and she was on his heels, fighting the urge to grab his arm.

"Well clearly, you can. I'm the one that's the problem, apparently."

"Jamie, you don't know that."

"Too bad we didn't check things out earlier, hey?"

She stopped chasing him and fell to her knees, and all the tiny rocks on the sidewalk dug into her shins. Jamie stopped at the corner of Prospect Street and looked up the hill at her.

"Fuck, Cleo." He raised both his hands in the air, they flopped back down to his sides. He was gone.

The woman had crossed the street and was hovering near the entrance to the store. She made her way to where Cleo was sitting on the ground.

"Don't you worry, my love. He's not worth it. You'll be all right," she said, and she reached down to squeeze Cleo's shoulder.

Cleo let the old woman believe that this was all Jamie's fault, and took whatever comfort she could get from the stranger until the cold from the sidewalk crept into her bones.

the thing that breaks us

CLEO THOUGHT NOTHING COULD BE WORSE THAN WHAT HAD happened with Jamie on the sidewalk in front of Halliday's, but here she was, moose roast going down in lumps while she sat across from Francis. Nalfie sat next to him, sipping her second glass of white wine, her soft wrinkled hand occasionally giving his a supportive squeeze. Joe and Maisie sat at either end of the dining room table, Maisie's eyes not leaving her husband, not even as she cut her meat.

Cleo had asked Nancy to come as a buffer and she'd agreed in an instant, not wanting to miss any of what was sure to be a historic night of family drama. When they'd come into the dining room, Joe had patted Francis on the back a little too hard and said, "You sit here next to me, my buddy." Cleo hoped having Nancy there might help Joe self-censor, or at the very least prevent him from reaching across the table and grabbing Francis by the throat.

The opening verse of Madonna's "Like a Virgin" kicked in on Maisie's dinner party playlist and Nancy gave a little snort, raising her wine glass to her lips, and shooting a sideways glance at Cleo.

"Thanks so much for having me over this evening, Mr. and Mrs. Best," Francis said. Cleo noticed the sheen of sweat on his upper lip and remembered how cocky he'd been the night they'd met. How he'd strolled on up to her stepfather with a beer and called him Joe.

"Oh, I'd say it's the least we could have done, seeing as how you so generously put a grandchild in our daughter," Joe said.

"Joe." Maisie, her first warning look down the table, fork and knife and a hunk of moose meat frozen in mid-air between her plate and mouth.

Nalfie, years beyond caring about decorum, laughed so hard Cleo thought this must be at least her third glass.

"Well, he's not wrong, Maisie," she said, reaching over to give Francis's hand another pat. He blanched so quickly it looked like he was going to fall out of his chair.

"Don't you mind the likes of Joe Best. I won't let him hurt you." She leaned ahead slightly and turned her attention to Cleo across the table. "Good for you, my dear, your young man is very handsome. If you're lucky the baby will get that fine head of hair. Your mother was completely bald until she was two and a half."

Joe put down his fork. His other hand still gripped the knife by the side of the plate, which Cleo found funny, then scary for a second, then back to funny because Nalfie wouldn't let him hurt Francis and everyone at the table knew it, especially Joe. He pointed hard at Francis with his fork hand.

"I'll tell you one thing right now, Skipper, the only thing stopping me from kicking your ass into next Easter is the fact that you're the father of my grandkid. Now Cleo's had a rough go of it and maybe you were a welcome distraction, I'm staying out of the goddamn sordid details."

"Oh Jesus, Joe." Cleo put her face in her hands.

"I'm no spring chicken, but I knows how it works. You two are adults, you figure out whether you're makin' a go of it or not. But there's one thing that's not gonna happen and that's you takin' off and being a complete deadbeat shithead, you get that?"

"Language, Joe," said Maisie.

"Whatever happens, you're gonna treat my daughter with respect, and be a father to this child, and I'm not just talking monthly child support, I'm talking shitty diapers and little league and art lessons, you get that? You get that and we don't have a fuckin' problem here."

"Jesus Christ, Joe. Language!" Maisie's fork and knife clattered to her plate.

"I get that, Joe. I get it." Francis looked across the table to Cleo. His colour gone from white to deep pink.

"Christ on a bike, Maisie," Nalfie chimed in, sing-songy. "If there's a time for swearing, it's now. Let everyone get it out of their systems."

"Maisie, I can't get over how tender this moose is. Wonderful." Nancy put her foot on Cleo's under the table. For once she had nothing to say and she was a shitty buffer choice.

"Thank you, Nancy."

"I know I've made a big mistake," Cleo said, loud enough that everybody put their forks down, even Nalfie. "No offence, Francis."

Francis nodded and shrugged. Nalfie reached for his hand but this time she didn't let go and held it tight.

"We're all so happy, dear. But if you were ten years older we'd be thrilled," she whispered loudly in his ear.

"Thanks, Nalfie," Francis said.

It was strange to hear him call Cleo's grandmother by her nickname. Cleo would have thought it premature if she wasn't carrying his baby in her belly.

"Look, I know this is weird and awkward and it's probably going to get worse before it gets better. But this can't be the thing that breaks everyone. I'd never survive it, okay? Joe? I can't do this by myself. I can't have it be this way."

Joe looked up from his plate and crossed his arms over his chest. He cleared his throat and looked at Cleo.

"You're not doing this by yourself," he said.

She thought he might be blinking his eyes a little too hard but that was impossible. Cleo had never seen Joe cry, not once.

"Francis." Joe uncrossed his arms. He wiped invisible crumbs off the tablecloth with his right hand. "Another beer?"

"Yes please, sir," said Francis.

"Now's not the time for *sir*, Francis. Those days are long gone." Joe got up from the table and walked into the kitchen.

Maisie dropped her shoulders and leaned back in her chair. Nalfie looked across the table at Cleo and winked, then picked up her fork and carried on eating.

there we are

CLEO MADE FRANCIS STAY HOME FOR THE FIRST ULTRASOUND, despite Joe's insistence. Francis had nodded dumbly at her and said, "Okay." Relieved perhaps, or afraid. A bit of both, most likely. Relieved to be off the hook and afraid Joe would think he backed out. Maisie wanted to go with her and Nancy had volunteered as well. They all thought she needed someone in the room with her, but Cleo insisted she had to do it on her own. At least the first ultrasound. She knew there'd be another further down the road, if she made it down that road at all. She might not get out the front door with her boots on, not at her age.

Cleo felt it would give her a sense of false hope if she took someone with her. She'd be doing this pretty much on her own for the rest of her life, so a solo ultrasound seemed fitting. Just her, the kidney bean inside her, and the stranger who got to tell her good news or bad. Cleo would be fine with both, she knew that. Relieved either way. She'd done so much drinking before she took the test the poor thing was probably floating in there like one lonely pickled egg left in a jar, sitting on a shelf behind the cash register of some seedy bar.

She was supposed to be there a half-hour before her appointment, but between trying to find parking and making her way through the maze of antiseptic corridors, she didn't arrive at the ultrasound desk until five minutes beforehand. She registered with the receptionist and followed another maze of corridors down to what she supposed was the actual official ultrasound waiting room. It was small and blue and sad. Cleo thought it might be one of the happier spots in the hospital, but nobody was talking or smiling. Just sitting in uncomfortable silence. There was no place for her to sit. Even some hugely pregnant women were leaning against the wall, while several ball-capped men in their twenties sat with their presumably pregnant girlfriends and stared at the floor or their phones without looking up, afraid they'd have to give up their seats.

After an hour's wait, Cleo's name was called. Her bladder was bursting but she wasn't allowed to pee, so said the instructions on her requisition sheet. Medical science could take out your heart and give you a new one but couldn't spot your baby without a full bladder. The little room she walked into was dark and the sonographer was a kind, middle-aged woman who reminded Cleo of her mom's oldest sister, Cora. Funny how Cleo thought of the woman as middle-aged when she wasn't really that far off herself. That awful term, "geriatric pregnancy." Nancy always said that if men suddenly started having babies they'd probably change the name to "distinguished pregnancy."

"I'll just get you to lay down on this table and undo your jeans. That's it, just pull down your underwear a little bit more. This will be cold." A squirt of jelly on Cleo's abdomen and she winced. She remembered when pulling down underwear and cold jelly in the dark meant something different, but she kept that thought to herself.

It was only in that moment, lying on the table in the dark room, Cleo remembered it wasn't her first time here. Doug had been out of town when Nancy had her early ultrasound on her second pregnancy. Cleo came with her and sat in the chair in the corner of the room, waiting to see the miniature human on the screen. What showed up was nothing: an empty black hole where the baby should have been. The sonographer's body stiffened, shifted ever so slightly without giving too much away, but just enough. She had told Nancy to sit tight while she got the doctor. Cleo could still recall the sound the chair made when she got up to grab Nancy's hand, how it had scraped so loud across the floor. Nancy's face was turned away from the screen and she was quiet, but tears ran sideways across her nose and down her face onto the paper-covered table.

Now Cleo craned her neck and forced herself to look at the screen that was turned away from her, waiting to see the same, or something mutant or not moving. But the sonographer was the only one who could see the full screen. So she could be the one to see the bad news first. Be the first person to see Cleo's poor little pickled egg before turning the screen to her face and yelling, *don't you see what you've done?*

Cleo waited for the shift in the sonographer and the summoning of the doctor.

The shift came then, but it wasn't from the woman at her side holding a wand to her belly. There was a flash of white at the corner of Cleo's eye, and something wriggled, something with a small black dot that was pulsing inside of it. It moved and jerked like an amoeba under a microscope.

"There we are. There's your baby." The sonographer turned the screen to Cleo and the flash of white with the dark spot was a fetus, the dark spot its beating heart.

Cleo got home in time to grab a quick lunch before returning to work for the afternoon. Before she opened the fridge, she took a set of three little black and white pictures out of her pocket that the sonographer had printed for her. Her baby, the size of a lime. In the last photo it looked like it was sucking its thumb, or playing the saxophone. She placed the little sheet of photos under a magnet on her fridge.

Then, the faintest flutter in her stomach, like she had swallowed a small bird, a chickadee, and it was trying to fly but kept hitting up against the cage of her insides.

Cleo's heart filled up, then sank like a stone, heavy with regret and bursting with love.

maisie

"I'VE BEEN THINKING," CLEO SAID, SITTING DOWN TO TEA IN her mother's kitchen.

It was a cold day in May, the first buds of spring on the tree outside the window stopped short by an overnight frost. The baby in Cleo's belly was just starting to make itself known to the general public in the form of a little pook under a pair of Nancy's maternity jeans.

"Uh-oh. That usually means something pretty big, these days. Although if news gets any more surprising you might put me in an early grave," Maisie said, but she glowed as she sipped her tea. Her shock had given way fairly early on to the unbridled joy of a first-time grandparent.

"I've been thinking about my father." Cleo said it plainly and simply. She didn't much care anymore how awkward things got.

Maisie's face didn't flinch, like she'd been expecting it all along. Her face gave nothing away behind the plume of steam rising from the mug.

"I don't really know how to begin to ask you this. I stopped trying a long time ago because I knew it hurt you," Cleo said. "But things are different now. I pretended not to care when I was a kid but I care more about this than anything in my whole life." Cleo was so calm she surprised herself. Everything had become so anticlimactic after she'd told Jamie she was pregnant.

Maisie looked past Cleo to the tree outside the kitchen window and smiled, and her smile was so warm and content Cleo had to look behind her to see what was going on.

"Cleo, you don't need any more stress in your life right now," Maisie said. Gentle and dismissive, like Cleo was a child again.

"I want to know his name. We never need to talk about him again, but I need to know who he is. Or who he was. This kid is going to have a pretty unconventional life and I want something to feel normal for them. I need to arm myself with some information. Just a name. That's all."

Maisie's wedding ring finger made a tap-tap-tap against her mug. They sat quietly for another minute, Maisie pondering consequences of her decision. She got up to turn on the sink, wetting the dishcloth hanging from the faucet, and began to wipe down the spotless kitchen counters.

"He's still alive." Maisie said, returning to the sink to rinse the dishcloth once more.

Cleo heard a car outside and prayed it wasn't Joe returning from the hardware store. The car pulled in the driveway next door. The neighbours.

"His name is Alexandre Joly." Maisie moved on to the stovetop now, lifting the elements and wiping the foil trays inside.

"Jesus, Mom."

"I need to tell you something else but I don't want to upset the baby."

One foil tray wasn't to Maisie's liking so she fished around in the cupboards looking for a clean one. Cleo thought of the day she told Jamie about the abortion, and how she focused on the coffee beans to help her through it. Seeing her mother do this made her panic a little.

"Upset the baby, what about me! The baby doesn't even understand English yet."

"God, Cleo, you are just like your grandmother. Can you just be serious for one second?"

"Fine. I can be serious. Tell me."

Maisie found a cardboard package of element trays under the sink and put a clean one under the top left burner of the stove before turning to look at Cleo.

"He never knew. Your father. He never knew I was pregnant. I just left."

Maisie took her tea from the kitchen table and dumped what was left in the sink. She rinsed and wrung out the dishcloth, hung it back on the faucet to dry, and left the kitchen to go upstairs.

Cleo sat in complete silence for ten minutes. Her head felt like it was encased in concrete. She heard Maisie running the bathroom sink upstairs, then padding across the floor to the bedroom. Then nothing. Complete silence from both floors of the house. Perhaps she had crawled into bed. Maybe she'd jumped out the window and run away.

After five more minutes, Cleo climbed the stairs. She walked down the hall and softly opened her mother's bedroom door without knocking. She hadn't done that since she was a child.

Maisie was sitting on the edge of the bed, staring out the window at the same tree she'd been so taken with in the kitchen. The bed was made but rumpled up, like she'd been lying down. She didn't turn around when she heard the door open. Cleo stood in the doorway for another minute before crossing the room and sitting next to her mother.

"Whatcha looking at."

"That little robin's nest in our maple. They're early this year. Not sure what the frost might have done to their eggs. They should have hatched by now."

"You sure are worried about an awful lot of babies."

"Cleo."

"I found a picture of him once."

"You didn't." Maisie finally turned to face Cleo, her eyes red and raw.

"I did. Before I went to France when I was sixteen. I snuck into the attic and went through your things. I found it in the bottom of a box and I kept it. I took it on the plane with me."

"Cleo Alfreda Best, you didn't! I searched for that photo for years. I cried for hours over that thing."

Cleo thought she was getting ready to melt down completely but her mother started to laugh.

Maisie moved across the bedroom to her vanity and sat down. She took out her messy bun and started to brush her hair. It wasn't as thick and long as it used to be, but it was still mostly blond, and only greying at the temples. Cleo had always been jealous of her mother's hair.

"I wasn't embarrassed about it, you know. I was thrilled. I was almost proud," Maisie said. She smoothed her hair down, redid it tightly in a ponytail high on her head. "I never told anyone. Not a soul. I thought I'd tell Alex, but then, you know. You get scared about having a baby in another country, without your family, on your own."

"I know," said Cleo, because she did.

"I just kept working until they told me I was gaining too much weight and then I left. I didn't even say goodbye." Maisie opened a little glass jar of cream and stuck her pinky finger in and dabbed under her eyes. Cleo sat on the bed, cross-legged. Like when she was a child, and they would chat when Maisie was doing her makeup before heading out to a party with Joe. Only making eye contact in between swipes of a mascara wand.

"Did you love him?"

Maisie screwed the lid back on the jar and reached for a pair of tweezers. Without looking at Cleo she leaned into the mirror, pulled taut the skin at her temple. "Yes," she said. And she plucked an eyebrow hair.

"That was it. I flew home. Nalfie told everyone I'd eloped in Paris and that my husband had died in an accident shortly after. Not that I was the first single mother on Carter's Hill, mind you. I don't know why she did that. I guess there were some pretty high hopes for me going off to Paris to dance. Maybe it softened the blow a little when everyone saw me marching around pregnant, I don't know."

They sat for a few more minutes, Cleo watching her mother finish her eyebrows, then apply the thinnest amount of eyeliner and mascara. The sound of Joe's pickup truck pulling into the driveway made Cleo start a little but Maisie's eyes didn't move from the mirror.

"I'm going to need to contact him," Cleo said, moving to the window and looking out. Her oblivious, beautiful stepfather stepping out of his truck and coming up the front path.

"I know. It's fine."

"What about Joe and Nalfie?"

"I'll figure it out." Maisie stood and straightened the items on her vanity table. She gave herself one more glance in the mirror, patting her cheeks and shaking her head a little. "You've got enough on your plate."

Maisie left the room, turning first in the doorway to look back at her daughter. "And I'd like that photo back, please," she said, before going downstairs to greet her husband.

like magic

Cleo had spent a week on a bus with a bunch of American and mainland Canadian teenagers during her first week in France. They were nice kids for the most part, all of them white, most of them rich, and everyone called her Newfie and asked her to "do an accent" whenever she talked with them. She kept to herself most days. Sitting at the back of the bus, watching the landscape change from city streets to July fields of sunflowers and lavender as they travelled north to south.

On her first day in Paris, the group was allowed an hour of free time in the morning before the planned trip to the Louvre. Cleo sat by herself at a café near their cheap hotel. She ordered an espresso in broken French and her cheeks started to flame when the waiter winked and called her Mademoiselle. She wanted to grab him by the collar and yell *You don't understand, I'm French, too! I just don't know how to speak it yet! This is supposed to be my life!* She drank bitter espresso that she hated, the picture she'd stolen from Maisie laid carefully on the table next to the cup. Not that it would help with identification, you couldn't really see the man's face buried in her mother's neck while they sat at a café not unlike the one Cleo found herself at now. It was a tortured romanticism, imagining her father would walk by and just *know* she was there, he would just *feel* it. Her eyes watched strangers on the street, lingering on every man of a certain age, thinking, *he could walk by, stuff like that happens, he could still be in Paris.* She did this for the better part of an hour, until she accidentally made eye contact a little too long with a man in his forties, who stopped and sat at her table. He said, "Bonjour, ma belle! Que fait une jolie Américaine toute seule à Paris?" and Cleo grabbed the picture and her backpack and ran inside to pay her bill. She was disappointed she didn't get to leave her francs on the table under her espresso cup like she'd seen in the movies. And disappointed the man thought she was American, and not a half-Canadian waiting for her French father to walk by.

bonjour

Cleo sat with her laptop at the small kitchen table. It was getting harder now, to do that. In the way it was harder to lean up against the sink to do dishes. She usually liked to work on the sofa in front of a muted television, computer sitting in the circle of her crossed legs and up against her belly. Now she had to worry about radioactive waves finding their way into her uterus and brain-damaging the baby or predestining it to be a bad reader or a serial killer just by checking her email.

Her inbox had thirty-seven unread emails and none of them mattered to her. Everyone was a bit more patient with her now. She'd been slayed by morning sickness, she'd been tired, emails could sit for a week unanswered until Cleo pasted the same generic apology at the beginning of every reply, thanking so-and-so for their understanding. She'd never played any kind of card like that at work, but she let herself do it with the pregnancy because she was too tired to care.

She typed "Alexandre Joly, dance" into Google and took a deep breath.

He had his own Wikipedia page. There wasn't a page full of Alexandres or a list of LinkedIn profiles, this was him. She could see right away it was him, that familiarity. She could pass him in the street without a second glance, but if they met at a party, spent more than twenty minutes in a room together, it would become eerily apparent to anyone in a circle of conversation with them.

She'd spent hours as a teenager daydreaming of her mother's life in Paris. Maisie leaving her quaint apartment in Montmartre in the morning to buy baguettes, Maisie drinking coffee and smoking at an outdoor café, or walking arm in arm with Cleo's mysterious father along the Seine. In all those years of romanticizing her mother's life and wondering what her father looked like, she was too afraid to make a face for him in her head. And now here he was.

His page said he was sixty-four and "semi-retraité" but was known to instruct and choreograph on occasion for several companies, mostly in the south. He lived in Toulon.

Cleo had stayed with a family in Toulon for a month when she was sixteen, as a summer exchange student. Maisie had met Alexandre in Paris in the seventies: how long had he lived in Toulon? Did her host family know who he was, or even know him personally? Had she passed him on the street? Cleo's heart hammered in her chest at the possibility of it all. The baby started moving in mini jolts, like little electric shocks shaking Cleo's belly. With her hands shaking she opened a new window on her laptop to search "baby hiccups during pregnancy" to be sure this was all normal and not the result of a shock to the baby.

Alexandre's grandchild.

~~~

She waited three days to email him. Let what she'd found out settle a little in her head, not mentioning her discovery to anyone, not even Nancy. Certainly not Maisie.

Cleo spent every evening after work at the kitchen table, eating supper in front of the laptop, reading endless articles about Alexandre's work. They were in French so she took away what she could.
~~~

Mostly she looked for clips of his work on dance sites and YouTube.

When she was a child she'd always thought of her mother in a tutu and feathers, spotlights bathing her in soft light among a crowd of slender, pale-skinned, dark-haired beauties. Maisie always front and centre, and always the most beautiful, her hair like sunshine making her stand out from the rest. Pirouetting across the stage, being lifted in the air by men in tights and fancy embroidered jackets. There were nights when Cleo lay in bed after Maisie had tucked her in, staring at the ceiling for an hour and worrying herself to sleep with grief and guilt that she had effectively ended her mother's glamorous life. Some nights angry tears that her mother had left at all and hadn't raised her in Paris.

But this wasn't the dance of Cleo's childhood daydreams, what Alexandre did now. Bodies of dancers contorted into positions Cleo never thought possible, like they were sad and in pain, a violence you couldn't look away from. Strains of scratchy irritating violins and screeching flutes accompanying women dancing in pantsuits, hair slicked back like Wall Street financiers. Sinewy bodies leaping off chairs or each other. It was as far from Swan Lake as you could get. It was beautiful. Cleo wondered if her mother had ever danced like that.

She'd emailed a random dance company he'd worked with and asked if they could put her in contact. "My mother was a dancer in Paris in the '70s . . . she's going to be in France . . . would like to contact Alexandre . . . he was such a great influence on her . . . is it possible you have his email address?" Cleo omitted "he got her pregnant and I'm the daughter trying to find him." She wasn't sure that would fly. But it was France, after all. Maybe this kind of thing wasn't terribly uncommon for handsome choreographers in the '70s. Cleo might have a whole network of half-brothers and -sisters splattered across Europe and the rest of the world.

She considered writing the email in her broken French but she wasn't even sure how to get all the accents right on the keyboard. He must speak some English, to have been able to speak to Maisie all those years ago, to be a choreographer working with dancers from everywhere. She would write to Alexandre in English, risk having him get someone to translate, rather than risk his mortification at her grammar, along with the shock of discovering a daughter.

The nightmare scenario crossed her mind of him casually calling his English-speaking wife over to the computer to ask her what the email said.

She only had to start writing. She didn't have to send anything.

Cleo sat at the kitchen table for three hours and wrote a long, rambling email. *Bonjour and Surprise! You have a daughter! My mother was pregnant when she left you . . . I didn't even know your name until last week . . . hey guess what I was in Toulon one time, imagine if we passed each other in the street, I bet we did . . . I googled you and you're definitely my dad, I have your eyes and your cowlick . . . when I was a kid I dreamed of spending summers with you in France eating peaches with juice running down my arms instead of dropping rocks on jellyfish off the wharf in Wesleyville . . . P.S. you're going to be a grandfather! Maybe we can meet someday, or you can ignore this email and get on with your life, no worries . . . I just thought you'd like to know that you have a relative across the pond, two relatives soon, fingers crossed . . .* and on and on until she realized she'd written the equivalent of a diary entry of a thirteen-year-old girl. She dumped the email in her drafts folder and crawled into bed at midnight.

jump

Cleo met her host family in Toulon after her week-long tour and she thought she'd won the lottery. They were all tanned and lovely and owned a sailboat. Their house had a pool and she had a bedroom with her very own bathroom. There was a terrace covered in bougainvillea where they ate supper every evening, and they let Cleo have champagne when they hosted parties. They took her on overnight sailing trips to islands in the Mediterranean and her life was, for a month, what she dreamed it should have been all along.

Her host sister, Delphine, was a year older than Cleo. A Brigitte Bardot lookalike with sun-kissed hair who smoked and drank and swore in broken English, she was the most beautiful creature Cleo had ever seen. They would have summer afternoon pool parties when Delphine's parents were at work. Everyone greeted Cleo with a kiss on the cheek, and she would watch as the girls stripped off their bikini tops before swimming, while the boys smoked and drank with their legs dangling in the pool, not clocking what would have caused multiple teenage cardiac arrests back home. Cleo ignored the boys, who she knew would have no interest in a pale Canadian sitting poolside, burning with Catholic shame in her shorts and Northern

Reflections T-shirt. She pretended to read a book in a deck chair, staring at the stunning tan-lineless torsos in the pool for as long as she could without seeming weird. The backs of her legs were hot and sweaty and they stuck to the plastic deck chairs and squeaked when Cleo moved to try and get more comfortable. Which was impossible.

She'd always regretted that. Not stripping off and jumping in the pool.

To: Alexandre Joly (apjoly@yahoo.fr)
From: Cleo Best (cleobest@gmail.com)
Sent: June-3-17 3:02 PM
Subject:

Dear Alexandre,

My name is Cleo Best and I am emailing you from Canada. More specifically, from St. John's in Newfoundland. You worked with my mother, Maisie Hancock, in the seventies while she was a dancer at the Paris Opera Ballet. I have reason to believe you are my biological father. I'm very sorry to email you what I'm sure is surprising news. I've only recently found out your name and I felt I had an obligation to inform you. If you would like to make contact, feel free to respond to this email. I look forward to hearing from you, but I will understand if you decide not to get in touch.

Sincerely,
Cleo Best

The email took her ten minutes and she sent it without a proofread. She closed her laptop, promising herself she wouldn't open it for the rest of the day.

He responded four days later, after she'd given up hope of an answer. When she opened her inbox and saw his name she felt sick to her stomach, and for a second wished she had never made contact. The baby kicked so hard Cleo thought it was her fault, like it could sense a sudden disruption in the rhythm of its house.

To: Cleo Best (cleobest@gmail.com)
From: Alexandre Joly (apjoly@yahoo.fr)
Sent: June-7-17 10:30 AM
Subject: Hello

Dearest Cleo,

I am very sorry for my late response. I do not check my email many times. You might understand that I was very shocked and surprised to read it. Of course I am answering you. I think it's better to talk on the telephone. Can you give me your phone number? I would like to talk with you. I apologize because my English is not good when I talk on the phone. Pardon me if this is impolite, but is it possible to send a picture? I am curious to see what you look like.

Yours truly,
Alexandre

Cleo wrote back immediately. There was no particular set of etiquette rules for this one. No need to be coy, or fear being seen as too eager. She *was* eager, it was impossible to be anything else. She didn't care if he knew.

To: Alexandre Joly (apjoly@yahoo.fr)
From: Cleo Best (cleobest@gmail.com)
Sent: June-7-17 6:17 PM
Subject: Phone number and photo

Dear Alexandre,

Thank you for your response. My phone number, including the country code is: 001 709 746 0259.

I have attached a photograph, although I look a little different now, as I am almost five months pregnant.

Call me anytime that's convenient for you. If you cannot reach me, please leave me a message and I will return your call as soon as I can. I am looking forward to talking with you. I don't mind if your English isn't very good, I would like to hear your voice. I speak a little French, so we will be okay.

Sincerely,

Cleo

She struggled with what photo to attach, finally settling on one that was two years old. Jamie had taken it on Middle Cove Beach two summers earlier. It was flattering, but she didn't look like she was trying too hard. She worried the email was too familiar, if it was too soon for that. But the man had had sex with her mother, after all. Cleo shared half his DNA, what harm was a familiar email now?

She hit Send.

an ocean between them

THE CALL CAME WHEN SHE WAS AT WORK, BARELY ONE DAY later. Cleo had left her phone on her desk when she went into a meeting, and the screen was flashing a voicemail message from an overseas number when she returned an hour later. She cursed loud enough for a few people to look up from their cubicles in mild interest. Everyone bristled a bit now when she swore, like she shouldn't because she was with child, or she was raising some kind of premature labour alarm. Rishi leaned back in his chair.

"You okay?" He looked excited.

"Yep, just missed a phone call, thanks Rish."

Cleo took her phone to the bathroom, checking under the stalls to make sure they were empty. She locked herself into the last one, went into her voicemail and held the phone to her ear with shaking hands.

"Hello. Ahhh, hello. This is Alexandre Joly, calling for Miss Cleo Best. Cleo, I am sorry to miss you, I hope we can speak soon. Perhaps it's hard with the change, the time change. I'm quite terrible on the phone in English, so maybe I will email you . . . ah . . . I'm using Skype sometimes for my work, perhaps this is possible for us. I will email you the Skype contact? I hope we can see each other. Okay, so you can call me, or we can prepare a Skype if that is a good idea. If that is better for you. Okay, that's good. Au revoir, bye bye."

The sound of his broken English in her ear melted Cleo's heart. She sat on the toilet and played the message three more times before heading back to her desk.

They set up a Skype chat for late Saturday morning Cleo's time. She woke at seven, unable to fall back asleep, so she got dressed and walked around the lake. Showered, forced herself to eat breakfast even though she was too nervous to be hungry. There was still an hour and a half to go, so she looked at her email again to double-check the time of their prearranged date. She left the computer open on the kitchen table and paced the living room, did the dishes, gutted the fridge. With five minutes to go she decided to get changed; it hadn't registered that she should make an effort to look half-decent when she was only puttering around her apartment, but her birth father was about to see her for the first time and she was wearing maternity leggings and an old T-shirt. He would only see her from the waist up, but still. What if he wanted to see her belly? His grandkid? That would be weird, though. Would it? She took off her T-shirt and pulled on a casual black maternity dress, one that was flattering and showed off her bump without making her look frumpy. She put on a bit of eyeliner and mascara. Was she trying too hard to look French?

The last coat of mascara was going on when Cleo heard Skype dinging from the kitchen. She dropped the wand in the bathroom sink and raced over to the kitchen table, feeling her neck and face starting to flush before she'd even touched the computer. She took a deep breath, fluffed her hair. Clicked the answer call button.

The pause before the image appeared on the screen, dear God let it work, of all times for the internet to quit, let it not be now.

There he was, and there was five seconds of them looking at each other. Knowing without a doubt. Even if he had doubted, he couldn't now.

"Hello, Cleo."

"Hello, Alexandre."

She was too embarrassed to say it properly with a French accent, and that morphed in an instant to wishing she had. What came out sounded stupid, like an old American tourist too lazy to try.

"How are you? How is the weather? I hear Newfoundland is a bit, ahhh . . . hard for weather."

He'd asked about the weather. Thank God.

"It's actually very beautiful today. It's our first warm day of the year, it feels like summer. But who knows, maybe snow tomorrow."

Cleo found herself slipping into the slow and simple teacher talk she used when she lived in Korea and she hated herself for it, but he laughed.

"That's good. You need fresh air now, especially."

"I do." The baby, he was talking about the baby. She felt like crying already.

"How are you feeling these days?"

His English was great, what was he worried about on the phone?

"Very well. I was sick for a couple of months, but I'm good now. Always hungry."

He laughed again. He had a low voice, rich and clear. His laugh came deep, from his belly, or so it seemed with two computer screens and an ocean between them.

"Is your husband taking good care of you?"

Fuck fuck fuck fuck fuck.

"Umm, actually . . ." Cleo fell out of her teacher-speak as quick as she'd fallen in. "I'm not married, and it's a bit of a complicated situation."

Jesus, could he be religious? If he was, she was fucked.

Alexandre's face fell. It was over, two minutes in.

"Oh, Cleo, I'm sorry for asking you. We just met, it's very early.

I'm sorry. Please forgive me. That question is a mistake."

"Oh, that's totally fine. It's okay!" Relief flooded through her. Why was she trying to please him already? He was a stranger. Why was she even doing this. "The father and I are very good friends. He's a good man. It's a long story."

"Ah yes, well. I hope someday you will tell me the story."

"I would like that."

ma fille perdue

CLEO AND ALEXANDRE DECIDED ON A WEEKLY SKYPE DATE, AND they kept the same Saturday time to make it easy. If one of them had anything to do they would message each other to reschedule, or simply wait until the following Saturday. It got easier for Cleo each time, with less blushing and wondering what to wear. She quit with the eye makeup after the second call. They prepared coffee and called it their "coffee date" to make it feel like they weren't so far away. As Cleo's belly grew, so did her regret that this man, who wasn't yet her father but was becoming a friend, would be so far away when her child decided to show up.

The fourth Saturday in, Alexandre took his laptop out to the table in the garden.

"So we can have our coffee outside," he said.

"I wish I could do the same, it's so cold and rainy here today." Cleo was wrapped in a sweater, sitting on her couch. They were paying for their beautiful June in July, apparently.

Cleo hadn't seen much of Alexandre's place and didn't feel comfortable enough yet to ask for a tour of his house. He lived alone, from what she could gather. He had briefly mentioned having a partner for fifteen years, but that had ended five years ago. Part of Cleo was relieved she'd imposed herself on a man who was unmarried, with no children. There was no need for him to tell anyone, if that's what he wished. He appeared to call from what looked to be a study or an office. It was cluttered, but not in a hoarder kind of way. It looked comfortable and airy and there was a lot of abstract art on the walls. Cleo could see a few espresso cups lying around. His cleaner had popped into the frame once, and he'd exclaimed without hesitation or embarrassment, "Mathilde! J'ai retrouvé ma fille perdue de vue! Viens la rencontrer!" And Cleo had stumbled through a conversation in broken French with her father's cleaning lady, who appeared pleased and not surprised in the least that her employer suddenly had a daughter in Canada.

When Alex, as he'd asked her to call him, had discovered she could speak French, she felt obligated to put in the effort. They went back and forth and it seemed to put him at ease, though his English was far better.

Alex placed the computer on the little table and adjusted it until he was to the left of the screen. Cleo could see a stone wall and some trees that enclosed the garden, and the tiniest sliver of what appeared to be the ocean.

"Voilà. You can see my ocean view, yes?" He laughed and looked back, making a grand sweeping gesture with his left hand.

"I think it's beautiful. You must spend a lot of time out there. I can hear the cicadas."

"The little bastards. So noisy they make you deaf."

"I was in France when I was sixteen. In Toulon, on an exchange trip. I stayed with a family there. Have you been in Toulon many years?" Cleo didn't know why she'd waited a month to tell him that.

"Cleo! C'est vrai? I am a little outside the city, but yes, I have this place for twenty-five years. We were so close. Imagine passing each other, without knowing."

"I thought a lot about you when I was there. I knew you were French, but that was it. I didn't know what city."

Alex didn't know what to say to this. He put his elbow on the table and turned to look at his little piece of the ocean. They were both comfortably quiet for a couple of minutes, drinking their coffee and thinking of the possibility of having passed each other on the street, in the market, at a restaurant.

"Maisie. How is she?" He was still looking at the ocean.

Cleo's heart skipped a beat when he said her mother's name. Like Maisie's must have the first time she heard him say it, *Mai-Zee*, the "zee" coming out long and musical, harder than in English. Her name must have sounded so boring when she returned to Newfoundland.

"She's well. She's been married to my stepfather, Joe, since I was two."

"Ah."

"Alex. I'm sorry. I'm sorry for what she did. I don't know why she did it."

"Cleo, it is not your fault. We were very young and foolish. It was, how do you say, a very whirlwind thing."

"I think she must have been very scared."

"Yes."

"And I think she loved you very much."

"Yes. I loved her as well."

summer II

CLEO WAS LYING ON HER BACK, STRETCHED OUT ON A BLANKET. It was so hot, even in the shade of the tree where they had set up, her back was soaked with sweat and her sundress stuck to her uncomfortably.

"Jesus, I feel like a beached whale."

"You look like it," said Nancy, lying at the other end of the blanket. Her leg was crossed over the other and she wriggled her bare toes.

Donna was unpacking the picnic basket and reached over to flick Nancy on the leg.

"Don't mind this one, you're gorgeous." She took a giant Mason jar out of the basket and handed it over to Cleo. It was filled with ice and slices of lemon and cucumber and it sparkled like stained glass in the scraps of sun beating through the trees. "I knew you couldn't have any rosé so I brought you a jar of fizzy water. Oh wait, I brought a straw too, it's in here somewhere. One of those environmentally friendly paper ones. You have to worry about that kind of stuff now, you know."

"People with no kids don't worry about that stuff?" Cleo heaved herself up to a sitting position.

"Not really, nope."

Donna rummaged around in the basket, unpacking the food while she looked for the straw. There were two baguettes and a bunch of grapes, and plastic containers filled with salads. She took out a wooden board and two kinds of cheese, then a couple of portable plastic wine glasses.

"Ah! Found it." Donna waved the straw in the air.

"My God, Donna. You're like Mary Poppins with the carpet bag," Nancy said. She sat up and started to tear off the end of a baguette.

"This is amazing, you're amazing." Cleo unscrewed the cap of the Mason jar and put the straw in. She couldn't think of anything better to drink in the world, not even a glass of rosé. She took a long sip and the bubbles burned down her throat and into her chest. She'd pay for this picnic in a few hours with wicked heartburn. Everything she loved to eat was rejected and sent back to the kitchen by whatever it was she was growing in there.

"Remind me again why we only do this once a summer?" Nancy was into the rosé now, pouring for herself and Donna.

"I know. Poor Reg. I made him buy this fancy basket for my birthday and I only use it once a year," Donna said, taking a cheese knife out of the basket and cutting up the wheel of camembert into triangles.

"Don't you two ever use it?"

"God, no. Reg hates eating outdoors."

"Reg only likes eating wings in a darkened room, doesn't he."

"Pretty much."

Cleo laughed at her two friends and their easy back and forth, wondering how it would all change, how the three of them would change when the baby came. They were just back to a new kind of normal after Nancy's Mack, and now this.

A group of teenaged girls walked by them, all bare bellies and short shorts. Their heads were down into their phones, but they were laughing and carrying on with their conversation, walking a sure path like they'd grown eyes in their shins. They passed by so close Cleo could smell their shampoo. She thought again about how old her hands had looked holding that pregnancy test. How much older they would look when her baby turned into a teenager.

"My God, how much shorter can the shorts get?" Donna said through a mouthful of bread, shaking her head as she watched the girls walk away.

"I know." Nancy sighed. "Aren't they gorgeous? And they don't even know it. Don't you wish you knew how great your body was at that age? I want to take them and shake them and tell them how beautiful they are and how all the boys are dickheads."

"Well, there's still no need for shorts that short, no matter how gorgeous they are."

"Oh, Donna, give up. They're stunning, let them enjoy it. We did when we were that age. They'll be old and wrinkly like us someday."

"And we'll be dead," said Cleo.

"Or not quite and they'll be changing our diapers in an under-funded nursing home. Cheers, ladies!" Nancy said it so loud the teenagers looked back at them and started laughing, shaking their freshly washed heads at the women who could be their mothers.

"Their poor parents, though. I'm so glad I had a boy," Nancy said, lying back down on her side this time, propped up on an elbow. "Apparently the boys are harder first and then they mellow out, but the sweet baby girls turn hellish when they get older."

"I've heard the same," said Donna. "And puberty happens now at eight instead of twelve like it did when we were kids."

"And this one still won't find out what she's having," Nancy nudged Cleo with her foot. "So annoying. Now I have to hold on to all of Mack's hand-me-downs until you squeeze out your youngster."

"I know. I'm sorry. It's not like I haven't had enough surprises this year already. I don't know, I just really don't want to find out."

The truth was Cleo wanted to avoid more fanfare. Telling everyone she was pregnant was hard enough. Telling everyone what she was having would be a Round Two she didn't need.

"Well, if you have a girl you'll just be delaying the nervous breakdown by a few years. A boy, and it'll be over in four to five," Nancy said, and she laughed.

Cleo knew Nancy wasn't entirely joking. She'd had a hard time when Mack came. Cleo thought about that often, how she'd watched her best friend work her way through that first year of motherhood like a zombie. The memory of it was always at the back of Cleo's brain: how would she manage without someone like Doug around? Or someone like Jamie.

The baby kicked and rolled so hard Cleo had to put down her jar of water and stretch out on her back. Nancy tried to catch the kicks with her hands and Donna's head moved down to Cleo's belly, listening intently. They both kept quiet, as if their silence would lure the creature into movement.

"I don't care what it is," Cleo said. Staring up into the leaves of the tree above them, the hands and head of her two friends still on her belly. "I just don't want it to be an asshole."

The baby kicked Donna in the face, and the women howled.

getting the fuck out

THE TRICK TO SURVIVING WALMART WAS TO PRETEND YOU WERE on one of those supermarket game shows. If you ran around and got what you needed as fast as you could, you won the prize. In this case, Cleo's prize was getting the fuck out of Walmart.

It took her fifteen minutes to track down a plunger. Another ten to find someone to ask if they had shower curtains to fit shower stalls and not full-size tubs. The teenager had no idea what she was talking about, was clearly still living with his parents in the suburbs somewhere in a sprawling three-and-a-half-bathroom house and had never had to worry about fitting a shower stall with a curtain.

"Never mind," said Cleo. "I'll buy one of these and cut it." The kid shrugged and took his phone out of the front of his blue smock.

She gave up on finding anyone else remotely useful and wandered the store for another twenty minutes until she found a pair of scissors.

Cleo only had three items but the express line snaked around the partitions and spilled into the aisles, so she took her chances and got in one of the regular lines. The woman in front of her looked vaguely familiar. She was standing back on, but there was something in the way she held herself, the way her purse was slung over the crook in her elbow, wrist upturned, that made Cleo think they'd met before. Cleo's phone went off in her coat pocket and she juggled her plunger, shower curtain, and scissors, the plunger stuck out from under her arm, and she had to be careful not to hit the woman in front of her with the end of it.

She put the pair of scissors under her chin and managed to unzip her pocket and grab the phone. "Mom" popped up on call display. Normally Cleo would ignore a call in a checkout line and call back later, but when she didn't answer the phone these days, Maisie worried. Cleo took the scissors from under her chin and shoved them under her arm with the shower curtain and plunger.

"Hey Mom, how's it going. I'm okay. I'm picking up some stuff at Walmart . . . I know, I know, but I didn't know where else to get a plunger, Jesus, Maisie."

The woman in front bristled when Cleo started speaking and turned around at the mention of Maisie's name.

Evelyn.

Evelyn, who wasn't quite recognizable because her hair was short now and she'd lost weight. Cleo's mouth dropped open and her chest got hot and the heat crawled up her neck and cheeks until her whole face was on fire.

"Cleo?" From somewhere behind the ringing in her ears Cleo heard her mother.

"Cleo, honey are you okay? Are you there?"

"Just a second, Mom," Cleo squeaked out, and she wanted to say hi to Evelyn to give a scrap of normalcy to the situation, but the words wouldn't come.

She looked from Cleo's face down to her eight-month belly and back to her face again. Evelyn's eyes filled with tears first, then panic, and with shaking hands, but very calmly, she bent and placed her shopping basket right there on the floor next to the magazine rack. She shouldered her way past the people ahead of her in line, not saying a word, physically moving them out of her way, pushing past like she was going to be sick and maybe she was.

"Evelyn," Cleo called, but Evelyn didn't look back, just crossed her arms in front of her and hurried out the front entrance of the store.

All eyes turned to look at Cleo, her face flaming, a plunger stuck out from under her arm.

goddamn

THE CONTRACTIONS STARTED WHILE CLEO WAS WATCHING television. Some stupid reality show, so it felt like God's way of punishing her for watching shit TV. Perhaps if she'd been reading *War and Peace* there would have been a gentler start. The kind of start Cleo had heard about, where you get to labour at home for two days while the father of your baby, the one you were married to, rubbed your back and held your elbow while you paced the kitchen floor, fed you orange segments, brewed cups of chamomile tea and wiped your forehead with a damp cloth in between highly manageable contractions that were almost beautiful in their pain, almost orgasmic if you breathed the right way and had taken all those hypnotic birthing classes.

Fuck fuck fuck fuck fuck fuck *fuuuuuuuuuuuuuuuuuuuuuuuuuuuuuuuuck.*

Fuck all those fucking hippies and their fucking . . .

FUCK.

It wasn't supposed to be like this, this didn't feel right.

She was alone in her apartment and it was two weeks early, too early, she was alone. In a pair of Francis's oversized track pants and her rattiest maternity T-shirt, a hand-me-down from Nancy. She couldn't be seen like this, not by anyone at the hospital, she didn't care if they had to take her clothes off and take a baby out of her, she had to get a shower and get changed. Nalfie's words in her ears as the second contraction brought her to her hands and knees: "If you ever ends up at the hospital with dirty drawers on, you better not tell them you belongs to me, Missy."

Cleo tried to breathe through it like they told her in that useless prenatal class at the Health Sciences Centre. "We won't really get into the breathing here today, you'll know what to do," they'd said. *Oh, you'll get the epidural, all right* what they really meant. Smiling down at the terrified looking fathers and rosy-cheeked mothers who all had such high hopes for a natural childbirth. The same women who would be begging for a needle in their spine before they made it across the hospital parking lot.

Phone. Where was the fucking phone.

Maisie. She needed her mother. She didn't care if she ever saw Francis again. She wanted her mother and she wanted Nancy. Cleo felt so stupid for letting this happen to herself, she was a stupid, stupid woman wearing track pants and crying for her mother like a child.

Cleo spied the phone under the sofa when she laid her face on the floor, collapsing off her hands and knees when the contraction subsided. For two beautiful minutes there was no pain, just long enough to call a cab. She couldn't shower, it hurt too much, she didn't even have it in her to speak a fully formed sentence, just the two words of her address that she shouted at the dispatcher. She had to be calm when the cab got here or he might not let her in; Cleo had heard stories of cabbies afraid of water breaking and ruining upholstery. That couldn't be right, she would sue if that happened. She would jump in as soon as the car pulled up and then there'd be nothing they could do except drive.

She sent Maisie, Nancy, and Francis a group text.

Contractions started i'm in cab see you at hospital soon please

One of them was bound to see it and contact the others.

Thank God Nancy had packed her hospital bag last week. Cleo managed to get on her coat and boots before another contraction came and she had to lean over the back of the sofa, head on her arms.

"How the fuck do people do this without druuuuuuuuuuuuuugs."

She lowed it like a cow in a barn, no one in the world to help her.

Sudden movement upstairs, quick footsteps crossing the floor. Marsha had heard her yelling through the ceiling. The last thing she needed right now and everything she was secretly hoping for the minute the contractions started. By the time Cleo had made it to her hands and knees again, Marsha's key was in the door. That was fast, Cleo thought. In whatever lucid seconds her body let her have as she lowered herself to the floor, she imagined a whole wall of video monitors upstairs on the living room wall, Marsha sitting in her recliner and watching with a bowl of popcorn and a glass of sherry on the end table.

"Can you make it to the car," Marsha said. She was on the floor now too, her voice strangely calm and kind. Like she'd been waiting for a tenant to go into labour her entire life.

"It's okay, I called a cab."

"Cleo, get up, take my arm, we have to get to the car."

"But the cab will—"

"Cleo I'm not sending my pregnant tenant to the hospital in a goddamn Jiffy Cab." Marsha took her cell out of her jacket pocket and called the cab company, pulled Cleo up off the floor, and cancelled the taxi with the phone sandwiched between her ear and shoulder.

"Let's get you out of here before your water breaks, this laminate floor is only two years old."

hello

The baby comes twelve hours after Cleo arrives at the hospital. Marsha gets her to the case room lobby, where Maisie and Joe are already waiting. Nancy arrives behind her, running around the corner just as Maisie shuffles Cleo through the entrance, and she shouts, "I love you!" before the door shuts. It occurs to Cleo days after the birth that Nancy and Joe plunked themselves down outside for twelve hours straight, only going as far as the cafeteria to get sandwiches and coffee.

Francis bursts in through the birthing room door two hours later, breathless with apology, "There was a fire, I'm so sorry, what did I miss." Cleo has had the morphine and epidural by this point. Takes quick naps and eats endless popsicles, waits the few centimetres more she needs to dilate before the pushing can begin. She is high and jokes with the nurses, "This is goddamn great, you guys must love it when women get epidurals, can I get another pineapple popsicle, please."

At ten in the morning, she's ready to start pushing. The epidural deadened the waves of contractions just enough for her to feel when it's time to push, bracing against Francis and Maisie holding a leg each. Cleo marvels at the wonder of the drugs, how she can feel the push of everything and how hard it is but she doesn't want to die like she thought she would, she feels strong enough to do this, to push this baby out and still be able to joke with the nurses apologetically when she pushes and the smell of her own shit hits her nose. She looks back at Francis, "I bet you wish you were still at that fire." The women laugh and Francis turns green.

The nurses stay with her for hours, they do all the work, while the doctor comes in at the last minute to go through the motions. The hardest push to get the head out. "We have the head, we have the head, you can do it, one more push, that's it, good girl, we have a baby."

No one says what it is, they hold it in the air so Cleo can see for herself, an offering with a high-pitched wail. Nothing tucked in neat, everything out in the world for all to see.

A boy.

Francis and Maisie cry. They sob like children, Francis with his forehead on Cleo's head. "A son, that's our son, that's our son, I'm so proud of you."

This little creature gets placed on her chest, his dark hair slick and his clenched fists still purple. Quiet in the bustle around him, contemplating his next move, big eyes open and terrified. Cleo wraps her arms around the baby and breathes up and down, slow and sure to calm him because he looks so scared.

"It's okay, buddy": the first words she says to her son.

perfect pancake

Cleo woke up in the too-early morning light from a short and broken sleep. Her mother was holding Timothy in the chair where Francis had been before Cleo had fallen asleep.

"Good morning, love," Maisie said, without taking her eyes from the baby.

"Morning. Where's Francis?"

"I snuck in an hour ago and sent him home. He looked exhausted. They're not meant to handle it, you know."

"I don't exactly feel meant to handle it either." Cleo sat up as slowly and tenderly as she could. Her whole body felt like broken bits and pieces, especially from the waist down.

"I know. It'll get better," Maisie said. She stroked the top of Timothy's head with the lightest touch, like he was a newborn kitten instead of a child. "You did great. He's so perfect. He's so much like you when you were born. That hair. My goodness."

"I think he looks exactly like Francis."

"That'll change. They always look like their fathers when they're born."

"Did I?"

Maisie finally looked over at Cleo.

"You did."

what about us over here

THERE WAS A SOFT KNOCK ON THE DOOR AND CLEO HOISTED herself up off the couch, still too sore to imagine ever walking normally again, and hobbled across the room to let Donna in.

"Oh, sweetheart, hi. Oh my, you look great."

"Lies. I look like a bag of shit."

"Okay, well maybe a little tired, but your boobs look great."

Cleo lingered in Donna's hug for as long as she could. She smelled like freshly washed hair, a soft warm breeze of coconut.

I will never smell good again, Cleo thought. "Don't squeeze too hard, I might leak all over you."

"Seriously, you look good. How's the breastfeeding going?" Donna held Cleo out at arm's length and looked her up and down.

"A nightmare. Timothy hates me. Too soon to think about formula?"

"Not at all. Keep at it, it'll get easier. But if it doesn't, just do what you have to do to survive the first month, and for God's sake don't ask anybody about breastfeeding on Facebook. How are your bits?"

"Terrible. I can't believe women do this more than once. And who has sex after six weeks? Jesus Christ."

"That's a load of horseshit," Donna said, as she brought an enormous reusable grocery bag over to the kitchen table. "I have clients who've had to wait up to a year. That's mostly what they say so the husbands don't get scared. You sit down now and relax, I'll make us some coffee."

"Thank you for asking, nobody really cares about my vagina now the baby is out." Cleo gently lowered herself back onto the couch, gratefully accepting the chance to sit down baby-free for a few minutes. She hoped Timothy would sleep for longer than fifteen minutes on his own.

It hit her then that Donna was the first person to visit who hadn't thrown her aside after a quick hug to search for the baby, to hold the baby, to smell the baby's head, to have a turn rocking the baby in the glider. Donna put the coffee on and started unpacking what she'd brought, laying out the contents on the table.

"Okay, here's a couple of lasagnas." She carried the cling-wrapped pans to the freezer and stored them, returning to the pile of food she'd brought. "Here are your favourite coffee beans, I can grind them for you before I leave, I won't do it now in case I wake Timothy. I made some bran muffins to make things a bit easier for you. Chocolate chip so you can at least pretend they're a treat. Even Reg liked them, although I didn't tell him they were bran, so that should be interesting. They'll be all right left out for a couple of days."

Donna had only been in Cleo's apartment once, but she buzzed around the kitchen like she'd lived there twenty years. "Here's some fresh bread from the bakery and I've got pâté and a nice bottle of my mom's homemade chutney. Have you had lunch? Let me do a little plate for you."

Donna took coffee cream out of the fridge and reached into the cupboard for two mugs. Cleo watched as she dug out a wooden cutting board, preparing it with bread, pâté, and chutney. She placed the board on the table in front of Cleo, along with a cup of hot coffee and a giant glass of water. She went back to the kitchen again and turned on the sink, filling it with hot soapy water to do the dishes.

"Will I wake the baby if I do these dishes?" Donna snapped on a pair of pink rubber gloves that she'd found under the sink.

"Oh my God, Donna, sit down and have coffee with me, you don't have to—"

"Oh, stop it. Will I wake him?"

"No, he should be fine."

"Good. It's best not to tiptoe around them, or so they say. How's Francis doing with it all?"

"Good. He's good. He's here when he's not working. Spends the night when he can, to help with diaper changes and stuff. Not much he can do in the way of feeding until I start pumping or whatever. Mom's here whenever she's not teaching or looking after Nalfie." Cleo spread a hunk of bread with pâté. It tasted so good she could have wept. All she wanted in her life right now was carbs and sleep.

"How's the sleeping?"

"Not great. He does okay in bed with me. I know I'm not supposed to, but it's the only way I can sleep. I haven't rolled over on him yet, so that's good."

"You won't. He'll be fine. He's so scared to be on the outside, being close helps him sleep. The nurses at the hospital just aren't allowed to tell you that." She turned from the dishes and winked at Cleo.

She finished up whatever dishes were there and came and sat with Cleo on the couch, a cup of coffee curled in her hands.

"Donna, thank you. This is great. You didn't need to clean up, though."

"Don't be silly. It's the least I can do. It's killing Nancy that she can't be here all the time because of work and Mack. It's nothing for me to come over and help, you know that. My days off are yours."

Timothy started howling from Cleo's bedroom.

"Party time's over. Forty-five minutes on his own, a new record." Cleo made a move to get up.

"You stay there. I'll go get him for you." Donna put down her coffee, and the spring in her step belied how much she'd been trying to control herself when she'd first arrived.

"Oh, hello. Hello baby, hello you, it's okay my sweetie, you're okay, I'll bring you to your mom. There you go, there you go," Donna cooed from the bedroom. Cleo heard Timothy's screeches subside and she leaned back on the sofa, hoping he'd settle with Donna long enough that she could finish her coffee and food.

Donna came out of the bedroom with Timothy huddled on her shoulder. She was patting him on the back and bouncing him gently into complete submission. Magic nurse moves Cleo could never dream of mastering.

"Are you kidding me? He never settles for me like that. He never settles for anyone like that, not even Mom."

"Oh, Cleo. He's so perfect. Look at all his hair! He looks just like you."

"He's the spit of Francis."

"Oh, but he has your eyes, oh, just look at him." Donna sat down in the glider and began rocking the baby, his little eyes beginning to droop.

Donna looked so much more capable than Cleo, so much more like a mother. She was all curves, all soft freckled skin, blond hair, and blue eyes. Like one of those Virgin Marys hanging in a museum. Timothy was asleep on her already.

"Can I maybe bring Reg over to meet him? When you're settled in a bit more?"

"Yeah, of course! Hold on, Reg wants to meet a baby? I thought he didn't like kids. Didn't you have to drag him to Mack's christening?" Cleo thought of him sitting next to a beaming Donna in the pews at the Basilica, arms crossed over a plaid shirt, looking like he wanted to be anywhere else in the world.

"Oh no, Reg adores kids. We tried for years to have one and it didn't work out," Donna said, like she was talking to one of her colleagues about someone else at work. She rubbed Timothy's back and stuck her nose in his dark hair.

Cleo didn't know if it was the hormones, the lack of sleep, or the surprise of finding out that one of her best friends had wanted kids and she'd never, ever known it until Donna was holding a new baby that wasn't hers, a baby that hadn't been expected or even wanted at first. Donna was holding a baby that Cleo had thought about not having.

Cleo sat up, placed her mug on the coffee table, dropped her face in her hands and started sobbing uncontrollably. Huge, ugly post-partum sobs from a place Cleo hadn't even known existed until a week and a half ago.

"Oh fuck, oh fuck, Donna, how could I not have known? I'm sorry, I'm so sorry, I'm a such a terrible friend. Timothy was a surprise, I didn't even think I wanted him, and now, oh God . . ."

"Cleo, Cleo, it's okay! I didn't say that to make you feel bad. Oh, stop now, I can't even come over and hug you, the baby's gone to sleep." Donna's eyes were misting over now, too.

There was a box of tissues on the end table next to the couch and Cleo reached over and grabbed one, blowing her nose so loudly the baby jumped a little in his sleep.

"If I wake that kid because I just blew my nose I'm going to kill myself." Cleo's words came out broken and in between gulps of air and she blew her nose again, quietly this time.

"Don't say that kind of thing, I'm a nurse, I'll have to report you." But Donna was laughing and patting Timothy on the back, rocking the glider a little harder to lull him back into sleep.

"How did we never know that? Me and Nanc, I mean. That you were trying and couldn't?"

"Oh, I don't know," Donna sighed and looked up at the ceiling, her head resting on the glider. "We just thought it would happen. Like you do. And then it didn't. Then we felt like we would jinx ourselves if we talked about it with anyone, like that would be acknowledging we had a problem. And Nancy had all her troubles so I didn't want it to seem like, hey what about us over here, look at us! We're trying, too!

You know, I didn't want to make it about us when she was going through all that heartache."

"Did you ever . . . see a doctor or anything?"

"Oh, of course. We both checked out fine. We're in the 'we have no idea what's wrong with you' twenty per cent of infertile couples."

Cleo looked over at the little dark-haired bundle and wondered if she would have been able to make one with Jamie, if only she hadn't been so stubborn and scared.

"Are you two okay, is there any chance—"

"We're done, and we're pretty good with it. I've seen so many women go through so much heartache with in vitro and I knew I didn't have the constitution for it. We thought about adopting for a while, but Reg's heart really isn't in it. We love our nieces and nephews. And this guy, of course. I know it sounds trite, but I think it was meant to be. Like Timothy."

Donna looked over the baby's head and smiled at her. She was the only one of Cleo's friends who could never tell a lie, the truth was always laid bare on her face. There was no trace of anger, resentment, or jealousy.

"We're both very lucky to have you, Donna. You know that." Cleo felt a fresh wave of hormones let go, gathering in her throat, willing the dam to burst again. Then the sound of a huge wet fart and a shriek from the rocking chair.

"You mean you're lucky your kid just shit in my hand and not yours," said Donna, standing up with Timothy, yellow liquid leaking through his sleeper and onto her hand.

"Oh, Jesus, that too." Cleo launched herself off the couch and hobbled as fast as she could across the room to the laundry closet and the fresh stack of receiving blankets piled on top of the dryer.

prisoner of war

CLEO CAN'T BELIEVE ANYTHING IN HER LIFE USED TO MATTER that wasn't related to sleep. She can't believe she ever thought she was exhausted because she never truly was, not like this. She finally gets why parents are always tired and how they can't stop talking about being tired and she is mad at herself for ever rolling her eyes at them when they weren't looking. But now she understands that no one understands tired like a mother. Maybe a prisoner of war, maybe one of those obsessed interns in Manhattan working for Goldman Sachs who doesn't sleep and drinks too much Red Bull and jumps off a building one day or just straight-up dies from exhaustion. People like that might know what it's like, but fuck everyone else. Fuck all the people like Cleo who thought she knew tired before she had a baby. She can't believe people care about the internet or what kind of car to buy or world peace when all that really matters is sleep. She took it for granted before; she never realized how lucky she was to lounge in bed until eleven on a Saturday morning, curled into Jamie, him getting out of bed to go make her a cup of coffee. Now all she can think about, after keeping the baby alive, is sleep. This must be what it feels like to be obsessed with something, like being a serial killer and all you can think about is killing people. Cleo could kill somebody right now if it meant eight hours of sleep. Maybe she *should* kill somebody because then she could go to prison and get a full night's sleep. They must let you get at least six or seven hours of uninterrupted sleep in jail. She can't believe she ever liked sex. She can't believe she ever let anyone do that ridiculous thing to her that's resulted in her getting only an hour and half of sleep a night. Cleo used to have a recurring sexual fantasy about Gerard Butler being helicoptered in to her at a remote cabin in the Scottish Highlands. He would come in on one of those ladders hanging from the chopper like 007 and burst through the door and it was raucous up-against-the-wall sex and sex-on-bearskin-rugs and blah blah blah. Now, when Timothy is crying and trying to latch on and kicking his legs and screaming, all she fantasizes about is sleep. Instead of Gerard Butler there's a giant wooden crate filled with booze and food hanging from the helicopter. Some person, maybe Gerard Butler, maybe not, who cares, comes in for five minutes to unpack everything and then leaves. Cleo takes a long bath and puts on silk pyjamas and crawls into a king-size bed with sheets that are four hundred thread count Egyptian cotton. She gets under the covers with still-damp hair and sleeps for a full uninterrupted eight hours and when she wakes up, she eats and drinks and goes back to bed. This is what she does forever, until the end of time. She wants to be alone forever with a king-size bed and someone to bring her food and leave her the fuck alone. How do people do this, she can't do this, she hates this life, she hates Jamie, she hates Francis, she thinks she might hate her baby, why can't she be alone and sleep.

There are tears in Timothy's hair, he's asleep at her breast, finally, and now she can't move, she's too afraid to wake him, so she stays in the rocker and cries and cries and cries but she tries not to let her chest heave too much because if the baby wakes now she might die. She sits there holding Timothy and imagines herself in a king-size bed, alone, with clean wet hair.

tripping downstairs

Cleo was laid out on the couch at her parents' house. Maisie held Timothy to her chest and walked him back and forth, back and forth and in a loop. Through the living room, through the kitchen and dining room, over and over. Maisie had been doing this so long, an hour? An hour and a half? Cleo thought her mother might leave permanent tracks in the hardwood floor.

She fell in and out of sleep on the couch, dozing half-in, half-out to the sound of Maisie padding around in her sock feet and the soft strains of a "Mozart for Babies" playlist her mother had been so delighted to find on Spotify. Cleo dreamed she was holding Timothy and walking down a steep flight of stairs. In the dream she tripped and started to fall and her legs made a sudden movement to try and catch herself, like she was riding a bike down the flight of stairs, and it jolted her awake.

There was no sound of crying, only the sound of feet and Mozart, so Timothy was still asleep. Her mother was so content when she walked the floor with the baby, it was like she could do it forever and by the way things were going she'd probably have to. Of course Maisie was content. Of course she was. Because at the end of the day, or the night, or the week, or whenever Cleo was able to wrench herself away to attempt a day or two of this on her own, the baby was hers, and not her mother's. Cleo was the one who had to go home with him and deal with him for the rest of her life, not Maisie. Maisie had had her turn with a baby and a toddler and a teenager and she was done. Of fucking course she was content. She got to do all the fun stuff and then wave good bye.

Cleo was lulled back into a half-sleep but she had the same tripping-downstairs dream and her legs shocked her awake once more.

She was never going to sleep again.

Cleo gave up and sat upright on the couch, wrapping herself in the quilt Maisie had brought downstairs for her. Her mother came out of the dining room for the thousandth time that evening. This time Timothy was fussing.

"You're awake."

"I'm always awake."

"You'll be awake till he's five and then you'll have to drag him out of bed in the mornings for school."

"Shoot me."

"After you feed him."

Maisie handed over the squealing bundle. The baby howled till he was red in the face as Cleo struggled to release her breast from the nursing bra. Timothy latched on like he hadn't been fed in days, and he gummed Cleo's nipple so hard she yelped. This startled him into a second and a half of silence. Then he unlatched and started screaming.

"Jesus Christ, Jesus Christ, Mom, take him, please take him." Cleo stood up, wobbly with exhaustion, and tried to hand the baby off to her mother.

"He needs to eat, Cleo, just take a deep breath and try again."

"I can't. I can't do this. He hates me."

Maisie put one hand on Cleo's shoulder and the other under the elbow that was supporting Timothy and eased them both back onto the couch. She lifted the baby's head and gently guided him to Cleo's nipple, just like the nurse had done on the day he was born. He started suckling immediately, and Cleo's head flopped back on the couch. She made no sound, but fat tears rolled down her face. Timothy arched his back and stiffened his legs, but kept on with the feeding, sputtering and crying in between gulps of milk.

"Just feed him for as long as you can manage," Maisie said, rising from the couch. "I'm going to warm some formula."

"You bought formula?" Cleo feigned indignation as hard as her exhaustion would allow, but secretly her insides melted with relief.

"And bottles. They're already sterilized. Just give me a few minutes."

"Mom, I—"

"Cleo, you're miserable. It's supposed to be hard, but not like this. Let me help you."

It was the permission she needed. Cleo nodded at Maisie and let her go to the kitchen without another word of protest.

A half-hour later, Timothy was fed, burped, freshly changed, and plopped into the bassinet that Maisie and Joe kept for him in their spare bedroom. He was sound asleep. Maisie sat in the rocking chair next to the fireplace, drinking a cup of herbal tea, her job for the evening complete. Cleo sat on the edge of the couch and pushed her hands through her hair, then bowed her head and covered her eyes. Her hair was so greasy. She hadn't showered in days, she was afraid to wash her hair, it was going to start falling out in lumps soon like Nancy said it would.

"How did you do this? What's wrong with me? How does everyone make this look so fucking easy?" She couldn't look her mother in the eye.

"You just need to stay off Facebook. Everyone has a hard time, but it's only the good stuff they like to show off about."

"Sometimes I feel like I ruined your life. I think about that a lot because there are days when I feel like Timothy has ruined mine."

Cleo's head still hung low. The only sound was the squeak of the ancient rocking chair and the crackling spit of the fire. She was glad

Joe was working nights. He was at the station right now, and so was Francis.

"Did I ever, even once, give you reason to think that? Can you think of one time you ever felt unwanted or unloved?"

The tone of Maisie's voice forced Cleo's head out of her hands. She folded them like she was in prayer, resting her chin on them so she could make eye contact with her mother.

"I'm not like you. I'm not as good. I got pregnant in Korea and had an abortion. I couldn't do what you did."

"You're doing it now." Maisie looked out the window. The wind whipped up outside and rain and wet leaves blew against the panes of glass.

"Cleo, you have this fantasy in your head, this romantic thing about France and this shiny, exotic life. Life's not like that, it never turns out the way you expect. I hated Paris, I hated work, I hated not being able to eat. The only thing I loved about it was Alex. I had a shitty apartment, everyone was mean to me, I was hungry and cold all the time, and I missed my mother. When I got pregnant, I realized how much I goddamn hated the place."

Maisie got up and placed her mug of tea on the mantel. She closed the curtains and walked to the couch and tucked Cleo in under Nalfie's homemade quilt.

"You're allowed to think your baby's ruined your life when you're only getting two hours sleep a night, you know." Maisie bent and kissed her on the forehead. "I'll get up with Timothy if he wakes. You get some rest. Two of you stay here for a few days, until you get your head on straight."

"Okay." Cleo started to fade. "Mom, if anything happened to him I would want to die."

"I know, my darling. Don't I know it." Maisie switched off the lamp in the living room and went to the kitchen to turn off the lights before heading to bed.

explosive

"All right, Timothy. Let's do this. Mommy and me first solo trip to the grocery store. Please don't poop right now because I forgot your diaper bag at home. Okay, sweetface?"

Timothy stared up at Cleo and gave her what she thought might be his first genuine grin. One that wasn't motivated by gas.

"You're definitely going to shit your pants aren't you." She tickled his stomach and he grinned again.

Cleo still didn't understand how the car seat carrier was supposed to click onto the shopping cart, and she was so paranoid about Timothy falling she placed carrier and all into the cart and put whatever groceries she needed around him. He looked like a little Baby Jesus in a nest of fruit and vegetables instead of a manger.

"Here's our Christmas card, buddy. Nalfie will kill us, but come on, look how sweet you look!"

Cleo had just fished her phone out of her purse and held it up to take a picture when she saw him at the other end of the baking aisle. A basket hanging off one arm, looking down at a grocery list on his phone.

What was he doing in the baking aisle? He didn't bake. They hadn't even shopped at this store when they were together. She fumbled to put her phone back in her purse.

And fucking dropped it. Like a grenade, waiting to explode on the floor next to the giant bags of whole wheat flour.

Jamie looked up at the sound from the other end of the aisle and when he saw her Cleo's heart started to beat so fast she could feel it in her head, behind her left eye, a sudden, awful tremor. He smiled and looked away, as if he hadn't really seen her, only shared a moment with a stranger and given a polite smile.

Cleo bent over to pick up her phone and it still hurt to do that, she had to do it so slowly and gently, like if she didn't her insides would fall out. Goddammit, goddammit why did it still hurt so much. She couldn't even run away now if she wanted to.

Timothy started to fuss because he was better than a cat at smelling and sensing fear, at picking up from across a room or a grocery aisle when Cleo's heart started to beat faster. She looked at him and smiled and cooed and stroked his cheek, trying her best to keep calm, if only long enough to get him out to the car. She was in no mood to breastfeed in Dominion.

"All right. Take two, buddy. We can go home soon, okay?" She rocked the shopping cart back and forth, back and forth, until Timothy's eyes glazed over long enough that Cleo thought she might just have time to grab the remaining things she needed and get the hell out of the store without running into Jamie again.

Cleo moved aisle to aisle, peeking carefully into each one to make sure it was safe, only to find that Jamie was doing the same thing. They smiled awkwardly at each other at either end of crackers, of canned meat and fish, toilet paper, dog food, cleaning supplies. Cleo cursed him under her breath every time she looked up; she was the one with the baby, she needed to get groceries now, while the baby wasn't fussing. Why didn't he duck out gracefully and go to the grocery store across town, or at least sit in his car and wait for her to finish? If he had any class, that's what he'd do. *And if I had any class I wouldn't have slept with a twenty-five-year-old and gotten pregnant*, she thought.

They'd both doubled back hoping to avoid each other, but Jamie was standing at the end of the condiment aisle, looking her way and clearly unsure of what to do.

Cleo took a deep breath and started to roll Timothy and her cart towards him. It had to happen sometime. Let it be now and get it over with. Nothing could be worse than seeing Evelyn at Walmart when she was full-on pregnant.

The walk down the length of the aisle gave her time to think of what to say; it was like the hiss of air when you climbed on top of an air mattress to deflate it, full body weight forcing the long, slow, satisfying hiss of air out until your nose touched the floor. She passed the jars of olives and thought about stopping to grab the one she needed, but realized that might give him the chance for a quick getaway and she wanted this done. She pulled her cart alongside him.

"Hello there," she said. "That was silly, wasn't it? I'm sorry."

"It was silly. I'm sorry, too. So, this is the little guy?" Jamie came around to her end of the cart and peered down at Timothy. They both grinned at each other.

Even for this baby, Jamie was smiling. And Cleo's heart broke for the hundredth time since they'd parted ways. Everything was fresh and she was so sore and hormonal and was likely to burst into tears over anything, but she couldn't do it now. She believed her life depended on it; on keeping her shit together in the condiment aisle, for both their sakes.

"Timothy, right?" He looked at her and smiled but she could see behind it.

"Yes. Yeah. I didn't want to call or text or anything after he was born it felt like it would have been—"

"Of course. Yeah, no, of course. I ran into Doug a few weeks ago, he told me. Cleo, he's gorgeous. He looks just like you."

"Oh God, no he looks like—"

Jamie looked down at his shoes. There was such a silence, Cleo wanted to run away or die or both.

"Well, I think he has your eyes. Definitely your eyes."

"He does. You're right, he really does. Thanks. No one really says that, so . . ." And she wanted so badly to tell him about finding her father and how Timothy actually had *his* eyes, but it was too much all at the one time.

"How are your parents?" She knew it was the wrong question because Jamie's eyes got bigger and it was almost as if he had to stifle a laugh.

"I guess your mom told you I ran into her at Walmart a couple months ago," she barrelled on before he had a chance to interject. "It was pretty fucking awful."

"Yeah, she told me. She felt really bad afterwards."

"There was no need at all for her to feel bad. Can you tell her . . . tell her I'm sorry for everything. And that I love her and . . . I miss her." She could feel herself losing it and made a move to wheel the cart away.

"Cleo, you don't have to be sorry, can you—"

For as long as she lived, she would remember how grateful she was for her son and the sound of an explosive shit emanating from him in that moment when she needed one the most.

"I gotta go, I forgot the diaper bag, I gotta go." Cleo wheeled away from Jamie and wanted to look back when she got to the end of the aisle to wave at him in apology or regret or something that would make it all better, but she'd already started to cry.

A few days later, Cleo was returning from walking Timothy around the lake. He still hated the stroller so he was snuggled up against her in the carrier, his face squished against her chest, sound asleep.

Marsha opened the front door when she saw Cleo coming down the front path.

"You had a delivery. Some fella was down pounding at your door with a ratty old armchair. I didn't want to open your door and let him in with it, just in case he was a nut job or something. I told him to leave it outside your door. Were you expecting it? It doesn't really fit in with the other furniture. I can get George to bring it in for you, or bring it to the dump, it's up to you."

"I wasn't expecting it, no. But it's my chair. Well, it was my grandfather's."

"Ah. Right. Takes all kinds, I suppose. I'll send George down when he gets home from work, get him to take it in for you."

"Thanks, Marsha."

Cleo rounded the corner and the chair was next to her front door. She never realized how old and worn it had become; like it had been sitting right there in the sun and rain for years.

Timothy was sound asleep and she knew once she opened the front door he'd wake up. He already knew the sound of the doorknob and the lock clicking in place, the difference between fresh air and being inside.

She sat in her grandfather's chair, in the late fall sun, with her son pressed against her and looked out at the lake for an hour, until Timothy woke up.

later

sunday dinner II

It wasn't a Flavour-of-the-Week Sunday, it was turkey with all the traditional Jiggs' dinner fixings, but Cleo didn't mind so much. Timothy was getting a bit hard to please these days, after the short and sweet honeymoon of *My Baby Eats Everything!* Last week he'd flung a Thai fishcake so far across the table it had hit Joe in the face, much to the delight of everyone in the dining room.

But he loved a Jiggs' dinner. He sat in his high chair, shovelling fistfuls of pease pudding into his mouth like someone was ready to snatch it if he looked away for a second. There were bits of carrot and dressing in his hair and he was humming and kicking his legs.

"Just like his mother," Nalfie said, and she took a spoonful of her pease pudding to plop on his plate when he finished. "He looks like his father, but my God, Cleo how much is he like you when he eats. Sure you still hums when you eats now and you're forty-one."

"Oh, wow," said Abby. Francis's new girlfriend was sitting next to Cleo and she made a point of putting down her fork to touch Cleo's arm.

"You look really great."

"Thanks," said Cleo. "Use sunscreen and don't forget to moisturize your neck. And if you have a kid when you're twenty-seven instead of thirty-nine you'll look even better at my age."

Abby laughed a little too hard and Cleo caught Francis's eye and threw him a wink, knowing that his new lady was a fan of tanning beds. He rolled his eyes at her, the way a kid brother would, and got up from the table for a second helping of dinner.

It was no trouble to see where Timothy got his appetite.

"Want some more, little man?" Francis leaned in to Timothy, and reached for his little plastic plate. It was cream-coloured and covered in a circle of miniature brown rabbits, from a set of baby dinnerware Alexandre had sent from France when Timothy was born.

"Mmmm, mmmm, mmm," Timothy grunted in response, kicking his legs harder and banging his sticky fists on the high chair table.

"I'll take that as a yes," Francis said, taking the plate and heading into the kitchen for refills for them both.

"Grab us another beer while you're in there, will you Francis?" Joe called out, his plate empty too, but he liked to pace himself and breathe a bit before seconds. "One of the dark Belgians on the bottom shelf of the fridge."

"Sure thing, Joe."

"My God, what a state he's in," Maisie said, jumping up from the table. "Let me give him a wipe down before he starts in on his seconds."

"No point, Mom. Just wait till after dessert," Cleo said.

"That's a sin for you, Cleo. You'll have to get at him with a chisel if you leave that mess for too long." Maisie was halfway to the kitchen to wet down a cloth.

"Sure it's not a bad day out, just bring him out back and we'll hose him off," Nalfie chimed in, reaching over to feed the baby a spoonful of her dressing while he waited for his second plate.

Timothy's dark hair was stuck off in all directions; some strands of it pasted to his forehead with gravy. He looked towards the kitchen and Francis, and screamed with impatience for his second plate.

"Timothy, sweetheart. No screaming for food. What do we say?" Cleo looked at him with a raised eyebrow across the table.

He looked back at Cleo and grinned, his eyes crinkling at the corners, chin jutting out proudly. Two perfect white teeth sticking out of his bottom gums.

"Peeeeeeaaaaase."

"That's better."

Cleo sat back in her chair and looked at her son, sitting in his chair in the spot where she'd once imagined him.

It was starting to feel a bit like home again.

in a heartbeat

IT WAS THEIR FIRST REAL WALK AROUND THE LAKE WITHOUT having to trudge through snow or mud. Timothy was too restless for his stroller these days, so she'd take him by the hand and they'd walk through the tall grass coming down the hill from their place until they hit the main path. Cleo let him run ahead, keeping an eye that he didn't bolt for the water, or the road when they came around the north side. He could walk the full length of the lake now, sleeping like a stone at night on the days they did.

She'd put him in his little rubber boots today, but the path was mostly dry and she wondered if she shouldn't go back and get his sneakers. He walked more easily in them and took fewer tumbles. But he was already bounding down the hill, and dragging him out of the sun and back inside would be asking for a tantrum. One that could ruin a perfectly beautiful sunny day in a heartbeat.

It was late April, the first day of the year when the city poked its head out the front door and took its first tentative steps outside in the hopes that this was it. Winter had been brutal. If it hadn't been for George upstairs, Francis and Joe, Cleo and Timothy would still be shovelling their way out of the apartment. The only good thing about winter was how much Timothy had loved it; that huge backyard had saved her sanity, and she thanked whatever lucky stars she had left that she'd grabbed this place before she'd gotten pregnant, and not a tiny spot downtown.

Timothy was running down the path like a greyhound just let loose out of its pen, yelling at the top of his lungs and tearing off his hat and mittens for Cleo to pick up after him as she ran yelling, "Slow down, buddy, hat on, please." But she didn't have the heart to follow through and be Stern Mom today. It was warm, and he was so happy to have his face in the sun and his hair in the wind and out from under the winter hat he'd been forced to wear for seven months. He looked back at her and laughed, veering across the path towards the ditch.

"Eyes in front, buddy, eyes in front!" She watched him stumble and catch himself, then continue like a rocket down the path. If he tripped he'd skin his face out for sure. But Cleo forced herself to shut her mouth and put all worries of skinned noses and ear infections and falling in ditches out of her head. Today she wouldn't worry about the cold, or sunscreen. Today she would just let him run.

They were nearing the dog park and Timothy had tired a bit and slowed down to walk with Cleo. She knew he was only resting up before the next sprint, so she savoured his warm hand in hers, his fingers not as fat as they'd been even one month earlier.

There was a playground on one side of the path where a dad and his toddler were playing. The dark-haired girl looked to be a couple of years older than Timothy, and when she spied him walking down the path she broke away from her dad and came running at him.

"Hello, baby!" She ran up to them and stopped, taking Timothy by the hand like she'd known him all her life and leading him to the little clearing. Timothy went along without question, as if she were his big sister.

Cleo was so taken with the little girl that she didn't realize until she followed the kids that the man standing there wasn't the girl's father, it was Jamie.

"Well hello there, stranger," he said, and he took Cleo genuinely and with no hesitation into a hug before she even had time to think.

"Hi," she said, and she felt his beard brush past her cheek on the way into the embrace. He still smelled exactly the same.

He looked good. Like he was healthier, or shinier or had lost weight or something. Cleo couldn't put her finger on it. She was still ten pounds over her pre-baby weight and had never felt it more than she did now, standing in front of him.

"Look at him go," Jamie said, laughing at Timothy running around with the dark-haired girl.

"Who's this little one?" Cleo asked, trying to keep her voice as even as Jamie's. She was only beginning to crawl out of the insanity of the past two years, only ready now to peek into the sun. She wasn't ready for this. Wouldn't be for a long time, and yet here she was. Here they all were.

"This is Rosie. I've been with her mother for about a year and a half. She had to run some errands, so Rosie and I are hanging out for a few hours. You know what's it's like trying to get anything done with one of these monsters running around."

"Yep. Do I ever."

She remembered Nancy telling her when Timothy was a couple months old that Jamie was seeing someone. But Cleo was so tired she didn't care, hadn't even asked who the woman was.

Thank God she wasn't here. Thank you thank you thank fuck.

They sat on a bench facing the lake and watched the kids play in the grass. Timothy was so enamoured with Rosie at this point Cleo knew he wasn't going anywhere.

"We're actually headed off to Andrew and Fran's for a playdate with Clara Jane after this."

"Oh, wow. That's great. So . . . Andrew and Fran? They're doing okay? And Clara Jane?"

"They're best kind. And C.J. is perfect. I thought the baby would break them, if I'm being completely honest, but it seems to have had the opposite effect. They're in a good place."

Cleo opened her mouth to say *Isn't it funny how they made it and we didn't?* but she thought better of it.

"Good for them," she said.

"So how have you been? How's motherhood?" Jamie slung his arm over the back of the bench and his hand brushed Cleo's shoulder.

"I'm good. It's been insane, and hard. Really hard, but we're good. Had a super rough start, but we're in a nice rhythm now, with work and Timothy's daycare and he loves it. He's a great kid, he's so much fun."

"Is his father in the picture?" Jamie asked the question so easily it took Cleo a little by surprise.

"He is. He's a great help. Francis takes him every second weekend if he's not working."

"Yeah, Doug told me he's one of Joe's firefighters."

"He is. Sometimes I wonder if he's only in the picture because Joe scared the living shit out of him. I mean, I gave him the option. But then I look at him with Timothy, and they're both mad about each other."

Cleo didn't feel the need to say anything else, about how old Francis was, or how it had been such a meaningless fling. It was nothing that mattered now, and nothing he hadn't heard from their mutual friends.

"How about you? How did you meet your lady?" Like she wanted to know, but she had to be polite.

"It's a bit strange, actually." Jamie looked away from her and laughed a little uncomfortably, the first crack since they'd run into each other. "I met Paula at the airport, ages ago. You sort of met her, too. One time when you dropped me off for a work trip. Rosie was a baby and I was giving Paula a hand at check-in."

Were you ever giving her a fucking hand at check-in. He met her when he was with me. He met her when he was with me, I met her, I met this kid.

Cleo stared at the little girl, that chocolate hair, that beautiful porcelain skin just like her mother's, and Cleo with the too-tight jeans from Christmas cheese. Jamie kissing her goodbye with future daughter in his arms in front of the woman who was now his.

"Oh." Cleo kept her eyes on one duck, following its path back and forth along the bank, Timothy in her peripheral vision. He was still holding Rosie's hand.

"We ran into each other randomly at Bowring Park the fall before last. She was with Rosie, I had Sophie with me. We were all feeding the ducks. Things kind of went from there."

"Small city," she said.

"Too small, sometimes." Jamie looked her way and smiled. A bit sadly, if she was being honest with herself.

He'd done nothing wrong, not really, but he felt guilty about it. It made Cleo feel smug and strangely happy. Like they were even, somehow.

"I found my father," Cleo blurted out, not wanting to hear anything else about Paula, and wanting to tell Jamie the news he deserved to know. And it might be years before they saw each other again unless they made the effort, and they wouldn't.

"Jesus, what? Oh my God, Cleo. What is he, I mean, are you . . . I thought Maisie would never say. Have you met him?"

"Only on Skype. But yes, we've met. He's seen Timothy. We're going to visit him in June." She felt like she'd won, she was like a selfish teenager because she'd trumped his new girlfriend news.

"Is he still in France?"

"Yep, in the south. He's semi-retired, he has a little house in Provence. We're going for a month. I mean, if it doesn't work out, we'll get an Airbnb, but he seems like a good guy."

"Is Maisie okay with it? And Joe?"

"Maisie's okay. Joe is great with it. We're figuring it out. Turns out she didn't tell my father she was pregnant, she just left the country. He didn't even know I existed."

"Jesus Christ, Cleo. I'm so sorry."

"The women in my family aren't the best communicators, I guess."

Jamie turned to say something but Rosie gave a shout and started running back across the grass to their bench, dragging Timothy in one hand and holding something clear and plastic in her other.

"Come on, baby," Rosie turned and yelled at Timothy who was struggling to keep up. When they reached the bench, she let him go—the momentum propelled him forward and he fell on his hands and knees. Cleo braced herself for the worst, but Timothy stood, brushed himself off, and wedged himself between her legs, facing out with his hands on her upper thighs.

"Jamie look, Jamie look what I found," Rosie shouted at them in a panic.

"It's okay, sweetie, calm down. What do you have there?" Jamie leaned forward on the park bench, giving the child his full attention.

There was something about his tone of voice with Rosie, and being there with him and two kids they never had together. It almost made Cleo double over.

Rosie held her hand high in the air, the plastic rings from a six-pack dangling off one finger.

"Someone didn't cut the rings, we have to cut the rings or the birdies will get hurt."

"That's right," Jamie said. "But I don't have scissors on me right now, so how about we take these home and we'll cut them up and put them in the garbage properly, okay?"

"Okay!"

Rosie waited until Jamie had folded the rings and zipped them into the inner pocket of his jacket. Satisfied, she grabbed Timothy by the arm again and they both ran off across the grass.

Cleo looked across at Jamie and laughed. An easy, comfortable, true laugh filled with longing and loss, from a pocket inside of her that had been emptied of tears many months ago.

"I'm assuming you didn't tell her the birds might choke and die."

"Nah. She'll figure it out when she's older."

That's how they sat for a while longer, watching their children play in the grass. Rosie throwing rocks as far as she could until they hit the water, sending Timothy into fits of laughter when one made the tiniest splash. Pointing at Jamie's dark-haired girl and looking back at Cleo and laughing each time, his eyes squinting against the glare of the midday sun.

recommencer

Cleo pulled over once during the drive, at a little fruit and vegetable stand on the side of the road, to ask the owner for directions. The woman was so taken with Timothy that Cleo let him out of the car to visit for ten minutes. They conversed in French, Cleo with the relative ease of someone who'd been completely immersed in the language for two weeks. She spoke some English at home with Alexandre, but they went back and forth, to try and get Timothy used to it.

The woman, Martine, sent them on their way with a brown paper bag of peaches, refusing to take money for them. Cleo made a mental note to try and make it back there again before they returned to St. John's.

She pulled down the dirt road, and into the grove of pine trees, quite pleased with herself for finding the spot. There was lots of room in the small parking lot, only one other car in the tiny dirt clearing. She turned off the car and got out, leaving Timothy in his car seat with the door open so she could get their gear ready for the hike.

She took out Timothy's carrier and placed it on a picnic table next to the car, then some water and food, including two peaches from the fruit stand. She wasn't sure if they'd last the hike but they looked too good to leave behind. They were so ripe the soft flesh gave way beneath Cleo's fingers and perfumed the air as she zipped them into the pouch on the carrier, along with some bread and cheese and a large bottle of water.

Timothy was next. She put him in the carrier and he screamed at the injustice of being moved from a car seat directly to the confines of another device, but the screams turned into giggles as soon as Cleo hoisted the carrier in the air and swung him up onto her back. He thought the funniest thing in the world was being able to see over his mother's head.

Cleo locked the car and put the keys into the small pouch on the side of the backpack. Before she tucked her phone away with the keys, she took a selfie of the two of them to send to Maisie. She sent at least one photo a day, unsure at first if it was something her mother wanted to see. But Maisie had been adamant that they loved receiving them, even Joe. Cleo had accidentally sent one last night of herself and Alexandre drinking wine in the garden after Timothy had gone to bed. Before she'd had a chance to text and apologize Maisie had answered, "Tell him I said hello and that he looks wonderful."

The hike was meant to cover part of the coast and then loop back around to the parking lot. It would take them an hour and a half, depending on Timothy's mood and whether there were spots where she could let him out to walk himself. This would be the easy part of the day; Cleo had managed to get here, driving a stick shift for the first time in years, navigating roads she'd never driven on. She laughed at herself now for being afraid to parallel-park on Prospect Street. Having Timothy with her was a lesson in bravery every day.

The trail was narrow and went through the woods briefly before opening up to the Mediterranean. The shock of it made Cleo gasp, and she stopped for several minutes to take it all in, standing still and breathing for as long as Timothy would allow before becoming restless.

The sparse vegetation on the scrubbed cliffs reminded Cleo of hiking at home, but it was the colour of the sea that gave it away. This blue never happened at home. The sea she was used to was temperamental, mostly green and grey. As beautiful as it was, it was never this pure and calm and clear.

They walked for an hour before the trail snaked back into the woods, so Cleo let Timothy out to run for a bit. After another fifteen minutes, they found a bench and sat down to have lunch. There was only the sound of birds and the distant sea as they ate their bread and cheese, Timothy sucking on the end of the chewy baguette until it became soft enough for him to tear off with his teeth. He devoured his bruised peach like a monkey, juice on his cheeks, his forehead, running down his arms. He cried when Cleo took the pit away from him, then comforted himself by licking juice off his wrists.

After they finished eating, Cleo packed up and they carried on. The last part of the trail became rocky, so she slung Timothy up onto her back again. He was full from lunch and tired from his run, so there were no complaints this time.

The way she held her body with her son on her back reminded her of backpacking in her twenties. The way her chest jutted forward, how her legs burned. Excited and a little scared of what was coming at her next. It was a different kind of weight on her now, a different kind of excitement mixed with fear.

But it was good.

ACKNOWLEDGEMENTS

Huge thanks to Rebecca Rose, Nicole Haldoupis, Rhonda Molloy, and the entire team at Breakwater Books for being so welcoming, and for making this a reality for me. To my wonderful editor, Marnie Parsons, thank you for your kindness, patience, and support. Claire Wilkshire, I am very grateful for your copyediting, I learned so much.

To my parents, Wendy Porter and Lloyd Kean, thank you for not flinching, years ago when I said I wanted to be an actor, and then a writer. Thank you to my sisters, Robin and Jade. You are everywhere in here.

Janet McNaughton championed this book from the very beginning, when it was in its roughest, earliest draft. Thank you for being so generous with your time.

Many excellent human beings read various early drafts of my manuscript. I have huge gratitude for Brian Marler, Paul Rowe, Allison Moira Kelly, Robin Kean, Michael Crummey, and Michelle Butler Hallett. Thank you for your kind, honest, creative, and thoughtful notes.

I would like to acknowledge the generous support of the City of St. John's and the Newfoundland and Labrador Arts Council. Thank you to the Writers' Alliance of Newfoundland and Labrador and to Alisha Morrissey.

Thanks to Amelia Curran and to Six Shooter Records. The epigraph is from "Years" by Amelia Curran, from the album *Spectators*, published by Girl on a Horse (SOCAN) © 2012.

I threw a lot of questions and panicked emails over the years at a lot of friends and writers and I was never made to feel like the pain in the ass I most certainly was. For the advice and help and everything in between I would like to thank Robert Chafe, Bernardine Stapleton, Wanda Nolan, Terry Doyle, and Bridget Canning. The writing community in this place cannot be beat.

Big thanks to Susie Taylor for the support, advice, rhubarb delivery, recipes, and just everything.

Celine Schneider, thank you for being my "France French" consultant.

Thank you to Anita Best, Peg Norman, and Melanie Caines for the beautiful spaces to write.

Love and thanks to the women who've offered inspiration and support when I've needed it the most. Deidre Gillard-Rowlings, Melanie Gale, Joanne Middleton, Renée Hackett, Nell Leyshon, Alison Woolridge, Renée Hillier, Nicole Rousseau, Dana Warren, Heather Huybregts, Wendy Chambers, Marquita Walsh, Sandy Gow, and all those I've missed.

To the amazing Duncan Major, for taking my clumsy thoughts and turning them into a beautiful book cover. There is no way to adequately thank you for your time, your enthusiasm, and your thoughtfulness.

The generosity of my in-laws, Randy and Florence Simms, is unparalleled. An extra heaping of gratitude for Florence; I don't exaggerate when I say that without her unending supply of childcare, this book would never have been completed. Thank you from the bottom of my heart.

For Geraldine Porter, who was the inspiration for Nalfie. I miss you every day.

Justin Simms, this book would not exist without you. Thank you for the days and weekends of solo parenting that allowed me to get this done, for the love and encouragement, and for everything that would take another ten pages to list.

Biggest thanks of all to Jude Abram Simms, our second pancake. I'm so glad you're here. I love you very much.

WILLOW KEAN is an actor and writer originally from Labrador West. She's co-written several children's plays that have toured provincially, and her five-woman comedy *Supper Club* premiered at the LSPU Hall in 2021. She's been shortlisted for the Cuffer Prize, longlisted for the NLCU Fresh Fish Award, and won the Percy Janes First Novel Award in 2018. Willow lives in St. John's with her partner, the filmmaker Justin Simms, and their son, Jude. She gets angry, cooks, and writes about it at *thelittleredchicken.substack.com*